Praise for *Raise Your Other Right Hand*

"Jody Weiner's *Raise Your Other Right Hand* is funny, wry, and so thrilling you can't stop turning the pages. Weiner's tale of a superstar caught up in a bizarre double shooting will keep the reader guessing but riveted until the very end."
   —**Frances Dinkelspiel:** Award-winning Author of *Tangled Vines: Greed, Murder, Obsession, and an Arsonist in the Vineyards of California*

"In his seriocomic, fast-paced novel, *Raise Your Other Right Hand*, Jody Weiner tells the story of Radon Jaalaba, a reckless, charismatic NBA superstar who stumbles into a double murder while scoring drugs. Weiner sets his tale in San Francisco and he knows the city intimately: its natural splendor and rogue history, its gossip and intrigues. He creates a wide kaleidoscope of colorful characters and, being a veteran attorney, offers an insider's keen understanding of law and order, city politics and jurisprudence."
   —**Edward Guthmann:** Author of *Wild Seed, Searching for my Brother Dan* and past film/book critic for the San Francisco Chronicle

"Former Rookie of the Year Radon Jaalaba finds himself on the hook for two murders and could end up playing for the San Quentin Warriors. It's up to Archie Krafter, the hero of Jody Weiner's funny and wise legal thriller, *Raise Your Other Right Hand,* to see that he doesn't. Archie and his wife, Lora, balance their high-wire romance against the assortment of upper echelon world-beaters who swirl around them competing for a piece of Radon. Drugs, sex, hoops, romance, betrayal, and no refs in sight; Nick and Nora Charles meet The Lincoln Lawyer in this slam-dunk novel."
   —**Byron Spooner** Author of *Rounding Up a Bison: Stories,* Pushcart Prize Nominee, winner of *Dillydoun International Fiction Prize*

Books by Jody Weiner

The Krafters: Partners in Time
Book 1: Raise Your Other Right Hand

Coming Soon!
The Krafters: Partners in Time
Book 2: Crime Therapy

Prisoners of Truth

For more information
visit: www.SpeakingVolumes.us

Raise Your Other Right Hand

SPEAKING VOLUMES, LLC
NAPLES, FLORIDA
2025

Raise Your Other Right Hand

Copyright © 2025 by Jody Weiner

All rights reserved. No part of this book may be reproduced or transmitted in any form or by any means without written permission.

This is a work of fiction. Names, characters, places, and incidents are either the product of the author's imagination or are used fictitiously. Any resemblance to actual persons, living or dead, is entirely coincidental or satirical.

The publisher does not bear any responsibility for the information by the author or third parties and does not have any control over, nor assume any responsibility for, the contained information.

"One For The Road" words and music by Harold Arlen and Johnny Mercer for the movie musical, *The Sky's the Limit* (1943); "I Only Have Eyes For You" words and music by The Flamingos; "Price On My Head", "Daughter of Rain" and "Pro Bono Man" words and music by Nancy Calef.

ISBN 979-8-89022-250-3

Raise Your Other Right Hand

Jody Weiner

To Nancy
My Partner in Time

"In Nature there are neither rewards nor punishments;
there are consequences."
—Robert G. Ingersoll (1833-99)
American lawyer, orator and writer

Chapter One

Integrity

"Hello, Archie Krafter!"

He turned to see a fashionably dressed young woman navigating through the holiday crowd gathered at this iconic hotel bar, backlit by neon-mirrored shelves stocked with every spirit on the market. Archie was thinking of the smoothest way to tell his wife, Lora, that their tile contractor was trying to screw them on the sauna conversion in the upstairs guest bath. And while this looming lady's crimson-tinted curls and big dark eyes were clearly familiar to him, her name and their connection eluded him.

"You don't remember me? Marina Ramirez? Bryan and Susan? She *just* texted me your number and here you are." Marina plowed on without acknowledgement from him. "Obviously it was meant to be . . . Look," after more silence, "I would never intrude on Christmas Eve unless this was important."

Archie was waiting for Lora in the Redwood Room, where they traditionally met up following their separate last minute holiday shopping, surrounded this year by rather subdued crowds in soggy Union Square. Considering Archie's plate already overflowed with other people's problems, he remained disinterested in any new matters not involving his wife, his *Naked Lawyer* blog, or their vengeful rescue tabby ironically named "Swami." Nonetheless, his former law partner Bryan Marten's spouse had sent this sinewy siren, so he was slightly curious to hear what Ms. Ramirez had to say.

"Radon's gone missing," Marina said *sotto voce,* preventing nearby patrons from hearing about whom she was speaking.

"I'm not a detective. Wait a minute . . . Radon Jaalaba on the Worriers? Oh, *of course!* You're Radon's partner."

"We're going on eight years together."

"It's coming back to me."

"You really aren't a detective," Marina said.

"What's coming back to you, Archie?" Lora appeared at his side, shopping bags dangling from her nicely toned arms, her timing perfect, as usual. "Happy Holidays, Marina," Lora said as they embraced. "We haven't seen you in a while. Is everything alright?"

"I haven't been able to reach Radon in three days. I'm worried something's happened to him."

"Tomorrow evening's game is on national television," Krafter said, his curiosity finally aroused. "There would've been reports from practice if anything was wrong."

"Not necessarily," Marina responded defensively.

"Did he miss another practice?"

"Don't cross-examine the poor girl," Lora butted in. "Can't you see she's upset?"

"Sweetheart, do I ever tell you how to run your charities?"

"Don't be glib, Archie."

"I'm not, Dear. I simply can't get the facts if you interrupt my *Chi'*."

"I hope you don't think *Kraftworks* is a charity?"

"Lora, I'm happy the theater almost breaks even."

"Now that's condescending."

"Radon is addicted to painkillers and who knows what else," Marina blurted out, apparently unable to withstand their bickering anymore. "I have to get him help."

"There've been rumors for a couple years now," Archie said, reacting like a fan. "Starting with physical therapy following his second knee surgery."

"You don't know how much Radon endures," Marina replied. "I watch him sacrifice his body every waking minute to play another game. Lately, though, he's out of control, and he's on the way to destroying everything he's worked for."

"Radon has played great the first six weeks of the season," Archie said. "I'm sure he's been drug tested."

"Not necessarily," Marina repeated. "Isn't there something you can do to find him?"

"Maybe he doesn't want to be found."

"Oh, hush, Archie," Lora piped in again. "What about Mike Prey?"

"It's Christmas Eve, "Archie implored her.

"Mike's a Worriers fan," Lora persisted. "He'll know where to look."

"Mike's a Bulls fan," Krafter corrected her while handing Marina his business card. "Lora and I have to go home and feed our cat," he added. "If you haven't heard from Radon by tomorrow morning let me know."

"Oh, thank you *so* much." Marina hugged Archie and soon Lora was in between them and the sweet-smelling, desperate beauty was hugging Lora, too. "God Bless you both," Marina said, as Archie and Lora finally managed to escape into the rainy San Francisco night.

"That poor girl needs your help," Lora pronounced in her way of assessing their future, as they walked toward the parking garage shielded from the steady drizzle under their over-sized umbrella bearing the *K*raftworks logo.

Withholding his skepticism about Marina Ramirez's bona fides, Archie did not discourage Lora from pursuing her missions once they'd moved her. He drove silently up deserted Russian Hill, reaching the turn into their dead-end lane.

"You up for one more?" Archie asked, having realized he'd hurried Lora out of the bar before she'd finished her drink. She nodded in approval, and he continued on down the north side of the hill. "I told Swami we'd be home by seven."

"He's a pretty smart cat," Lora replied. "But I doubt he knows what time it is once the sun goes down."

Chapter Two

Motivation

Radon Jaalaba hid behind thick Manzanita bushes that rimmed the manicured park across the street from Marina Ramirez's freshly painted white deco apartment building. His head pounded, his heart raced, and his body felt clammy all over. A smothering fear had crawled up his neck and spread to the back of his parched throat, in waves, repeatedly choking off the instinct to survive this horror into which his life had just plummeted.

After wandering around furtively for nearly two hours, in shock, really, Radon cowered in wait for Marina to come home, not knowing where else to go. A rag fashioned from his shirt sleeve was wrapped around the heel of his right hand, caked with blood from the gash he'd sustained while fleeing through the already shattered, sliding-glass patio door off the dining room in some dude named "Alonzo's" railroad flat. Having panicked at the sight of his dear friend Russell Marchetti lying face down on the grimy linoleum floor with a gaping hole in the back of his head, Radon bolted out the patio and slipped away across the weed-filled backyard.

This time there was no escape. Radon had screwed up beyond his wildest machinations, leaving not the slightest hint of salvation. Whatever faith he'd held in doing acts of selflessness—something his precious mother preached constantly—had just deserted him. His undeniable cowardice had been exposed and he found himself unable to seek faith in Allah, Buddha, Jesus, or any other *Truth*. For as much as Radon did not want to think about his mother at this moment, his life had suddenly become a cliché of the American Dream. More than anyone else in the world, Lieutenant Commander Michelle Garroway had led the way to Radon's phenomenal success, and she deserved a world of better from her only child.

Michelle and her precocious, mocha-colored five-year-old had come home to South LA at the end of `86, following Michelle's service with distinction in the Middle Eastern Sector of US Naval Intelligence. Radon's father, Ramin Jaalaba, a Moroccan captain in the French Air Force, had accompanied them to California on a "Sweetheart's visa." Sadly, though, Ramin could not cope with being house husband to a female American triple threat: a returning local military hero, helicopter mom and assistant director of communications at the Torrance City Manager's Office. Ramin had failed to thrive on his own or adjust to what he believed was his subservient role in the family, and eventually he'd embarked on his final bender as far as Michelle was concerned.

The couple had met at an underground officer's club in Riyadh during the run up to the Lebanon War. Based on Michelle's fairly fluent Farsi and her computer science skills, she had been assigned to a "big ship" monitoring the Persian Gulf. Captain Jaalaba was flying missions to assist the Israeli incursion. He had seriously deep green eyes and forever smiling teeth, and they'd hit it off. Their maiden encounter had blossomed into romantic assignations, eventually filling Michelle's belly with Radon. However unintended her pregnancy, not bearing Radon was never an option. Michelle had been raised Catholic and didn't tell Ramin until the end of the fourth month; even liberated Muslims disapproved of abortion after sixteen weeks. She was told to choose whether to have her baby in Saudi Arabia or at the Naval Hospital in Lanstuhl, Germany.

Lieutenant Garroway and her future NBA point guard had returned from Germany to a set of private rooms inside a prominent Saudi family's Riyadh complex, not far from her new desk assignment in a nondescript Intelligence office. Ramin was a doting if not sporadic father, frequently flying and living cleanly when he was in Saudi Arabia, as far as she knew. Michelle's only hint that Ramin might have had a substance abuse problem occurred the second time he'd arrived from Israel still buzzing on something he'd snorted with another pilot.

When her office was shut down partly on account of the Iran/Contra affair, Michelle had decided to retire and come home. At first, Ramin had eagerly followed mother and son to the Southern California tract home that Michelle's father had helped her maintain while she was in the Gulf. Yet, Michelle could not bring herself to close the marriage deal.

She had also flirted with Islam, seeing the influence of discipline through prayer; she'd accepted "Jaalaba" as her son's surname out of respect for the rainbow of cultures existing within that special boy. And while she'd sworn under penalty of perjury in Ramin's visa application that they were getting married, she had held everyone off, intuiting something wasn't right. Then on Radon's seventh birthday, during a backyard party for most of his school mates, featuring Barney the Dinosaur, Ramin was arrested at the local pharmacy trying to pay for a bogus Dilaudid prescription with Michelle's credit card.

"It is what it is, Ramin," had been Michelle's simple parting shot. Unless he agreed to promptly vacate her house and find another legal reason to remain in the country, the government might have to deport him. Apparently, one junkie in the family was more than Michelle could stand. And yet, twenty-three years later, Radon was hiding in the park, terrified, consumed with shame and the disgrace he was about to cast his mother's way.

"Why did this happen NOW?" Radon stifled an anguished cry at the vanishing Christmas sun. Just when he'd returned to form, quick as

ever off the dribble, a wiser, better player in every facet of his game. He had worked too *goddamn* hard for the last five-and-a-half years to heal his blown-out knee. *Twice!* The pain, too, had been conquered; well, definitely under control. Then he was slammed in the gut by the haunting vision of Russell's contorted body lying on the patio floor, shot dead while running away from a police officer! Now Radon wondered, had he really drawn a better fate by managing to escape?

He knew it was far too late to justify his actions. Yet, Radon couldn't stop replaying in his head the horrible events that had unfolded during a pit stop on the way to the Arena. He'd waited in the car at least fifteen minutes and Russell had not returned from the apartment. When Radon went inside to find him, he was met at the front door by Alonzo's frantic girlfriend—What the hell *was* her name? *Tanya!*—she had called 911 because she said Russell and Alonzo were arguing, and she was afraid "somebody was gonna get killed."

Why didn't I try to stop them? Radon's tardy and rather lame self-examination further sparked his memory, as Radon had witnessed part of the escalating scenario. Having followed Tanya down the narrow hallway to the living room, he'd seen Alonzo standing in the middle of the room, gripping a baseball bat in his right hand, pointing at Russell with his left, screaming: "Put the gun down, bitch!"

Radon had frozen in place, as more yelling from outside the ground floor flat turned out to be SFPD responding and, in the chaos, Tanya inexplicably hurried past him down the hall and out the rear patio. He'd started after her and retreated into the kitchen instead, not wanting to desert his friend. Within moments, though, Russell had come running down the hallway with a cop in pursuit, gun in hand, firing two shots at him, as Radon remembered seeing the patio glass door shatter and Russell literally hitting the deck.

Radon did not immediately recall that he'd rushed from the kitchen across the dining room, dodging another gunshot, and exited through the patio. But then the face of a second uniformed officer suddenly returned to his mind's eye, coming at him like a 3D movie, having advanced from the outside, firing *into* the dining room while Radon had barreled through the broken sliding door and escaped across the yard.

Russell was dead for no good reason. But when did he get a gun? Radon wondered. For, just as Radon's shock was receding, it occurred to him, again, how he had stupidly risked everything by going there in the first place. He hadn't slept in three days and if Russell had brought him an "eighth" yesterday, like he'd promised, Radon would have made it through the game today and none of this would have happened . . . There she is at last, he thought, spotting Marina's metallic blue Prius approach her apartment building. Sliding out from behind the hedges, Radon hurried across the street and followed her into the ground floor garage. Ever since he was drafted by the NBA, Radon's underwear model good-looks and custom wardrobe had been crafted to soften his streetwise swagger, rendering the total package relevant beyond basketball. Truth be told, though, Radon often worried that the optics concealed his weakness of character, something just obscenely displayed for the world to judge. Was he destined to follow his father's path, after all?

For sure Michelle Garroway had fiercely protected her talented son. Likely, she'd coddled him too much as well, having determined Radon would secure a proper formal education and its perks. A mother's vision had manifested during Radon's sophomore and junior years at Torrance High, most of all, because he had grown six-and-a-half inches taller and become a *Parade Magazine* All-American. So, Michelle had wisely assumed management of her highly recruited, suddenly famous, self-consumed and overwhelmed teenager. Having fielded over seventy scholarship offers, she had prevailed upon Radon to matriculate at Stanford, but he'd voiced concerns about having to also compete off the basketball court. They'd agreed on Cal Berkeley, where he'd met Russell Marchetti and Marina Ramirez under quite different circumstances.

"*Where have you been?*" Marina screeched, at wit's end, after exiting her hybrid, squeezed in among the compact parking spaces. "Oh my God! You look terrible . . . What's happened?"

They hurried across the deserted garage and ascended the small elevator to her fifth-floor apartment. Last night's rain had blown far down the peninsula leaving a clear azure sky visible through the living room bay windows, while billowing sails and metallic container ships moved along the choppy waterway inside the Golden Gate.

Marina Ramirez saw terror in Radon's eyes as they sat facing each other on the sofa. Radon's self-confidence usually bordered on arrogance, enough to turn off anyone unwilling to dig up his vulnerabilities, which it turns out were buried not too far beneath his gracefully toned surface. In the beginning, Marina had hopes for them. After entering Cal in pre-med, she'd eventually parlayed her BS into an RN, determined to help people and still have a life. Having trained nearby, she'd landed a floater position in the Berkeley hospital where she happened to be on duty when they'd met.

Radon was a rising superstar, recently named AP All-American, second team. On a spring weekend afternoon, two hours into a quiet hike up near Wild Cat Canyon Road with Russell Marchetti, tripping on mushrooms, Russell had fractured his radius in a nasty fall along the trail and Radon brought him into the emergency room. Three years earlier, Russell had been appointed special equipment manager to the Cal basketball team, assigned to greet Radon's heralded arrival on campus during freshman orientation week. That winter, having shared Radon's joint at the Maui Invitational, Russell had thereafter managed to share the coaches' intelligence on the drug-testing routine.

When Radon first noticed Nurse Ramirez taking Russell's pulse on the gurney, her sultry eyes and fiery curls exploded around her powder blue cap and Radon immediately knew that "Rina" was going to be his partner. Radon's intuition was often stronger than his experience back then, whether he was penetrating the lane or choosing his lovers.

As the sun sank on this fateful Christmas, Marina Ramirez held Radon tightly, steadying his breathing, easing his pain, protecting him from his demons. Then she gently led him toward the bathroom to address his wounds, strangely, recalling the first time they'd been naked together and Radon had sobbed, panicked by the honest tenderness of their emotions. Marina had come to love Radon deeply over the years.

Still, the clock was ticking on her own life's fulfillment, and Radon was not the missing piece in her long-term puzzle. It was time for her "to get off the pot," as her former mentor in pediatrics, Dr. Randall Mutton, had recently reminded her. Marina had held "Randy" off since she'd left the hospital to start the Jaalaba Foundation at Radon's urging. Last year she'd run out of excuses. Yet, she knew this was definitely not the time to bail on Radon. Especially when bailing him out of jail was the realistic agenda.

"Hold still," Marina implored him, standing over Radon, seated on the lidded toilet adjacent to the marble sink in her bathroom, while she deftly cleaned and bandaged his wounded hand.

"*Alhamdulillah!* What am I gonna *do?* The police will be looking for me."

"Here's Archie Krafter's number. Call him."

"You saw Krafter?"

"I was worried when you turned off your cell . . . You need treatment, Radon."

"Lady, you don't understand how serious this is. A cop killed Russell. Might as well be me," Radon whimpered a little. "Because they're gonna blame me for it."

"At least tell Bryan you're alive." Marina punched in his number, already in her phone, and handed it to Radon. "He's probably at the game right now. Radon? . . . They're all waiting on you."

Chapter Three

Eating While Reclining

Archie was comfortably propped up alone in the couple's king-size bed perusing the ever-shrinking daily *SF Chronicle* with a bowl of steel-cut oats and a mug of freshly pressed dark roast resting on the nearby nightstand. Looking out through the center window of their upstairs bedroom suite, the revolving searchlight on Alcatraz Island was disappearing into the spreading sunlight as Mt. Tamalpais peeked through. The "Today" show's Christmas Morning crew issued forth reverently from the flat screen hanging above their polished mahogany double dresser. The landline rang, announcing: "Call from Prey . . . M."

Krafter grabbed the phone and quipped: "You're up early."

"What's with that pouty seductive look on Savannah Guthrie's face? She's a lawyer, for God sakes," Mike replied, apparently watching the same program.

Mike Prey had been hunkered down in his hillside lair near the crest of Sausalito Boulevard for over two decades. Having survived law school together for a minute back in Chicago, they'd reconnected after Krafter relocated to San Francisco. However, Mike's brainwashing in the Socratic Method hadn't taken hold and he dropped out before the end of the first year, choosing instead to travel around the world along the guidebook version of the old "Hippie Trail."

Eventually, while trekking in India near the source of the Ganges, Michael Stephen Prey actually believed that he'd discovered his true calling to Buddha among the throngs of *Hindu* pilgrims in a Kumbh Mela celebration. Humbly, he'd returned to his mattress-on-the-floor studio apartment on the North Side of Chicago, thirty pounds lighter, mostly from dysentery, and every morning for the next six months, dressed in white linens, he ritualistically banged together brass Tibetan bells before lighting his bong.

"Where are Lauer and Roker anyway?" Mike groused into the phone, assuming his investigator stance. "Network anchors make enough to show up on Christmas."

For, as the mescal worm had turned, not long after Mike's sadhu epiphany wore off he'd moved to California and drifted up and down the coast, having settled in Carmel Valley to pursue a career in spiritual counseling. When complaints had eventually surfaced at Esalen concerning his constant state of arousal around the infinity pools, Mike fled to the Bay Area for another shot at the legal profession. In the end, though, despite finally obtaining his law degree, it wasn't meant to be. Following too many failed bar exam attempts, Mike abides these days on paralegal gigs, serving subpoenas and occasionally snooping through the trash of the rich and famous for newsworthy items.

"Archie, I hope you'll appreciate what I went through to discover that our pretty boy phoned in his practice yesterday," Mike crowed, having obviously reached his contact in the front office. "Just like the game he missed in Miami."

"I thought they held Radon out with a groin pull?"

"Officially, it's the flu this time," Mike replied, and Krafter could feel Mike grinning through the phone, as Prey often tried to bill him on a per-question basis. "*You know who* confided in me," Mike continued, adding his anonymous team source to seal the deal. "Nobody knows if Jaalaba will suit up today. And Radon's doorman hasn't seen him in three days, Archie."

"Well, I guess we'll have to wait 'till this afternoon with the rest of America to find out. Who're the Worriers playing? . . . Don't answer that unless it's free."

"The Trailblazers and their new phenom, LaMarcus Aldridge. Wish *I* could afford a ticket."

"Lora wants me to invite you to the house for dinner," Archie said, just as his telephone signaled "Bryan Marten" waiting, and Krafter flashed over before Mike could accept the invitation.

"Bryan?" Archie got up, surprised to hear from him, and padded across the thick tweed carpeting covering their upper-level rooms and hallways. Nestled among a row of ivy-covered houses near the crest of Russian Hill, the couple's renovated Victorian included a terraced rear garden with free-standing cottage, converted into a recording studio and occasional guest house. Ample space on multiple levels was afforded them to flourish or crash from project to project, individually and as a couple.

"Merry Christmas, Archie. How're things?"

"Things are fine. It's been a while."

"I've been kinda busy," Bryan hemmed. "Susan and I were saying we should come over the Bridge and meet you two for dinner."

"Whenever you're free."

"You know how it is," Bryan hawed.

"Lora's opening a new play," Archie changed the subject. "It's on a Wednesday in January, when people don't go out."

"Listen, Arch. I was . . . Would you be our guest at the game today? I realize you and Lora probably have other plans. I won't lie. I don't know what's happening with Radon lately and I'd feel a whole lot better if you were there in case anything goes wrong . . . You're better at dealing with these things," Bryan added, unnerved by Krafter's persisting silence.

"It's almost four years," Archie responded emotionally. "You need *my* help?"

"You blew *me* off! Remember? . . . Look, Archie. I'm sorry. What more do you want from me? Susan's looking forward to seeing you both."

"That's some rousing endorsement."

Krafter was stalling this time. He'd noticed his indecision had caught Lora's attention. She'd appeared at the entrance to their dressing room, having surmised what was going on. Then she sealed Archie's fate with a double horizontal-headshake and shoulder-shrug move, thereby releasing him from any shared Christmas activities—yet to be determined anyway—as long as Lora did not have to listen to Susan Marten's gluten-free whining for three hours.

"There's a holiday pre-party in Dunbar's suite, so we'll pick you up at four." Bryan confirmed it before Krafter could respond, reminding Archie of yet another reason why they were no longer partners. "I really appreciate this," Bryan added.

"We'll see," Krafter said, having endured their roller coaster friendship far too long, including two prior professional associations, a lot of which seemed to depend upon Bryan's degree of sobriety. Their last working relationship had ended on a sour note after Bryan had begun regularly cozying up to Perry Dunbar, the Worriers' minority owner and politically primordial mogul. Bryan has also been Radon's agent, manager and baby-sitter since his rookie contract, as well as the person behind Jaalaba's mounting fortune from branded merchandise. He owed Radon his unwavering loyalty and candor—fiduciary duties of which Bryan had too often been forced to be reminded.

Nevertheless, Perry Dunbar was an enticing philanthropist who, along with a group of civic-minded investors, had stepped in at the eleventh hour to keep the sad-sack Worriers from fleeing to a new arena in San Jose. Dunbar's group had vowed to maintain the Bay Area's proud NBA heritage since 1962, when the franchise had arrived in San Francisco from Philadelphia.

"Maybe you'll change your mind?" Archie prevailed upon Lora, as she watched him fuss over the proper attire for a prime-time game in Perry's private skybox.

Dunbar often hosted politicians and celebrities, usually accompanied by his curvaceous "cha ching" of the month, soliciting for her latest charitable cause. Deep into his seventies, Perry never married, preferring instead to roam around the world collecting businesses and younger women. The not-tall Brooklyn native from meager means was a self-taught chemist, who patented several surgical devices but made his first half-a-billion during the nineties on affordable battery-powered hearing aids he made in China. Perry resided mostly in San Francisco, using his wealth to fuel an ongoing empire of personally inspired offbeat products, as well as endowing foundations and hospital wings bearing his name.

In the aftermath of 9/11, Perry's "genius" niece, Felicia, had divorced her second husband in Connecticut and moved into her uncle Perry's Nob Hill apartment building as a perk for becoming COO of Dunbar Holdings LLC. For her big-splash maiden effort to elevate the Dunbar brand's visibility, Felicia had convinced her uncle to invest a chunk of his money in the "Save the Worriers Project." And despite the team's mostly dismal performance over the ensuing four seasons, Perry's huge civic donation—which the ever-mercurial Dunbar had once dubbed: "Felicia's fuckin' folly"—eventually turned to gold.

Radon Jaalaba had been a "lottery pick" from Cal and everything changed. The NBA Rookie of the Year took the Worriers from perennial losers to the second round of the playoffs in just two seasons. Fans returned, home games sold out, and Perry Dunbar was entertaining lawmakers and star-struck business associates in his glass-enclosed living room on the mezzanine level hanging above mid-court.

"I'm glad I decided to come, Archie," Lora admitted, eagerly fixing them a plate of jumbo shrimp and fried calamari off the festooned white-linen buffet conjured up by Felicia's caterer. "People are saying they'll come out to see the play on a weeknight," she added, concerned about a new drama from an unknown playwright that she'd agreed to stage. Rehearsals were imminent and Lora had reservations about its sheer nihilism, written by a young woman who also happened to be Lora's brother Dominic's latest girlfriend.

"Grab some marinara, too," Krafter replied, pointing at the cluster of cute little ceramic basketballs cradling the seafood sauces. "It doesn't matter when you open the play."

"What's *that* supposed to mean?"

They were hovering near the Christmas banquet table, set up on the entrance level of the private suite, looking out over the rapidly filling arena. Their cushioned seats were down near the glass, in two long rows, where the Martens had already staked their claim, including their demon son, Simon, noticeably amped up on the sugar from his plateful of pastries. Susan Marten and Felicia Dunbar stood at the end of the first row, likely discussing the benefits of Xanax versus Wellbutrin.

Back over at the well-stocked bar, opposite the buffet table, Perry chatted with Willie, Sid, Pasha, and Bryan, all of them seemingly oblivious to Radon Jaalaba's absence from the pregame warm-ups. The loyal fans, literally beneath them, had shelled out serious shekels for their seats, expecting Radon to pull off his third triple-double during this young season, and send the Worriers over the fearsome Portland Trailblazers.

"So, you think Andrea's play stinks all year round?"

"No, no, no, Lora. It all takes place *inside*. Doesn't matter when you do it. The couple's relationship is claustrophobic; it's intended to capture the audience."

"Very slick, mister. Manage to be supportive and still get in your dig."

"My mother, bless her soul, always told me, "Look your best, you never know who's looking at you.""

"Your mother sold clothes, Archie. What else would you expect her to say? You know you've disliked the idea from the moment my brother asked me to produce it. Will you at least support that I'm doing something nice for his girlfriend?"

"So, you admit the play isn't very good?"

"I admit you're being an *a-hole* . . . Now please think of something clever I can say to Felicia before she runs away from Susan."

"There's still time before the National Anthem. I'll hang here." Krafter was watching the players on both ends of the court gracefully dancing, twirling, and leaping through their lay-up drills to the timeless strains of "Sweet Georgia Brown." Trail Blazer teammates continuously snuck glances toward the Worriers' bench, obviously also wondering where the hell was Radon Jaalaba?

"Lora went to Sacred Heart, too," Susan Marten happened to say to Felicia just as Lora walked over.

"My mother was not a good Catholic," Felicia said, continuing her reflections on their shared religious education. "But she thought I needed to be one." Then she greeted Lora with a surprisingly warm hug, considering all the time that had passed since Lora was a blip on Felicia's radar. "How have *you* been Lora?"

"Very well, thanks. You're looking fit as ever, Felicia."

"It's definitely a chore; thanks . . . Did I hear you're producing a new play?"

"It's called *Bananafish Blackjack.* Maybe a little dark and controversial," Lora added rather awkwardly. "I hope you'll come and see for yourself."

She wanted to ask Felicia about the little theater off Avenue A, on the Lower East Side, that she'd love to wrangle for a run of several one-acts she had in hand, not the least of which was her autobiographic musical monologue in development. Immediately, though, Lora's body heat rose, and her sweat glands opened with a damp spot under her right armpit. She was often shy about promoting her art as opposed to performing it. "Thanks for including us, Felicia," she went on, opting instead for gratitude to stem her perspiration. "I hope Archie and I aren't intruding on your family party."

"It hasn't been *that* long. I've always supported *K*raftworks. Have you considered bringing any of your plays to New York? I'd be happy to put out some feelers."

"Wow! I sure appreciate you thinking of me," Lora sputtered, spooked that Felicia had apparently just read her mind. Remarkably, though, *this* Felicia Dunbar was not at all in character with the person Lora had encountered during the two years Archie was a partner in Bryan's firm, representing Radon together.

Felicia was still trim and toned from excessive energy; her big round eyes were deeply set in her big round head, topped with impossibly curly black hair that had since started to fleck with gray. Her posture remained perfect; no doubt having been formed much earlier in life by the silver stick planted firmly up her rear end. No, the old Felicia Dunbar would not have offered to do much of anything for Lora, who graciously forgave their past, while not forgetting it.

Archie happened over to the bar just as Perry Dunbar was cross-examining Willie, a former civic leader and bon vivant: "Why do I need a permit?" Dunbar demanded.

"It ain't only a permit," Willie replied with his devilish grin. "You're gonna need the Board of Supervisors to approve this cockamamie idea. Marten, you better strap 'em on, 'cause this fight will not be easy. Don't matter how much you're donating, Perry, a private homeless facility threatens the bureaucracy."

"I'm not Perry's lawyer," Bryan quickly corrected him. "But you're right. What major city has ever started a full-service residence for people living on the street?"

"What do you think, Krafter?" Dunbar addressed him for the first time.

"Sounds terrific as long as you privately manage it going forward. Once the city and county get involved, they'll make you put the whole project out to bid."

"That's ridiculous," Perry grumbled. He simply couldn't fathom why city managers would not immediately implement his genius idea to donate ten million dollars for a brick-and-mortar residential homeless re-entry center with detox, psychological treatment and vocational training all in one place. "Pasha," Perry called out to his slender young companion in a tight wool dress, accented by her faux Burberry bag. "Remind me to invite Jerry for lunch next week."

Bryan's pants suddenly emitted the theme from "Jaws", and he slinked out of earshot. Krafter watched Bryan's eyes grow large, listening to the caller. Bryan caught Archie's gaze, desperately signaling him to come over.

"Radon's hiding from the police," Bryan whispered, thrusting the phone at Krafter, despite his protestations. "He wants to talk to you."

". . . It's Archie, Radon. What's going on?"

"I could use your help . . . Right now . . . My buddy Russell was driving me to the arena," Radon's rapid-fire voice cracked with desperation. "He stopped at a dude's apartment . . . they got into a fight and the police showed up . . . I got away . . . except the cops *fucking shot* Russell . . . *Dead!* . . . What am I supposed to do now?"

"OK, calm down. Don't talk to anyone and be at my office in thirty minutes."

Chapter Four

A Subpoena Has You By The Balls

The Naked Lawyer
(Wednesday, January 26th)

Two months have passed since "Wikileaks" started disseminating embarrassing classified State Department and NSA cables about the Middle East and the sky hasn't fallen on America. Yet, according to Attorney General Eric Holder, Julian Assange and his source(s) have conspired to commit treason, while vast government resources are being well spent to prevent further promised leaks and bring the perpetrators to justice. This includes freezing Wikileaks' deposits and allegedly threatening to prosecute all major banks and credit card companies, worldwide, for aiding the enemy by processing any more supporters' donations. Here is Wikileaks' own summary on its website:

Wikileaks began on Sunday November 28th publishing 251,287 leaked United States embassy cables, which date from 1966 and contain confidential communications between 274 embassies in countries throughout the world and the State Department in Washington DC. 15,652 of the cables are classified 'Secret.' The embassy cables will be released in stages over the next year and show the extent of US spying on its allies and the UN; turning a blind eye to corruption and human rights abuse in 'client states,' 'backroom deals' with supposedly neutral countries, lobbying for US corporations, and the measures US diplomats take to advance those who have access to them. This document release reveals the contradictions between the US's public persona and what it says behind closed doors . . . if citizens in a democracy want their governments to reflect their wishes, they should ask to see what's going on behind the scenes.

"Archie, aren't you ready yet?" Lora's voice came over the intercom from the kitchen, one floor below, breaking the soothing tap-tap on the desktop keyboard in his study.

"Gimme five minutes," Archie tossed back, continuing to type away:

> *The Naked Lawyer* doesn't quibble with the substance of these illegally leaked revelations of unlawful conduct by the CIA and the State Department. Intelligence agencies worldwide, and the diplomats of nearly every country with the resources, act pretty much the same way: spying, dissembling, and trying to destabilize countries whose ideologies and system of government they disagree with or find threatening. Equally disturbing to me, though, the cables revealed just how cynical is the White House foreign brain trust about the entire Middle Eastern peace process.
>
> It is no coincidence an "Arab Spring" is suddenly upon us. This fresh media moniker describes pro-democracy protests in Tunisia, Algeria, and Egypt, where President Mubarak seems likely to resign and in Libya where Qaddafi could certainly follow. As more and more normally powerless citizens in the Middle East get connected over the internet, this may likely lead to the toppling of other leaders and governments throughout the region. Given the choice, who *wouldn't* prefer to vote for their country's leader in a democratic election rather than to salute the new military boss or mullah selected by the current dictator?
>
> If this Islamic insurgency continues to spread, Wikileaks' disclosures may help end one of America's longest wars, in Afghanistan, and help spur a worldwide free speech movement online. America needs rehab to cure its dependence on war as

much as it needs to protect the secrecy of its national defense. However, at what point does the democratic insurgency just become another form of mob rule? . . .

"Archie, we have to leave *now!*" Lora stood in the doorway, imploring him this time, fearing they would be late for the opening of *Bananafish Blackjack.*

"Relax, sweetheart." Archie shut down the computer, stood up and walked over to embrace her. "It's gonna go fine." While appearing a bit stressed, Lora looked delicious in a lavender mini dress accentuating her dark legs. Archie had long ago succumbed to Lora's dark round Mediterranean eyes and luminescent smile seductively working in tandem. He gently brushed aside her chestnut hair and kissed her perfumed neck, languorously, as he knew Lora simply wanted a little tenderness and support in the moment.

That's the way it was with them, no baloney, and no prisoners. Ever since they'd struck up a conversation in the popcorn line at a benefit screening of *Good Will Hunting*, and Lora wrote her number on a napkin. Their burgeoning mutual attraction quickly ran on all cylinders, organically, reaching deeper emotional levels as well.

One afternoon they'd stumbled upon a live-work commercial loft near Jackson Square and moved into the upstairs apartment together within the first hundred days, while Lora transformed the ground floor into *K*raftworks, a semi-repertory theater and sometime event space. Lora swore to him she had envisioned that logo long before the couple met and not because of any similarity to Archie's last name! Being lovers, best friends, and co-creators in mutual servitude, they'd married three years later and thereafter acquired their "cozy house on the hill"—so described by a local society columnist who often attended their seasonal soirees.

"Did you feed Swami?" Lora asked again, this time as Archie was backing out of the garage.

Archie couldn't help thinking that if she'd bothered to check the elaborate set-up in the corner, Lora would've noticed the tabby's time-release food dispenser was full, alongside the continuously recycling waterfall/drinking fountain and the self-cleaning, domed litter box, all of which, technically, would allow them a week out of town without running afoul of the Animal Care and Control police.

"Yes, dear," Archie repeated, uttering the one phrase he'd probably used most often during their relationship. He wasn't complaining, just deferring to his internal guide for selecting the battles in which to engage. He had more pressing priorities at hand than giving Lora grief for being a little manic over *Bananafish Blackjack*, which was opening in an hour-and-a-half to meager buzz and few advance ticket sales.

Krafter was awaiting a call from District Attorney, Cameron Wheatley. She'd personally taken over Radon Jaalaba's prosecution after Krafter had persuaded Radon to surrender to the authorities late on Christmas Night and the Honorable Raymond Chew, who also happened to be a Worriers fan, had granted bail on the State's hastily drawn felony-murder complaint the next morning with many conditions. In addition to posting the deed to his condo, Radon had been fitted for an ankle bracelet and allowed to remain in a private treatment facility, one that Krafter had scrambled to pre-arrange for him.

In response to Radon's frantic call during the game, Archie had directed him to meet at *Kraftworks*; Krafter had relocated his practice to the theater's back offices the last time he and Bryan had gone their separate ways over Radon's proper "handling," a word Archie hated and Bryan believed in. On the ride over, Krafter had tracked down an expert psychologist from a prior case to recommend a residential sanatorium that would admit Radon under the circumstances. Krafter had phoned

Cameron Wheatley's office and left a voice message offering to surrender Radon, accompanied by the Executive Director of the facility vouching for him. Wheatley had ignored Archie's request, but it had helped convince Judge Chew at the detention hearing.

Having slipped Radon into voluntary treatment at the same time he was being criminally charged, Krafter also counseled him to remain silent about what had occurred inside Alonzo Shenkman's apartment. Krafter was hoping to forestall the Worriers from legally terminating Radon's contract, relying on a clause in the soon-to-be-expiring NBA Players Union Agreement that permitted the players "one free bite" at substance-abuse treatment before they could be dismissed for positive drug samples. Considering that Radon Jaalaba was presumed innocent until proven guilty in court, the mere filing of felony charges without an incriminating statement from Radon might not provide sufficient legal cause for the team owners to dump his multi-million-dollar pact, especially if he successfully completed rehab.

Nevertheless, reality had arrived during the first week of Radon's in-patient residence at Brookhaven in the Napa Valley, when Cameron Wheatley's investigators served a Grand Jury subpoena ordering Jaalaba to explain under oath how Russell Marchetti *and* SFPD Officer Gino Trower had *both died* during an attempted *armed robbery* while Radon was present.

Consequently, Radon was about to be indicted on two counts of first-degree felony-murder: for the death of Russell Marchetti *and* the death of Patrolman Trower, who had actually chased down and shot Russell moments earlier. One relevant excerpt from the lead homicide detectives' report that was attached to Radon's Grand Jury subpoena stated:

> ". . . uniformed responding officers (ROs) Trower and Yancy, dispatched to a home invasion in progress, had fanned out to

surround the property; RO Trower proceeded to the front of the building and after knocking loudly and announcing his office, RO Trower entered Alonzo "Lonnie" Shenkman's unlocked ground floor apartment. RO Yancy had at the same time proceeded around the building to the rear yard. Within minutes of taking up a position, RO Yancy heard two shots fired and glass breaking in the ground floor patio. RO Yancy observed a light-skinned African American male exiting the patio in his direction; he yelled at the suspect to stop and discharged his weapon defensively after the suspect continued running toward him, missing the suspect and inadvertently striking RO Trower who was standing inside the dining room."

Officer Yancy had further recalled to investigators that the fleeing perpetrator: "looked a lot like the ballplayer on the `Camo Commanders' sneakers commercial," referring to Radon's signature, camouflage-style Pumas plastered all over the world. In the confusion, Yancy did not learn that the shot he fired at Radon had accidentally hit his own partner in the abdomen until Gino Trower was lying on the stretcher, about to be placed in the ambulance, conscious, but destined to die thirty-six hours later from a nasty bacterial infection caused by the bullet wound to his gut.

Officer Trower had managed to tell investigators at the scene that he had confronted Russell Marchetti brandishing a semi-automatic pistol in his right hand and immediately ordered him to drop it. Marchetti took off running down the hallway and Trower had pursued him, firing "when Marchetti turned back in my direction with the weapon in his hand."

But as far as Radon was concerned, the most incredible part of this nightmare had come from Alonzo Shenkman's recorded statement to homicide detectives that evening at central station, the lowlights of which Radon had vehemently denied to Krafter. For Shenkman claimed that Russell Marchetti had bullied his way into the apartment under the pretense of purchasing medical marijuana and they'd argued over the price and quality of the "Purple Kush." The volume and tone of their disagreement had accelerated until, according to the transcript of Shenkman's statement:

> "Russell's tall beefy friend in dark shades suddenly showed up—and I didn't know him—so I told them both to get out. But Marchetti pulls out a gun and grabs my entire stock of flowers off the dining room table. Then he threatened to shoot me if I tried to stop them." (SFPD later confirmed Shenkman was affiliated with a licensed medical cannabis dispensary at a commercial location certified under California HSC 11362.5.)"

"The Felony-Murder Rule goes back to Twelfth Century England," Krafter had first advised Radon in the holding cell at the station. By then, they had learned Officer Trower had also been shot and was in surgery. It was midnight, after Radon had been fingerprinted, processed, and they awaited a DA to approve the felony charges.

"Thirty-two states and England abolished the rule in the Seventies," Archie went on, explaining that Jaalaba could be criminally responsible under this archaic law of transferred intent, still being enforced in California. "Unfortunately, during the commission of a serious felony—for example, the armed robbery of five pounds of marijuana—when one of the robbers is killed by a cop while trying to escape, the robber's unarmed accomplice can be found guilty of his co-felon's murder. What's worse; if Officer Trower also happens to die in the hospital, the unarmed accomplice—that's you—can be found guilty of Trower's murder too, even though officer Yancy's bullet killed him."

"Are you shittin' me?" Radon had uttered in disbelief. "Nobody said *anything about the blow?*"

"Wait . . . What? . . . The police found a Hefty bag in the hallway containing multiple jars of sealed marijuana, in the spot where Marchetti had supposedly dropped it running away from Officer Trower. But Shenkman *never* mentioned cocaine in the police report, and none was inventoried during their search of the apartment."

"What about his girlfriend, Tanya? She must've told them I came in after she called 911."

"Ms. Radishoff's cell phone was recovered in the community gardens two blocks from Shenkman's apartment. She hasn't been located."

"So that dude is lying about the coke to save himself?"

"If you say so."

"They don't know why Russell brought me there." Radon had suddenly understood Krafter's advice not to say anything when he'd surrendered. "So, if I keep silent and the judge lets me go to rehab, maybe they won't be able to throw me off the team?"

That's when Radon Jaalaba had decided to make certain his mother would *never* see him in this condition. Radon refused to let down the only person who'd given up everything for him. He would leave the team for as long as it took to make this right. With no more boosts, no more pills or alcohol, and an electronic chain around his ankle, cold turkey was *nothing* if his blessed mother could be proud again. He was not like his father. *Inshallah.*

By the time Radon had received his Grand Jury subpoena he expected to be indicted. News outlets from around the world clamored for details after local broadcasts of his arrest had contained scant information about his earlier presence at the scene. The Worriers' management had declined comment on all the media speculation, vaguely deferring to the legal process, while failing to demonstrate any sign of support for Radon.

Presently, though, Archie Krafter's plan to avoid Radon's firing seemed to be working. Radon had dutifully resided within the secure and serene confines of Brookhaven for the past thirty-one consecutive days, and counting, not without pain and suffering, denial, bargaining and depression, all the while tethered to his tracking device.

While Radon was cleared to go home as soon as the judge signed off, Krafter feared that Radon would be stalked by the media whether or not he agreed to testify at his upcoming Grand Jury appearance. Was it better for Radon to admit he was a recovering addict who happened to be at the wrong place at the wrong time? Rather than risk being found guilty of murder for condoning Alonzo Shenkman's robbery gone-wild scenario by relying on his right not to testify?

Something was missing from the equation, leaving Archie wondering what Radon wasn't willing to disclose, as he drove Lora and him toward their parking space behind the theater. For at the very least, one juror would have to believe without explanation that Radon did not knowingly aid and abet Marchetti's armed robbery and then leap over his best friend's body to escape from the police.

Under the scrutiny of his doctors, therapists and counselors, Radon was doing well at clean and sober. He'd been itching to leave the facility for days. Krafter wasn't convinced Radon really understood that he could end up with fifteen years to life if he went to trial relying on the Fifth Amendment. Unless Radon explained his conduct, Archie thought it might be too late. But as long as Archie was on the subject of truthful introspection, he felt quite anxious over the prospect of conducting his first jury trial in four years.

Lately, he was living the high life with Lora, collaborating on creative projects and writing his *Naked Lawyer* blog, all because Krafter had managed to distill his law practice down to advising small businesses, nonprofits and helping his neighborhood artist friends with their legal problems. Now he'd been thrust back into the pit and couldn't help wondering how sharp he'd be.

"Nobody ever went to jail because their play sucks, right?" Archie mused out loud to Lora, trying to cheer her up, as they approached the tiny vestibule in front of *K*raftworks, its lighted marquee proclaiming: OPENING TONITE! *Bananafish Blackjack.*

Chapter Five

The Rapini King

"You can turn off the car, anytime," Lora said, piercing the fog enveloping Krafter's brain. She had been patiently waiting in the passenger seat, parked in their space behind the theater, while Archie silently grappled with the recent turn of events rudely intruding on his perfectly ordered life. "I know you're thinking about Radon's case," Lora continued. "Right now, you have to go inside and help me get through this opening. I can't believe my brother would bring our father here."

"Let's hope they aren't the only ones in the audience."

Entering through the garage, they avoided the lobby and went directly to Lora's office. Jill Banitch, Lora's theater manager for six years, in addition to being their personal assistant and Krafter's legal secretary for the last three, was on Krafter's line with a reporter asking whether Radon was going to appear before the Grand Jury.

"Not now, Jill," Krafter said in his most humble tone, gently gesturing with a finger slash across his throat, as Lora hurried to the curtained window built into the wall at the rear of the theater, allowing her to keep an eye on the house.

"Andrea's in the lobby with your father," Jill offered, having doted over Lora and Archie long enough to know practically everything about them.

Just a week behind forty, Jillian Banitch had big blue eyes and high cheekbones, accenting her slender, severely styled frame. Jill knew QuickBooks, Photoshop and In Design; she filed court documents and wrote a decent letter. Yet, Jill's shoulders were stooped, and her face usually displayed some measure of her chronic insecurity. Although she'd earned a degree in child and family counseling, lately Jill's been leaning toward therapy, having recently suffered a duo of disastrous romantic disentanglements. But when she got right down to it, working at *K*raftworks from nine to five-thirty, sometimes until the theater closed, managing the books, the website, the schedules, and publicity, not to mention Archie's law practice, she had nothing left for her own life. By the time she retreated upstairs to the biggest benefit of the job, her well-appointed loft apartment belonging to Lora and Archie before they'd acquired their house, all Jill could think about was making some brown rice, broccoli, and tofu, and watching the latest episodes of "Dexter" and "Parenthood" on cable.

"Where's Dominic?" Lora asked. Despite her younger brother's declared determination not to disappoint his current darling, Andrea Steiner, especially on the playwright's big opening night, his track record had left Lora justifiably suspicious. That Dominic had also failed to mention he'd invited their father was particularly insensitive, while par for the course.

"Is that a trick question?" Jill replied, a bit snarkily. "Mr. Sal came in the office eight minutes ago and Andrea took him to get some coffee four minutes later."

"Well played, Jill," Archie piped in. "Lora, let's go find your father. Maybe Dominic's here too."

Archie did not really know whether his father-in-law, Salvatore Dellacozzi, by then eighty-five years old and stroke-impaired, was a retired member of the West Coast Mafia. Archie had heard the legion of stories and learned many facts about Sal's colorful relatives spanning generations in California back to the late 1880's.

The Dellacozzi family had planted and acquired vineyards in Sonoma and Monterey Counties, farms in Castroville and Salinas, real estate in San Francisco, not to mention a piece of the Roman Catholic dioceses. Sal's father, Vincent Dellacozzi, allegedly ran whiskey down from Canada into the Monterey Peninsula during Prohibition. Vince's parents had emigrated from Calabria just before the turn of the Twentieth Century and landed in New York's Lower East Side. There Vincent happened to grow up on the block next to Charles "Lucky" Luciano, who went on to form the original nationwide syndicate of organized crime called "The Commission."

By 1931, Vince was married to Lora's grandmother, Sophia, and Sal was going on six years old. Temperance had exacerbated "The Great Depression" while Luciano had just orchestrated the killing of Sal Maranzano, consolidating the American Mafia's power into the "Five Families of New York." Fortunately, Vince earlier moved his new family out to California so he could work for his Calabrian uncles' rapidly expanding farm operations. His connection to Luciano had helped Vince rise to a West Coast underboss. Especially after Vince returned to the Catskills, New York, for one of the early Commission meetings near Lake Louise Marie (named for Al Capone's daughter), involving Luciano, Meyer Lansky, and Benjamin Siegel, who reportedly went nuts for Vince's turnip greens. Italians originally named it "Rapini."

Out of the array of California vegetables that Vince had brought in tribute from their flourishing Dellacozzi Farms, "Bugsy" Siegel had sworn that he'd never before tasted anything like these greens; what Americans would soon call "broccoli rabe." He asked Vince to immediately start shipping all they could grow to the Commission's newly formed East Coast Distribution Center in Bayonne, New Jersey. By the time Prohibition had ended, Dellacozzi Farms was distributing nearly as much rapini and other Italian vegetables as the wine and whiskey they could start selling legit.

Consequently, Salvatore Dellacozzi had big cement shoes to fill. Being streetwise in San Francisco before he could legally obtain a driver's license, Sal was apparently wholesaling pilfered stock from the family farms on the Peninsula to the Mission Street produce markets. Despite rarely attending classes, he'd been allowed to graduate from Catholic prep school, reinforcing his sense of entitlement. A bony, fearless loudmouth, Sal had tried to enlist in the Air Force after the Allies landed at Normandy. Rejected on account of a droopy eye, he was inducted into the Army instead and wound up working procurement in Berlin at the end of the war. Never having fired a shot, the only action Sal saw had involved liberating the *frauleins*.

Barely twenty-one, Sal had come home a swaggering, paper-thin hero in a pressed khaki suit, with one lone bar hanging over his rather scrawny chest, itching for some real excitement. However, Vince had reason not to regard his son too highly after catching him skimming from the Oakland warehouse, and Salvatore refused to apologize. Instead, he'd begun spending more time at the racetracks, in the pool halls and the girlie clubs springing up around Northern California. Eventually, Vince had been compelled to test his son's filial loyalty by ordering him to shut down a roadhouse brothel and gambling joint on the outskirts of Sacramento. Knowing the place was frequented by statehouse politicians, Vince was forced to intercede after the "Oriental" owners had defied his family's territorial rights to whorehouse concessions and gambling protection.

Following what must have passed for soul searching, Sal had decided to fulfill his father's command and dispatched the "Filmore Gang" to solve the problem. In fact, they'd done such a fine job taking over the operation that Speaker Roger Collingsforth of the State Assembly, a regular roadhouse patron, had openly remarked: "The new music is great, and the colored girls are much more fun."

After all, though, the sudden disappearance of a popular immigrant owner along with his reputed dominatrix wife had to be investigated. Luckily for Sal, Korea had just imploded. Before the local police could finger Sal's two button men, he had managed to re-up as a non-com US Army officer and got stationed on the American base in Manila. At the tender age of twenty-six, Sergeant Salvatore Dellacozzi had stepped onto a low rung in the ladder of command. Based on his supply experience in Germany, he'd been made a supervisor in the largest military procurement center in Southeast Asia, not unlike a well-oiled, super-sized Amazon warehouse of yesteryear. Sal's connections had always delivered, and his methods were tolerated until the war ended in '53. He came home a two-time paper hero, with another thin row of braids on his still scrawny chest, still never having fired a shot.

One of the Filmore assassins had agreed to take the heat for the Sacramento roadhouse couple, confessing that he killed them in a sex-fueled rage when one of their regular kinky triads had gone awry. Having pleaded guilty to manslaughter in exchange for a paltry three-year sentence, he was paroled on good behavior in time to meet Sal at the airport, returning from active duty, and drive him to his parents' house.

Sophia Dellacozzi (nee Trapani) had greeted her son warmly, while wisely wary of him. For Sophia had essentially suffered in silence since Sal was only a year old. When Vincent abruptly informed her they were leaving her family's home on Sullivan Street in Lower Manhattan, moving way out to Carmel Valley, California, in *ten days,* to live on a farm settled by Vincent's great uncles from Calabria, Sophia had followed her husband, and she'd pampered their only son, praying against all hope that Salvatore would not develop into a self-involved *Mafiosi* like his father. This was Sophia's lot, however, having defied her own father by marrying a non-Sicilian.

Vince, on the other hand, had positively glowed at the sight of Sergeant Dellacozzi marching home, droopy eye and all, having finally received his son into the family business with respect. For Sal had moved more munitions, mufflers, and meat in Manila, monthly, than his family farms had shipped in a year. As Dellacozzi Wine and Spirits had expanded production through national distribution channels, Sal had easily slipped into a venerated role beside his father. Sal had also begun slipping it into the beautiful young women he was able to convince with his money and not so subtle charm. Until he'd met Lora and Dominic's mother, Olivia Newcomb, on Thanksgiving Day.

By all accounts, Olivia had class. Born in Ohio, the child of an Episcopalian mother with ties to "the Colonies" and her father, a Cuyahoga Bank and Trust executive, she'd graduated from a Massachusetts women's college where she performed in the theater club and often sung in the church choir. On her drama teacher's recommendation, Olivia had successfully auditioned for the road company of *Damn Yankees* and happened to meet Salvatore while the Marines Memorial Theater was dark for the Holiday.

She had wandered over to Washington Square Park, having once seen photographs of Marilyn Monroe and Joe DiMaggio visiting St Peter and Paul's church on their wedding day, and Olivia heard musicians playing outside the nearby Italian Athletic Club. Sal had happened to be volunteering at the annual Veterans turkey feed, spooning potatoes au gratin that he couldn't help bragging about, in addition to all the food he'd donated every year since his first hitch during WWII. He had spotted Olivia watching the tarantella in front of the bandstand and struck up a conversation. Soon he was smitten, determined to possess her, especially after she'd coolly informed him "traveling in the musical chorus doesn't make me an exotic dancer."

Yet, Sal had eventually worn Olivia down with flowers, high falutin promises and assorted gems of increasing value, and despite the whispers and looks whenever they were out together—she was four inches taller—it had been a timely American story of beauty and the powerfully rich beast. They'd married within a year, after Olivia became pregnant. Sadly, their first born, Anthony, had died from a congenitally deformed heart before his first birthday. They had waited eight years, through two miscarriages, to have Lora, then another six and a half for Dominic.

As it happened, Lora had found the only joy she'd known with her mother during those early years. She remembered most the private times in Olivia's bedroom suite, sitting on the velvet settee alongside her mother's opulent dressing table before being sent off to bed. Lora had listened attentively to her mother's stories about the theater, feeling her smile radiate over Lora like a warm furry blanket. Dazzling in her silk dressing gowns and smelling of Halston, Olivia brushed out her own thick, shiny, black hair before the oval mirror while reciting to Lora lines from plays she'd performed on stage, promising unicorns and rainbows. Then her mother suddenly went into the hospital to prematurely deliver Dominic and departed in a hearse bound for the Perino Brothers Mortuary.

Salvatore had trouble dealing with deaths over which he had no control. Before long he came to blame little Dominic, rarely speaking to him until he was four, openly resenting him thereafter, and thus helping to explain Lora's role looking after her sibling as they grew up. Between the nannies, the cooks, and crazy Aunt Rose—her mother's dotty older sister had been dispatched from Long Island to help Sal with both children—Lora's family experience became transactional, without much parental love or guidance. She still missed her mother terribly. Back then, though, she rarely missed her mostly absent father, whose reputed underworld notoriety she had harshly discovered not long after her mother's passing. For grandfather Vince had suddenly croaked three months later from choking on a sweet and sour pork rib in Chinatown and one of the nuns at school had left the newspaper obituary for Lora to find. While detailing her grandfather's history with organized crime, the article had also mentioned her father's anointment as the new "Rapini King."

Archie couldn't help marveling at how "normal" Lora turned out. Aside from her inclination to micro-manage and the occasional insecurity about her musical artistry, Lora's principal compulsion was to overstock the house with paper goods, particularly toilet paper, which she pilfered from hotels instead of towels. Make no mistake, Archie knew he was a lucky man. Lora was principled, kind, and whip smart. She'd inherited her mother's legs and tiger-striped eyes, along with none of her father's malice. Archie had convinced himself, however naively, that Sal must've maintained a speck of empathy toward Lora; despite knowing how little she thought of him.

In Lora's defense, she had pretended to be an orphan from the age of ten. Sal had been unwilling to face her questions, and then her accusations, so she'd begun avoiding him. In turn, her father had rarely sought her out, and the discipline of isolation kept Lora far ahead in music, poetry, and history. At seventeen, she'd put her last semester on hold and escaped to Italy and Greece for fourteen months. She had returned to the city, found a studio apartment and a waitressing job while obtaining her equivalency degree and enrolling in a performing arts college.

Whilst Olivia's will had provided Lora and Dominic with inheritances, Sal had remained trustee of their mother's estate, in charge of the amount they received until each of them reached age thirty-five. Lora had taken out student loans rather than ask her father for the money and, upon earning her MFA, she'd sent Sal her sheepskin and a note thanking him for inspiring her to accomplish it without his help. Sal must've carefully considered this slam, for he proudly hung her diploma in his den, and Lora had since managed to remain beyond his influence.

Having landed a job at the downtown city cultural center, Lora had eventually been hired as the assistant manager of the theater arts complex. Every night she came home from work and played her almost new Kimball upright piano, squeezed into the long narrow hallway of her apartment, acquired for the cost of moving it. In due course, she had avoided Sal long enough not to feel guilty over acknowledging his occasional handwritten notes accompanied by unsolicited gifts. Eventually, she had learned to accept her predicament, the best she could, as an accident of birth over which she had no power.

Lora had confided her lineage to Archie soon after they'd met. Despite his pestering, not until they'd moved in together did she reluctantly agree to introduce Archie to her father at Sal's favorite North Beach restaurant. Archie had acquitted himself graciously, answering Sal's questions about his law practice, and Sal had thereafter sought Krafter's advice in private over macchiato at the same restaurant. However, Archie had delicately turned down Sal's generous offer to retain him, citing his writing aspirations at the time and, ironically, his devotion to Lora. Sal had never asked again.

Lora and Archie had married in a Lake Tahoe roadside chapel, having eloped to avoid a celebration involving her father. When she had reached thirty-five and the time came to request her trust accounting from Sal, Lora penned a polite note to her father inquiring about distribution of the funds due her. Having grown dismayed by his failure to respond, rather than hire some estate law firm to pry open a can of spaghetti, she had asked Krafter to draft a legal letter respectfully requesting that Sal comply with her mother's wishes, while delicately explaining her rights. Following five nail-biting days, incredibly, Sal had sent a messenger with an envelope containing a list of trust assets worth way more than enough to pay for their house, including a huge check made to the order of: "Archie Krafter and wife." The accompanying handwritten note to Lora simply read: "I'm glad you got a smart husband who can take care of you from now on."

Perhaps what followed was karma, as Sal had suffered a stroke exactly two years before the opening night of *Bananafish Blackjack*. He had been stricken, not smote, as biblically warranted, while Dominic was traveling in the Loire Valley, ostensibly studying its enology. Yet, unbeknownst to Lora and Archie at the time, and being none of their concern, "Dom" had also been looking after the family's export business, including offshore distribution operations in Africa. As a result, Lora had been summoned to the hospital, where she was shocked, but not too moved, upon seeing her father reduced to a state of mental and physical drooling. Sal's left side had been paralyzed and who knew how much of his brain was impaired at the time.

Mostly by default, Lora and Archie had been sucked into visiting her father. But their compassionate mistake had compounded one day after Lora, frustrated with the entire situation, had strongly advised Sal to stop feeling sorry for himself, having declared: "Do the friggin physical therapy, already!"

As if Satan himself had been listening, following the next year and a half of rigorous rehabilitation, Sal had managed to resume going out on his own, to light his cigar with one good arm, and he'd come to believe that Lora was his angel of salvation. Presently, he limped along, dragging his left leg, a drooping shoulder to go with his droopy eye. While prone to emotional outbursts, Salvatore Dellacozzi's mind remained clear and strong; still a force of nature so long as he could sign his name and wipe his own ass.

"Hello, Dad," Lora said, while she and Archie approached Sal standing with Andrea Steiner in the carpeted lobby, among a thin bunch of attendees, fifteen minutes before curtain.

"Hello, Booful," Sal crowed, his upper lip quivering, his mouth forming a crooked half-smile. "When's . . . your . . . brofa coming?"

"Dominic's not coming," Andrea Steiner answered instead, repressing her well-earned wave of panic. Greeting Lora and Archie warmly, Andrea was relieved to relinquish responsibility for entertaining Sal, who'd arrived alone. The playwright could finally focus on the sound and, yes, the fury of her characters about to be brought to life for the next ninety-seven minutes, despite just forty-one folks in the audience. Indeed, Andrea held out hope that the guy in the tortoise shell glasses, waiting at the counter for a bottle of fizzy water, really was theater critic Jonathan Herwitz.

Fuchsia streaks snaked through Andrea Steiner's coal black, shoulder-length hair. The tramp-stamped millennial from Valley Stream, Long Island had written *Bananafish Blackjack* in just five weeks. Not long after her permanent break-up with a handsome geek programmer and card-counting gambling addict named Gabe, he'd lost all his money at the crap table and ended up holding her hostage inside their fantasy hotel room in Las Vegas.

Gabe had eventually committed suicide with a little help from the Clark County SWAT team—thus giving away the surprise ending of *Bananafish Blackjack*. And while probably suffering from PTSD, Andrea had descended upon the Mission District and temporarily crashed with a friend she hadn't seen since college, rather than go back to New York and her part-time editing gig at *Taste This* magazine. Instead, she'd found her playwright's voice inside a cafe with a hotspot on

Valencia Street. Having also found an ad on Craigslist for sharing a nearby apartment, she'd shipped her stuff from Brooklyn, and that's where Andrea's has remained for the last two-and-a-half years.

Andrea and Dominic met in a Dogpatch karaoke bar. Having traded Jell-O shots over the last two verses of "Rocky Raccoon," Dominic had suggested getting together another time at a quieter place. Andrea had *Googled* him and, despite his mundane corporate credentials as "Vice President of Food Services," couldn't help finding him soft-spoken and sexy, like a younger Adrien Brody. During their second dinner out together, Andrea had disclosed she'd written a three-character play about her ex-boyfriend's meltdown in Las Vegas. Dominic had raced back to Andrea's apartment, read the first ten pages, and promised her that his sister would produce it.

After hanging out together nearly ten months, Andrea had learned that Dominic often did impulsive things. He had disappeared from time to time and was probably into shit that Andrea did not want to know about. As it happened, Andrea wasn't too troubled by his last-minute text that two dozen roses were on their way to the theater instead of him. Andrea also knew how much Dominic disliked his father. Nonetheless, as soon as the house lights went down, Andrea slumped in her seat on the aisle, next to Archie, with Lora beside him, as Sal fidgeted on the other side of his daughter in the otherwise empty row.

The stage lights went up, illuminating a garishly decorated Las Vegas hotel suite that featured a heart-shaped revolving bed, on which the clearly pubescent, curly-haired and scantily clad SHARON LIPSCHMERTZ was cheerily chucking copious stacks of currency into the air.

Upstage right, the salt-and-pepper-haired WOODY POLARSKI was sitting in a sunken Roman bath, brandishing a revolver in one hand and a TV remote in the other. Andrea's heart sank. This was simply too much to comprehend—especially at forty dollars a ticket. The adrenaline surge of experiencing her wildest fantasy come true was finally giving way to being called to account for the quality of her work. What Andrea had penned as a reflexive act, a leaky, cathartic lark, really, was about to be unleashed on the world and would forever be identified with *her*. How could anyone possibly enjoy this crap? Her tortured silence was suddenly broken by the blaring: *DING-DONG, DING-DONG* sound of the onstage doorbell:

WOODY
I'll kill those fucks if they don't stop ringing
the fuckin' doorbell!

SHARON
You ordered room service.

WOODY
Are you fuckin' kidding me? I ordered room service?

SHARON
Yeah. The Asian pussy? Remember?

WOODY
Well, fuck me if I did. Answer the fuckin' door, already!

SHARON
Honey, my toenails are totally wet, and I got fourteen
kills on the Sling-Box. *Pleeease*?

(DING DONG—DING DONG)

WOODY
All right!! I'll get the fuckin' door.

(WOODY STANDS UP IN THE TUB NAKED AND POINTS HIS PISTOL AT SHARON—CONT)

Don't you fuckin' flip on me. 'Cause, I'll blow you up good, if I find out you fuckin' flipped on me.

Andrea Steiner lamented most of what she had written before the final curtain that evening. "Be careful what you wish for" reverberated in her head a long time thereafter. For it really was Jonathan Herwitz in the tortoise shell glasses, and his review the next day sealed the fate of *Bananafish Blackjack.* Mercifully, two performances later, they put it down.

Chapter Six

Stuff "The Lady"

Over the course of the NBA's grueling regular season, Radon Jaalaba had obsessively studied video of the Los Angeles Lakers' tendencies, all in preparation for this defining moment: The fourth quarter of Game Six, Western Conference Finals against the reigning champion, Lakers, who have the ball following the time out; thirty seconds remain, Worriers down four points, and Radon resolves that Andrew Bynum will post-up for the inbounds pass while Kobe Bryant acts as a decoy.

Ron Artest, who was in the process of changing his name to "Metta World Peace," stands at the mid-court line, out-of-bounds, holding the globe over his head; he's clicking off the options for inbounding the ball within the required five seconds to a teammate in the best scoring position. Between Artest's third and fourth counts, Bynum rushes to the top of the key and Radon slacks-off guarding Kobe, anticipating their predesigned play, and Jaalaba intercepts Artest's pass. He reaches midcourt in the other direction unmolested, his homework rewarded. The rest is "French pastry," a twisting dunk for the capacity crowd in the arena and especially for his mother, who has been on her feet screaming since the opening tip-off . . . Still, the clock is running out for the home team. Twenty-one seconds left, two points down, desperately in need of another big defensive play . . .

"Radon, wake up, please," Elias Dewhauser, MD, PhD said rather monotonously, while tugging on the bushy caterpillar of hair above his upper lip, the only indication he was irked. Dr. Dewhauser had experienced reservations about taking on Mr. Jaalaba when Dr. Joshin had asked him to consult. And yet, soon after the patient's in-residence treatment had begun, they'd hit it off. Radon had been candid about his history of addiction since he was an adolescent latchkey, cigarette-smoking "player" around the Torrance schoolyards.

Clinically speaking, of course, Dewhauser had opined to himself that Radon was a classic case: his foreign national father had departed under a cloud during Radon's most formidable years, and his dominating mother, a former naval officer with a stressful full-time job in government, had essentially left her only child to grow up on his own. Hardly a surprise that Radon was so screwed up.

Dewhauser shifted in his Danish Modern analyst's chair, purchased with a Freudian wink at Dr. Bob Hartley. The wall behind his desk was filled with framed diplomas and certificates attesting to his superior knowledge in matters of mental infirmity, including the neurological pathways affecting behavior. Yet, Dewhauser personally believed Radon was far from over his long-term addiction to opioid painkillers.

Following Radon's seemingly smooth transition out of residential rehab to home monitoring, Dewhauser had not been impressed during their four weekly office sessions since. Despite Radon's professed continuing sobriety (a condition of his bail), he showed early signs of motor impairment in his speech and reaction time, in addition to occasionally nodding off while he reclined on Dr. Dewhauser's thick leather couch.

"So sorry, Doc." Radon had spaced out during the imaginary play-off game taking place in his head. He'd closed his eyes and meditated into a doze-off; the only way he could stop his cranium from exploding over his ongoing suspension without pay imposed just forty-eight hours after the charges had been filed. The moment the news broke, rumors had begun swirling, especially with Radon's continuing refusal to publicly deny or comment. The local media started calling him an "affluent thug", so Perry Dunbar and his cronies had quickly banned Radon from practicing with the team or sitting on the bench during games. Notably, though, once he had been allowed to enter rehab and granted bail with an ankle-monitor, the team had declined to release him from his contract.

After Radon had appeared at his Arraignment and pled not guilty, Krafter whisked him away via the Hall of Justice basement, protecting Radon from fanatical fans and the press sticking microphones in his face pursuing him for more sad news. Unfortunately, the team had not fared well since his absence. Having struggled through two losing streaks, hovering below five hundred, they were slipping off the edge of contending for the playoffs without Radon. When his case had been assigned to the Honorable Judge Deena Norwell, she set his trial for the third week in August, sticking a fork in any glimmer of hope he'd return this season. Radon's anxiety attack in Dr. Dewhauser's office was triggered by the reoccurring pain of this newest development.

"Please *hear me!*" Radon desperately tried to be understood. "Winning is all I concentrate on in my life. I don't spend time worrying about 'masking my feelings,' like you said . . . When LeBron runs over you 'cause you're taking a charge to help your team, those pills soothe a whole lotta pain."

Given this patient's history of extreme physical fitness, Dr. Dewhauser had determined to utilize Radon's controlled routine in residence, while encouraging him to focus on the root causes of addiction and dependence. Radon had responded favorably until he returned home and started attending these office sessions. Dewhauser found him less engaged lately, often agitated, disoriented, and possibly relapsed, despite his denials. He'd ordered a brain scan and an MRI: "to assess the patient's measurable loss of motor function response to opiate analgesics and psychotropic's long term use." Having also reviewed the team doctors' medical records, Dewhauser had discovered more nails in the professional enabling coffin. He asked Radon for confirmation all the same: "How many years has Dr. Leavitt prescribed painkillers for you?"

"He started me on Percocet way back during the playoffs before my first surgery. We switched to Oxy and Vicodin, which was better for my back; it helped me sleep from getting pounded on the court . . . You understand those guys are all way bigger than me? But then he doubled up because he had to register every refill . . . I'm not gonna' lie to you. By the time I had the second surgery and physical therapy, I was also getting whatever I needed on the street. Is Leavitt any more to blame than I am?"

"You were already hooked by then."

"Look, Doc; I took charge of my life on the playground the first time I ever dunked a basketball." Radon was agitated again. "Whatchu all want, anyway? I got a ride to Cal and went to school like a *good boy* before I was Rookie of the Year."

"That's exactly what I meant about masking your feelings."

"Man; my picture is on a billboard in Ginza."

An interminable pause followed while Dewhauser made some notes about mood swings possibly related to sexual identity, and Radon calmed down until, finally, he could no longer stand the silence. "Truth is, I've been between worlds as long as I can remember. My oldest friends either died on the streets or they're living off my celebrity."

"Maybe your talent has allowed you to deflect things from who you really are?"

"The only place I don't have to pretend is on the basketball court. Every time I put on my superhero costume for the fans, I control my destiny."

"So, drugs don't have anything to do with hiding from reality?"

"Popping a pill aint nothing like popping a jumper from deep in the corner, fifteen thousand people screamin' your name. *Nobody*'s gonna take the ball away from me. I always played hurt, and I try to play injured as long as I can . . . It's the game," Radon added. "Three months ago, they were paying me way too much money just to like the pain. Now they're not. That's *my* reality as long as I'm playing."

. . . Nobody messed with Kobe. Being at least an inch-and-a-half shorter, Radon Jaalaba had to be quicker, trickier, more physical, and push beyond himself just to keep up with Kobe Bryant, son of an NBA player, and LA high school dropout, who'd become a two-time Olympic champion and earned his fifth NBA championship ring the previous year. Along with *only* his first league MVP trophy, but that's a different story about a superstar's long road to recovery from a tarnished reputation.

For tonight belonged to Radon. Anticipation and dogged determination provided the edge once more, as Jaalaba claimed the spot he knew Kobe would attack just inside the three-point arc, cutting Bryant off, causing him to kill his dribble and forcing him to give up the basketball. Fortuitously, or by genius, Radon feinted to the inside just when Kobe cocked his right arm to pass, and swiped at the ball, knocking it loose. Radon snatched up the star's dribble and headed back toward the hometown basket, disseminating a bit of in-your-face instruction.

Radon never elevated to the bucket from the free throw line like LeBron, or like Mike before him, leaping in full stride and swooping in for the jam. Instead Jaalaba always took an extra breakaway dribble, just enough time for Kobe to catch him from behind as Radon took off for the rim. Bryant hurtled himself into Jaalaba with a near cross-body block, vainly trying to swat Radon's arm away from the basket, but unable to stop the flight of the ball as it kissed the glass and spun through the net.

Radon didn't see the shot, having tumbled into the padded basket support after Bryant crashed into him, knocking Jaalaba's legs out from underneath him. Radon slowly rose to his feet and walked to the charity stripe, shaking off the throbbing pain in his left shoulder. He had slammed hard into the basket stanchion and the frenzied crowd cheered him on while he stood at the line bouncing the ball. If he completed the three-point play the Worriers would have the lead with fourteen seconds remaining in the game . . .

"Radon, have you considered," Dr. Dewhauser offered, objectively as possible, "that sometimes we self-destruct even as we justify our behavior for some higher purpose? . . . I suppose it's like playing hurt. You accept all that pain; maybe growing to expect it. Drugs often become a reward. Especially when someone feels unworthy of their accomplishments, they tear themselves down."

"Unworthy? . . . Wow! That's . . . You mean I busted ass all these years just to get *here*?"

. . . Jaalaba's concentration slipped for an instant and his free throw bounced off the back of the rim into Bynum's hands. Bynum flipped the rebound to Kobe, and they headed up the court—game tied. Radon bodied up to Bryant's left, forcing him to a right-hand dribble, trying not to foul. Radon's left arm throbbed. Unable to extend it, he decided to stop Kobe from penetrating into the middle, rather than risk a steal attempt. Ten seconds was a lifetime . . .

"You're here, Radon," Dewhauser said, "because you have a second chance to reestablish your life . . . Look, this is going to sound simplistic, mainly, since I accept that your tough guy basketball persona is necessary to compete at the professional level. You know how hard you've had to work to sustain it. But unless you address your personal life . . . equally valuing yourself as a person outside of basketball and work just as hard at being honest with whoever that person really is, I believe you will continue taking drugs."

. . . The instant Radon noticed Kobe slide toward the lane Radon signaled to his teammate, Monta Ellis, that Bryant would ultimately get the ball. Artest delivered the pass to Bynum, who muscled into the high post, his back to the basket, as the clock wound down to eight seconds. Artest cut to the basket, but Ellis drifted toward the baseline corner instead, responding to Radon's sign, just as Kobe popped out to receive Bynum's bounce pass. Ellis snatched the sphere from Kobe's outstretched hands and without pivoting around whipped the ball behind his back toward mid-court, where Radon caught up to it with nothing but daylight all the way to the Worriers' basket. The ecstatic hometown fans, screaming and stomping their feet the whole game, now counted down the clock in unison as Radon sped across the mid-court line toward victory in the lane . . . Three! . . .Two! . . . One!

It was the highest Radon had ever soared. A thundering jam, the sound of snapping net and reverberating backboard coincided with the game-ending buzzer. Radon stood under the basket for a moment, absorbing the wave of delirium resounding throughout the stands, shaking the very foundation of the building, ultimate satisfaction surging through his body. He strode toward his teammates, chest extended, and a broad grin spreading across his face for the first time in months. "I showed them! I showed them all!"

"Radon! . . . Wake up, Honey. You're talking in your sleep."

Marina wiped Radon's forehead with a corner of the grey Egyptian cotton top sheet that was twisted around his sweaty sculpted body. Marina was lying next to him in the platform bed, just her second night at Radon's condo in nearly a month since he'd come home from rehab. Radon was trying his best to win her over, having pulled off the big evening: private dinner in the backroom of a posh restaurant, backstage passes at the "Pink Martini" concert, and a walk along Crissy Field before they were recognized and had to jump into a cab to avoid exposing their location on social media.

Watching Radon settle under the covers and finally close his eyes, Marina wondered how she was ever going to get through this. How precarious everything had suddenly become. Yet, instead of turning to religion for life's deeper meaning, she often drew strength relying on what she called her "spiritual physics." Throughout her nursing career she'd asked for the terminal patients, those not expected to make it out of the hospital. She was able to look at death without much fear. Make no mistake, Marina was happy to be here, yet she also accepted that our present state of existence was simply one manifestation of our eternal consciousness.

Unquestionably, she'd gleaned much of this while growing up listening to her father, a Costa Rican trauma surgeon in South Florida, who possessed a slightly cynical view of the human condition. Yet, Marina remained an optimist. In the five and a half years since Radon had first urged her to establish the Jaalaba Foundation, it had become a nationally recognized non-profit seeking cures for pediatric brain disorders. Based on Radon's name and his sizeable endowment, along with the help and clout of Michelle Garroway, the foundation implements an impressive number of research and development programs at major universities. Consequently, Marina and Radon's business priorities have become intertwined with their personal lives, causing a lot more downs than ups lately.

"It's complicated" was the best rationalization Marina Ramirez could muster to the outside world about Radon's situation. Not to mention, the foundation's very existence was threatened by the loss of Radon's good name. Being pissed off at him was no help. Or feeling guilty for enabling him all these years. Marina could no longer afford to turn away. Unless Radon remained clean and sober, and Archie Krafter managed to keep him out of jail, funding will dry up and they'll never be able to save another kid. She had to continue supporting Radon as long as he didn't give in.

Chapter Seven

Recapitulation

"You're nuts, Krafter!" Bryan Marten derided him. "Unless Radon explains what he was doing in that apartment, tell me how he won't be convicted?"

"Don't you get it, Bryan? Reasonable doubt already exists in the court of public opinion because Radon hasn't said anything about what happened."

In truth, Krafter had no idea where this was heading. Radon's instructions to Archie had been clear from the get-go: No statements to the police or the prosecutor, and certainly not the press. Radon had specifically made Krafter promise to keep his treatment details secret from everyone in his life. And it *was* simpler for Krafter to say: "No comment" to requests coming in from all over the globe, rather than try explaining how Radon had been the victim of unsavory circumstances that tumbled into unintended consequences.

"Oh, I get it, alright," Bryan snorted out. They were standing at adjacent urinals in the men's room across the hall from Marten's twenty-seventh floor offices on California Street. "You don't think Radon's going to play again, so you've decided to bite the hand that's fed him all these years. But I really want to know what part of your brain came up with the notion to sue an NBA franchise while murder charges are pending?"

"Radon's health is the priority, Bryan."

"Who cares what Dunbar wants, right?" Marten dug in as they washed their hands in adjacent marble sinks along a well-lit mirrored row. "He's just the asshole who made Jaalaba a multi-millionaire."

"Wait until Radon gets here and ask him yourself."

Mike Prey was already seated at the long table in the glass-walled conference room when Krafter and Marten emerged from the restroom and waltzed over. Mike assumed he'd been summoned for an update, having been dispatched to locate Tanya Radishoff, along with the city and state police investigators, not to mention private media dicks and anyone else managing to access confidential SFPD homicide reports.

"Hey Bryan, long time no see," Prey said cheerfully enough.

"Yo, Mike," Bryan responded with a raised fist. "Don't bother getting up."

Mike Prey looked over at Krafter and raised his eyebrows. Mike hadn't thought too highly of Marten since he and Archie had met Bryan fifteen years earlier, scoping out the fried clams at Harry's Bar on a Friday night. After Brian had learned Archie was a newly transplanted Chicago trial lawyer, not yet licensed in California, he'd offered Krafter a glorified paralegal job in his boutique firm. According to Archie, by the time he had approached his first anniversary at Bellicose, Marten & Fang, he'd been underpaid to ghost-write complex legal briefs and silently second chair civil trials alongside the other two partners. As soon as Archie had passed the California bar exam, he realized Bryan was happier having him under his thumb, instead of eventually becoming his partner who'd receive a share of the profits. To the rest of the firm's surprise and disappointment, Krafter had declined their generous offer the next year, and opted to strike out on his own.

Radon Jaalaba hurried off the elevator looking serious and fresh, wearing the Michael Kors suit that *Vanity Fair* gave him last season after sitting for their "Athletes on $ Street" fall fashion edition. Radon knew that things were worse than they appeared. He had received his brain scan results, as if he didn't already have enough to worry about. Dr. Dewhauser had seen some cranial wave disturbance. But presently, seeing Mike Prey sitting in the leather swiveling chair at the head of the conference table really upset him.

"Who told you to visit my *mother?*" Radon brusquely confronted Prey without bothering to greet Bryan or Archie.

"I had to," Mike replied, rising timidly from the chair and backing away, while glancing toward Marten and Krafter for a little support. "Russ Marchetti's sister told me she saw Tanya Radishoff and Russell together before."

"What does my mother have to do with that?" Radon persisted.

"*I* told Mike to ask your mother if Russell ever brought Tanya around," Bryan admitted.

"What the *fuck!*" Radon answered everybody. Then he sank into the chair that Mike Prey had vacated, and he began swiveling to and fro. "I know you're plotting shit against me, Bryan," Radon went on after completely spinning around twice in the chair. "You been talking to Nellins behind my back, and now you sent this freak to harass my mother. You haven't believed me ever since I apologized for missing the Miami flight."

"I never discussed your treatment with management," Bryan insisted. "You're my most important client, Radon, you know that. I'd like to think we've become friends over the years."

"Maybe we should bring this down a little," Krafter interceded. "Mike, why don't you leave us to sort this out . . . I'll call you."

Mike Prey couldn't wait to exit the conference room, leaving Jaalaba and Krafter both swiveling in their chairs at one end of the table, while Bryan Marten stood defensively between them.

"Radon, you're a worldwide brand," Bryan went on, grabbing Radon's chair with both hands, stopping the swiveling. "You and me. We're tied in with too many people and their jobs; too many sponsors not to protect them."

"You, too, Krafter?"

"I didn't know about snooping on your family, Radon." Archie was contrite. "Bryan believes you should testify about what happened. He thinks the team will stand behind you."

"Sounds like you don't agree."

"We're the only ones who know your side of this," Krafter replied. "Your medical records and rehab reports are sealed by the Players' Union agreement with the NBA. The world thinks you participated in a marijuana deal gone sour. If you come forward, it's your word against Alonzo Shenkman's."

"Wait a minute," Bryan jumped in. "Shenkman has every reason to lie about selling cocaine. Whose gonna believe him if Radon admits that's what they came for?"

"You're exactly right, Bryan." Krafter then asked Radon directly, already knowing what his response will be, "Are you willing to say that's why you went to his apartment?"

"I'm saying this to both of you," Radon reacted, beyond perturbed. "That's not the only thing I'd have to admit, so please avoid any further misunderstanding of my position. Assert my *fucking Fifth Amendment right to remain silent*, and nothing can be used against me!"

Krafter eventually broke the long awkward silence. "I hate to change the subject when things are going so well," he said. "But I'm worried that even after you're acquitted you might not be reinstated if the team gets hold of your latest neurology test results."

"Whoa . . . Krafter. You joining the doubters, too?"

"A progressive brain condition affecting your performance could cause the underwriters to drop your insurance. Then the team could pull the plug on your contract."

"What condition?" Radon snarled back. "Dewhauser only said there was a minor change in my brain waves. Maybe, I might have a problem *someday*. You make it sound like I better retire or I'm gonna stroke out."

"C'mon, Radon," Bryan finally joined in, not so much in defense of Krafter, as Marten knew the billion-dollar career train he was conducting had just come off the rails. "Didn't Dr. Dewhauser explain the results of your map imaging?"

"My what?"

"The q-E-EG tests show measurable damage to several areas in the motor cortex of your brain."

"How's that measured, Bryan?" Radon testily replied. "One spoonful at a time?"

"Nobody knows for sure how much damage." Bryan tried to calm him. "You've been clean nearly four months, right? . . . Basically, Dewhauser believes it's scarring, caused by prolonged use of the painkillers, exacerbated by cocaine . . . You'd probably slow down any further damage if you don't do any more."

"That's cold, Bryan. You tell me the truth, Krafter. Am I ever gonna play again?"

"I don't know the truth, Radon. But two hundred and ten million painkillers were dispensed in the US last year. If the team doctor facilitated your addiction to keep you in the line-up all these years, we might be able to force them to live up to your contract. As long as you're acquitted, and you stay sober."

"You don't have any idea how to proceed with this," Bryan mocked him.

"We find an expert neuropharmacologist, preferably retired from the FDA, willing to testify there's a causal connection between Radon's long-term opioid abuse—beginning months before his first knee surgery—and the deteriorating cognitive skills indicated by his brain wave disturbances."

"Good luck with that, Archie," Bryan said. "I'm going to the club."

Krafter walked home through the crowded Chinatown streets wondering if he actually could mount a justiciable case based on the team doctor's malpractice. He became so distracted he mindlessly followed some young couple into a line waiting outside a tiny bakery on narrow Grant Avenue. Archie didn't come out of his trance until he'd shuffled inside, it was his turn, and the woman behind the counter began gesturing animatedly toward him, demanding his order in a Mandarin dialect he couldn't make out. Archie pointed at a row of yellow moon cakes and some chocolate-striped flaky-dough pastries, and he escaped with the beginnings of a gift pack that it never hurt bringing home to the wife.

Especially since Lora had phoned him earlier in the day about an unsettling call she'd received from her brother, hoping to speak with Archie about "some offshore internet business in Africa." Dominic had never asked for legal advice before, but Krafter wasn't shocked that his brother-in-law might be engaged in some shady affair. So Archie also stopped in the Hong Kong Bargain Bazaar, featuring the latest container shipment of household goods and souvenirs, and picked up two $1.99 multi-pronged wire scalp massagers that made your scalp tingle when you placed it on top of your head and pushed it up and down repeatedly, to go along with the surprise dessert.

When Archie finally made it up the hill and approached the arched stone entranceway to their front door, he could hear Lora singing and playing the piano in the parlor. He waited outside, listening, Lora's voice always enchanting him, whether she performed her own songs or standards from the *Ultimate Jazz Fakebook* she kept on the piano.

Lately, Archie has been reminding himself to simply stop and be present in mind and body during moments like this. He'd learned about meditation and awareness from Lora, how the stillness leads to everything. Sounding so corny to him at first, over the years, Archie had since taken up Pilates combined with yoga nearly every day. This exercise has become meditative, too, keeping his body fit, while bringing his most burning issues into perspective, relegating them to Archie and Lora's shared discussion during their afternoon walks along the Embarcadero.

Archie's has solved other people's problems for as long as he can remember. By three and a half, little Arthur had learned to count numbers and read the alphabet from the *Daily Racing Form*. An only child, he'd been left to his own devices since he was twelve, while his parents operated their department store on the other side of town all day and enjoyed going to the harness races at least four nights a week. Being responsible for his own survival had certainly kept Archie ahead of the hustle, likely accounting for his ability to empathize with the most unsavory clients while effortlessly slipping into society. Presently, though, Archie lingered outside their front parlor window, appreciating the moment, having shuttered Radon Jaalaba and Dominic Dellacozzi from his thoughts, leaving him free to revel in the wonder of Lora's music.

Chapter Eight

Revival

"Price On My Head"
Words and Music by Lora D (copyright 2011)

Verse 1
```
D    F#    A
Took A Vacation
D    F#    A
From my desperation
A    C#    E
Got a price on my head
A    C#    E
No one's paying up

AM
You should see me
Db   E    G
My head is turned around   # turn those heads
Db   E    G
And mine is upside down
Db   E    G
Inside out and upside down

D         Bb
Some say it's the way to go
D         Bb
Move through the door
D    F#   A
Leave the excess behind
D         Bb
Some say it's the way to live
D         Bb
Moving through on express time
D    F#   A
Leave it for the next life
Leave it for the next life
```

Verse 2
```
D    F#    A
In the curriculum of
D    F#    A
star and world school
A    C#    E
Then the clouds open up
A    C#    E
And feature the moon

AM
You should see me
Db   E    G
I turn those heads around
Db   E    G
But Mine is upside down
Db   E    G
Inside out and upside down
```

Chorus
```
D    A    F
There's war on TV
D    A    F
Comedy at three
D    A    F
Looking for a mate
D    A    F
Meetings with Heads of State

D    F    Ab   G
It's a  fool's  game
D    F    Ab   G
A man-made enterprise
D    F    Ab   G
Crisp and computerized
D    F    Ab   G
Plug it in and watch it rise

D    F    Ab   G
From zero to infinity
D    F    Ab   G
What's your version of reality
D    F    Ab   G
It's  a     fool's game
```

Verse 3
```
D    F#    A
Wrote another tune
D    F#    A
For my collection
A    C#    E
Seems so meaningless
A    C#    E
When the world is falling down

AM
You should see me
Db   E    G
Your head is turned around
Db   E    G
And Mine is upside down
Db   E    G
Inside out and upside down

D         Bb
Leave it for the next life
D         Bb
Does it really matter?
D    F#   A
Repeat D A F (it's a fools game)
B    G    D    B    G
Don't want to play the game no more
```

Most often Lora sang and composed on the baby grand. She had traded up not long after they'd moved into the house, having relegated her trusty upright piano to the backyard cottage. She usually played and vocalized for an hour or so, nearly every day, practicing her compositions, along with standards and contemporary songs that she'd admired enough to download sheet music and learn. Nevertheless, Lora's music discipline was eclipsed by her obsessive exercise routine. Every morning without fail, in sickness and in health, Lora worked out for an hour in front of the television, or her laptop screen while on the road, mixing in yoga, Zumba, kickboxing, step-aerobics, hip-hop and calisthenics, stretching back over twenty years.

Not just for vanity's sake, Lora's daily devotion to physical exertion helped redirect her hyper-energetic tendencies, as she approached her forty-second-year *sans* replacement hormones. Notably, the mindlessness of exercise often inspired Lora's songwriting. She'd composed "Price On My Head" about the helplessness that often accompanied artists: facing rejection, questioning the purpose of each imperfect work, having to monetize it just to keep on creating in a world demanding activism over imagination.

The song also has another meaning. Lora has recently fueled the notion of performing a musical comedy monologue about growing up in her notorious family. She'd envisioned portraying a plucky young professional—possibly a fitness trainer—making it on her own, with a little help from her underworld connections when things don't go her way. She has yet to seek her husband's input on the evolving libretto. Nevertheless, after Archie came into the parlor, sank into the sofa, and listened to her sing the song, Lora instead reported what her less than genius brother had said on the phone earlier that day.

"I'll try to repeat what Dom told me," Lora gingerly informed him. "The FBI subpoenaed company records at their building in Mauritius.

They showed up with Interpol, and Dominic hopes it's OK if he calls you for advice." Lora pressed on, watching Archie's expression turn dour. "Dominic wants you to—let me make sure I get this right," she read from her notes: 'Quash those Frog motherfuckers on the MPF already being paid to keep the DHS out of our ass.'"

"Humph," was all Archie could muster. "Where's Mauritius again?"

"I think it's off the southeastern coast of Africa—beyond Madagascar."

"What the heck is he doing there?"

"Seriously, Archie? You're asking me?"

"Tell me again why we agreed years ago to stay away from your family?"

"You already know how sorry I am. You certainly have no obligation to call my brother."

"Should I ignore him?"

"Do we really want to go there? I'm sure my father's involved."

"Before Sal's stroke, we didn't have anything to do with Dominic except for your occasional e-mails and holidays. Then he shows up asking you to stage his girlfriend's excrement . . . ."

". . . I get it. Of course, I should've turned him down . . . He was begging. It was pathetic. You're a *mench* Archie. Maybe, you'll hear Dominic out and then you'll turn him down."

"The FBI must believe they're doing something terrible, tracking him all the way to an African island."

"Don't call him back. I'm panko'ing chicken tenders, along with roasted potatoes and black kale. What time do you want to eat?"

"I'll think about calling him back another time."

Archie usually loved these mini moments, retreating to his den, allowing his brain to shift over to the other side. Constantly in search of fresh ways to nurture *The Naked Lawyer,* he tried to work on the penultimate short story in his *Thirteen Bill of Rights Collection*: fictionalized morality tales, one for each amendment, drawn from criminal cases he'd defended in his career. But it wasn't happening for him. Krafter was distracted by the specter of sparring with Cameron Wheatley at their looming settlement conference in the DA's office. Considering that Radon had remained resolute, refusing to reveal squat, Archie reckoned his meeting with Wheatley would likely not go well. He'd have to stonewall her; simply draw her out and reject any plea deal she offered.

With that in mind, five days later, Krafter resignedly walked up the grimy granite front steps of the criminal court building, passed through the metal detector and rode the elevator to the third floor. He strode down the wide, dimly lit hallway to the District Attorney's decorous outer office and announced himself to the receptionist.

Affectionately dubbed "Boss Wheatley" by her staff, Cameron promptly appeared through a door behind the front desk and marched over to him. Appearing seriously statuesque, Cameron sported short, straw-colored hair, southern-baked skin and a killer smile. "A*rr*chie, we have to talk," she said in her transplanted Arkansas drawl, while guiding him along the narrow corridor into a conference room. Two earnest-looking young assistant suits were already seated at an oblong table covered with leftover sandwich wrappings, paper plates, plastic cups, and a neatly laid out row of brown accordion folders.

"Chris and Nial are in the middle of the Vendini murder-for-hire trial." Cameron introduced them with a wave of her right arm, covered in the sage-colored jacket of her tailored pant suit. "I hope you don't mind if they join us?"

"As long as you don't gang up on me," Krafter answered, only half-joking, while he and Cameron sat down in adjacent conference chairs across the table from Chris and Nial.

"Don't worry, A*rr*chie." Cameron was charming him. "My boys are here to listen. Honestly, though, *they* know where the relevant documents are. Lord, I'm responsible for eight thousand felonies right now—plus community outreach just to keep this office viable. Forgive me for including them in our one-on-one."

Cameron's straight bright teeth flashed ahead of her no-nonsense law and order agenda, slyly customized to appease the most tolerant constituents, of which there were many in San Francisco. On the eve of her recent election to a second term as District Attorney, one alternative weekly's endorsement had proclaimed: "Wheatley is smokin' hot with brass balls and a big heart."

Cameron's story had really begun when her schoolteacher mother had left her abusive Baptist preacher father when she was thirteen and moved the two of them to Northern California to teach in a predominantly Muslim elementary school. Cameron thrived on public education and then state college, having sailed through Hastings Law School on a tuition grant, with honors. She'd worked for the City Attorney's civil office enforcing municipal ordinances with compassion for the poor and the disadvantaged until she'd found her calling, so to speak, representing the People of the State of California prosecuting the most pernicious criminals on the streets of San Francisco.

Over the next twelve years, having piled up impressive jury trial victories in a wide range of serious felonies, she'd risen within the ranks to First Assistant District Attorney, while keeping her nose clean and her eyes on the electoral prize. As far as Krafter was concerned she was a formidable adversary; Hell, he'd voted for her twice.

"I'm afraid you're going to be more reasonable about this than my client," Krafter confessed up front.

"That's exactly why I don't want to flim-flam with you." Cameron seemed candid while batting her eyelashes. "I do understand what you're going through. We've researched *everythin'* out there concerning Russell Marchetti and Alonzo Shenkman, for *goodness* sakes. I promise we are closing in on Tanya Radishoff's whereabouts . . . You already know she's an illegal from Croatia on a student visa expired long enough to be embarrassing. She could be anywhere. That doesn't make it easier."

"My client will not be reassured to hear this. He expects her testimony would absolve him."

"Please tell Mr. Jaalaba I am a *huge* Worriers fan. It would pain me deeply to send him to prison . . . We believe he likely didn't intend any harm to his friend, or to Officer Trower, for that matter. But your client set disastrous circumstances in motion when he walked into that apartment. He exacerbated them *exponentially* by running away."

"I'll tell him you're a fan, Ms. Wheatley. By the way, during your research, did you happen to uncover any prior drug transactions involving Alonzo Shenkman and Russell Marchetti?"

"It's Cameron, *please* . . . Y' see, Chris? Didn't I say: Don't underestimate Mr. Krafter? . . . Off the record, Archie. Is that your client's story? Marchetti took him there to buy cocaine? . . . 'Cause if it is, we might work something out that makes this case go away and, frankly, will benefit the entire Bay Area."

"Hold on a minute," Krafter replied. "That's not what I'm suggesting," he replied. "The evidence you have just as likely suggests that Radon was a bystander to whatever went down between Shenkman and Marchetti."

"Ha, Ha! That's marvelous, Mr. Krafter," Chris piped in. He was a hungry young power strip wrapped in a slim-fit charcoal suit, geeky carbonite glasses enhancing his look of predatory glee. "Hmm, let's see," Chris went on, "NBA superstar can't explain his presence during cop killing on Christmas?"

Wheatley shot her underling a silencing glance. "Now A*rr*chie, don't let Chris's foolishness upset you. I wouldn't allow a tiny compliment to go to your head `neither," the District Attorney added, retaking control of the discussion. "Alonzo Shenkman isn't a basketball fan. Between us girls, he told the Grand Jury he didn't recognize Mr. Jaalaba, and Russell Marchetti didn't bother introducing them. Shenkman also swore he was intimidated by your client's size and demeanor during Marchetti's assault and robbery. Mostly, the grand jury panel was swayed by Mr. Shenkman's legal authorization to dispense medical cannabis."

"Why on earth would Radon Jaalaba participate in a marijuana robbery?"

"Why did OJ Simpson strong-arm a bunch of memorabilia hustlers?" Nial spoke up, turning another screw. "We don't need a motive, but drug addiction works just fine."

Cameron quickly stepped in, deciding it was time to close the deal. "Mr. Jaalaba's personal life is not my main concern. We take our witnesses as they come to us in each situation, and Alonzo Shenkman has his share of warts. But Russell Marchetti's loaded weapon and a Hefty bag full of marijuana were recovered in the hall where Officer Trower, bless his soul, first encountered Marchetti."

Well, whaddaya know? In a rush of clarity, Krafter realized that Wheatley probably didn't believe Shenkman's story either. Yet, they were heading to a trial and there was no telling whether Radon would be acquitted even if he decided to testify. As if Cameron Wheatley happened to be tuned into Krafter's brain, she made a generous offer to avoid the upcoming public spectacle.

"If Mr. Jaalaba pleads guilty to attempted possession of a controlled substance and testifies truthfully, we'll consider dismissing the felony-murder charges and not recommend any prison time." She nodded approvingly. "He also must agree to stay clean, of course."

"I'll relay your offer," Krafter replied coolly while, inside, his liver high-fived his pancreas with relief. "We'll see what Radon thinks about pleading guilty to anything," he couldn't help adding.

"That's right proper of you, Mr. Krafter," Cameron Wheatley responded right properly herself, as she got up, preparing to move on to case number eight-thousand and one. "Please tell Mr. Jaalaba, if he rejects our magnanimous offer, we will seek to enforce our subpoena for his treatment records."

"Judge Norwell isn't going to allow the jury to see Radon's confidential medical files."

"You know the doctor-patient privilege is not absolute," she replied. "If those records prove your client was addicted to a controlled substance, I'm sure Judge Norwell will agree that the State's right to evidence in a forcible felony outweighs Mr. Jaalaba's privacy rights—especially when it causes a police officer's death. Now, A*rr*chie, I'm scooting to another appointment. Walk out with me while we finish our discussion."

Cameron slipped her cell phone into her suit jacket and started toward the door with a warm salute at Nial and Chris who beamed back in unison like puppies to their mistress. Krafter followed her along the office corridor and ended up watching the prosecutor's shapely fanny all the way down the back stairs of the Hall of Justice, out into the employee parking lot, where she finally stopped to address him.

"Between you and me, Archie?" Cameron went decidedly off script. "I know you hope Radon takes our offer. Despite what you may think, I am sensitive to your client's mental state. I can't imagine what it's like being a fallen hero to so many kids around the world . . . Here's a tip in case he wants to turn down the deal. Unofficially, I ran into Perry Dunbar at Sam's Grill last week and he seemed more interested in Radon's rehab files than whether he was guilty or innocent."

"I don't suppose Dunbar said anything about Dr. Leavitt's pain management of Radon's knee surgeries?"

"This is way out of my pulpit, Archie. I have no idea what's in your client's medical records. I'm just sayin', you pissed them off by sending Radon to an independent doctor."

"What if they knowingly facilitated his addiction just to keep him in the lineup?"

"Well, that evidence might interest the medical board, not to mention all the 'merch' companies sponsoring his brand. Dunbar was definitely concerned about your client's physical health . . . Who knows? Mr. Jaalaba might even salvage his career if he'd just come clean before it's too late."

Cameron smiled warmly and extended her right hand in a closing gesture. Krafter shook it respectfully and she disappeared into the back of a waiting town car. He left the parking lot and walked up toward Market Street, the afternoon sun still shining in the cerulean San Francisco sky. A faint light also shined at the end of Radon's tunnel, if only he would accept responsibility for what had happened that day. Krafter had to remind himself not to become personally involved. The myriad complications in Radon's personal life were way beyond his reach. How could he possibly know what was really going on in Radon's head?

Nevertheless, Radon had reacted negatively when Archie relayed the DA's offer over the phone on the walk home. Krafter was still reeling two hours later while Lora and he waited to be seated at the *Squawking Parrot* restaurant, the latest darling of sustainable small-plate world cuisine.

"Am I the crazy one here?" Archie was compelled to ask his wife. "I mean, this offer is fair and compassionate," he said, catching Lora up on highlights of the meeting with Ms. Wheatley. While Krafter knew there were ethical challenges to discussing his cases with Lora, they had long ago agreed that Lora was his legal assistant, and if that didn't work, they'd invoke the marital privilege forever more. For the record, no one had yet questioned their indiscretion.

From inside the tiny bar area, they watched the servers circulate among the tables with a variety of exotically sophisticated gut flora on reputedly well-timed dim sum-like carts. It was the last place they wanted to eat that night, but they'd made the reservation six months ago and weren't giving it up.

"You're not crazy, Archie," Lora reassured him once they were seated at the smallish linen covered table. "Radon is hiding from something you can't reach with a rational plan. Whatever makes him dazzle on the court probably drives his self-destruction, too."

"You're right. I can't make what happened go away. He has to be able to live with that. Or not . . . Wow, doesn't this menu seem a little precious? Listen to this, we can have guanciale chawan mushi for an appetizer. Can you believe they're serving guanciale? Wasn't it banned because of swine flu?"

"Wait . . . What's in it?"

"A Japanese egg custard topped with crispy Italian cured pork jowls."

"Jeezus, Archie. What am *I* gonna' eat?"

"Hey, you're the one who wanted the pro-biotic experience, reinvigorating your good intestinal bacteria . . . Brushed not washed, remember?"

"I wanted to come here last December," Lora grumbled as she watched a tattoo-necked waiter pass by, dressed in crisp, earth-toned overalls, wheeling a stainless steel cart neatly packed with square white plates of what eventually turned out to be beef tongue and horseradish-sourdough pancake, crab kimchi with spicy fried cauliflower, and smoked trout parfait with uni slaw. "I guess I'll cleanse with this," Lora acknowledged once the dishes were set before them. "From what you just told me about Radon, my gut also says you're going to try this case to a jury. Maybe we should invite Radon and Marina over for dinner, and ask Michelle to come?"

"Like an intervention? . . . Really? I dunno. That's risky. There's no confidentiality for whatever Radon might say to anyone there who becomes a trial witness . . . Wait a minute, Lora. I see what you're doing. This is a bait and switch. You asked me about Radon's case, so I'll talk with your brother about *his* legal problems, didn't you?"

Lora exposed a guilty grin as the waiter brought their dessert, and Archie stroked his chin in a combination of chagrin and acceptance. For as long as they'd been together, Archie has simply trusted Lora not to hurt him, having had no reason to deny any of her stated wants, needs and desires, while he was reasonably certain his unconditional love has been reciprocated. They were partners. Although Archie thought they would be better served staying far away from involvement in Dominic's legal problems, he simply couldn't say no to her.

Lora poked her dessert fork into a slice of cocoa hazelnut pound cake infused with coconut cream yogurt and mangosteen. "Dominic really wants to see you. He knows you won't take his case, Archie. He respects you and wants your opinion about what to do."

"Dominic said he respects me?" Archie raised his eyebrows, suspiciously.

"How can I refuse my baby brother?"

"*You* aren't refusing him. He wants to see me."

"He's in serious trouble. I hope you meet with him."

"Hmph," Archie said for the second time in a week, swallowing a tiny taste of resentment, as Lora's desire to help her brother hammered away at his better judgment.

Chapter Nine

Preparation H

On the first of July, fifty-two days before Radon Jaalaba's trial was scheduled to begin, the NBA Players Association declined to renew its Collective Bargaining Agreement. In turn, the owners shut the players out of their facilities, resulting in the fourth work stoppage in NBA history. The sides were mostly divided over revenue sharing and the structure of the "salary cap"—the maximum total salary amount each team can pay its active players on the roster. For the duration of the "lock-out," management could not trade, sign, or contact the players' agents. Likewise, the ballplayers couldn't access their team facilities, their trainers or any other staff members.

Surprisingly, though, Radon heard from Krafter that the strike could be good news for him. If he were to be acquitted while the lock-out went on, the owners could face pressure to reinstate him whenever the strike ended, as long as Radon also remained clean and sober. Krafter had challenged him to look inside himself for the right decision, assuring him that he might eventually find some distance from the tragedy of his bad judgment.

Yet, Radon felt more adrift than ever. Having convinced himself, however delusional it seemed, that he needed to be ready for training camp in the fall, his singular goal throughout this ongoing nightmare had been to stay sober and in playing condition until his trial was over. But this owners' lock-out? . . . Now? Since the seventh grade he'd been locked into a rigorous ritual of exercise and lifting, and Radon was physically prepared to weather the interruption however long it lasted.

Nevertheless, he was feeling relentless pressure to come forward and plead guilty. Even his lawyers wanted him to take the deal. Making matters worse, Radon had reason to worry that the insurance underwriters might get their hands on his brain scan results. And who knew when this labor dispute would end? Everything was slipping away from him no matter what he did, and he didn't know how much longer he could keep it together. As far as Radon could see, he was probably never going to play again. And if he was being honest with himself, deep inside, no matter how much he fought it, he was relieved that he finally may not have to hide from who he was any more.

"What are you saying, Radon?" Marina asked incredulously.

Marina Ramirez was shocked to hear him shutting her out. They were watching the ocean-kissed sunset from a window table in their favorite Carmel Highlands restaurant and Marina had not expected this. Radon had asked her to spend the weekend down the coast—he was allowed to travel within the state—for a quiet celebration thanking her for being there and acknowledging six and a half months clean and sober. Now he was suddenly disavowing their commitment to fight through this? "I don't understand," Marina said. "Don't you want me in the courtroom during the trial?"

"Look, Rina. My shrink was right. I need to figure out my personal shit. But I gotta do this on my own."

She had first described her big non-profit idea to him at this very table. Where they'd agreed to launch the Jaalaba Foundation for medical research into childhood diseases, from traumatic brain disorders to pediatric cancer. Marina's vision and determination, mixed with Michelle's unwavering support, and Radon's face on a million-dollar bill, had guided the foundation to plant the roots of its mission.

They'd cajoled USC to dedicate the first of four research labs, where ambitious, philanthropic professors and graduate students donated countless hours experimenting to find cures for afflicted kids. Radon's on-court PSA had gone viral—the one where he lifts up a six-year-old, helmet-clad, cerebral palsy sufferer, wheelchair, and all, and helps her drop a basketball through the hoop, raised awareness not to mention quite a few million dollars. Radon had always trusted and confided in Marina, so she had come to believe they would remain lifelong friends no matter what. It was simply not within her consciousness that Radon would emotionally turn away from her. Here of all places.

"I'm really struggling with this," Marina finally replied. "I'm there for you, Radon. You don't want me taking care of you anymore?"

"I'm not saying that."

Radon reached across the table, took both of her hands in his, tenderly, while Marina's forlorn face made his desperate eyes well up. "We're still partners, right? . . . I gotta go to the bathroom," he added, having spotted over Marina's shoulder a young woman in a short-sleeved tee shirt with a spidery tattoo crawling down her arm exiting one of the side-by-side restroom doors. Radon darted from his chair.

Inside the tiny room, he slid the bolt in place on the lacquered wood door and turned to face himself in the dim light above the sink mirror. "This is all a fraud," he said to the deprecated image staring back. He retrieved from his cashmere sock, wedged inside his tracking bracelet, a high tech, flat glassine vial containing white powder, into which Radon dipped a tiny, silver-plated spoon he'd pinched from one of Marina's hospital charity luncheon soirees. He extracted a snootful and ingested same with a soft salute. "You are great," Radon affirmed to his re-inflated reflection in the glass.

While Marina did not know exactly what Radon was up to that moment, she was the only person he had told about his test results. Watching him saunter back out of the restroom and stop to politely autograph a menu for some couple at the bar, Marina couldn't help thinking she should have known long before his first knee surgery that Radon's predilections plagued the sanctity of any commitment. Yet, she'd enabled him by her silence, turning away from confrontations while resentments built. She'd likely avoided the obvious all along, having surrendered to the safe distance of their mutually informed denial, never anticipating this day would inevitably arrive.

"Can you believe it?" Radon said as he sat down. "Two people in the world who don't hate me." He took a swig of apple cider from his wine glass—a condition of bail being no alcohol—and immediately began fidgeting with the fresh tableware set up, replaced during his absence. "No dessert for you?"

"I'm ready to go," Marina replied.

* * *

"Archie, I can't express how much this means," Dominic Dellacozzi said, a little too coolly, as far as Krafter was concerned, while he handed Archie a bottle of drinkable Loire Valley burgundy.

Krafter had suggested they meet at his office for lunch. Lora and Archie had reconfigured the rear suite off the *K*raftworks lobby, having created the inner sanctum for his law practice, Lora's think tank, and Jill Banitch's outer office, complete with a small conference room and library lining the rear wall. Archie or Lora occupied the conference room exclusively via reasonable notice to the other, posted on the monthly schedule attached to their main refrigerator at home, and also displayed on the big erasable whiteboard calendar tacked up behind the desk in Jill's office.

When Dominic had entered, he immediately spotted: "Dom - 12:30 PM?" blue-chalked into the schedule on the wall. Since Jill was off that day, Dominic walked over and began rubbing it out with the brown paper sleeve still housing the wine he'd brought as a gift.

"Who else needs to know I'm here," Dominic had sheepishly stated to Krafter who happened to walk in, mid-rub.

"Are you hungry, Dominic?"

"Didn't I come for lunch?" he replied with a prune-faced look, gesturing as if a listening device might be hovering somewhere nearby.

"OK," Krafter responded, concerned. He directed them out of Kraftworks and into the small, landscaped park across the street.

"You think I'm paranoid?" Dominic wondered, as they meandered along the paved path through an undulating lawn, passing, of all things, a group of primitive stone sculptures of prairie animals paying homage to the bust of Georgia O'Keefe. "The government's gotta be all over me; right?"

They were seated on a painted bench next to the path. "I hafta' say," Archie disclosed, "I had considered that you're being followed. My investigator got an earful about you from a friend at the Justice Department."

Mike Prey had apparently once shared a drunken Christmas party coupling with a female paralegal who'd gone on to work for the US Attorney's office in Sacramento. Consequently, Prey had managed to tap her for a draft copy of the criminal complaint circulating between DOJ in DC and the Eastern District CA office. The Feds were preparing to charge two East European onsite tenants in a Dellacozzi Farms Ltd office building in downtown Port Louis (the Capital of Mauritius) with conducting a continuing criminal enterprise by: "Defrauding no less than one hundred Californians (individual names redacted) out of their identity and their personal and real property valued at more than ten million dollars, by perpetrating a vast array of internet hacking schemes over the previous three years."

While Krafter read the litany of transgressions allegedly committed on the family's premises, his brother-in-law listened passively, almost bored. "If you're an unnamed co-conspirator, Dominic, they may be preparing similar charges against you. Money laundering, at least," Krafter added for emphasis.

"For what?" Dominic perked up.

"For running a cyber bank of Russian phishing thieves who made a hundred and fifty million Mauritian rupees from stolen property last year alone, according to this complaint. That's roughly four million dollars."

"I didn't run anything. I stopped at the island two, maybe three, times a year for a few days on the beach. Like, exactly, what were they *doing*?" Dominic finally seemed to grasp the seriousness of his predicament.

"*Like* hijacking e-mail accounts, stealing social security numbers and credit cards, key-logging bank accounts to transact electronic cash transfers and purchases of expensive art and consumer gadgets. *Like* creating fake passports, perpetuating stolen identities in order to file phony insurance claims, all the way to scamming the elderly out of their benefit checks." Krafter went on in gory detail. "Most damaging to you, as far as I can tell, anyway, the government claims they traced one-point-one million of that to your business bank account in the Outer Richmond."

"The account could be in my name, but it definitely isn't my money."

"Are you serious, dude? You can't be saying you had no idea what's been going on here?"

"I'll swear on my father's life, I had no clue."

"Hmph," Krafter grunted, yet again. Ironically, his verbal skills seemed to be decreasing in direct proportion to the increased time he'd been spending thinking about his in-laws.

After returning to his office and working on Jaalaba's trial brief for most of the afternoon, Archie came home to find Lora in the cottage studio. She'd been jamming earlier with George "B-flat" Hardy, Lora's musician friend and one-time-only lover back in graduate school. George was as close as it got to being a mentor to Lora, ever since they'd begun hanging out together in the tiny urban park next to their computer lab during breaks in their separate projects. They had discovered their mutual admiration for jazz and taken their collaboration to the next level over the years, performing standards and their own songs on piano and vocals in neighborhood venues and at house parties, between the lines of their busy lives.

George Hardy was a rock and roll legend, of sorts, having engineered recording sessions for some of the big stadium acts during the 90's. He played studio piano and guitar on four platinum and two Grammy-winning albums, while continuing to compose on both instruments. Being a geek as well as a musician, B-flat had capitalized on his digital mastering skills just when sound was converting from analog, and he'd become the darling of the West Coast recording industry.

Archie and George had bonded soon after Lora introduced them, and she'd let Archie know that sex with B-flat had been so bad they never tried it again. Archie appreciated Lora and George's relationship, and George's support was critical to Lora's confidence. Archie did mildly resent those times when Lora and B-flat were jamming in the cottage and didn't invite him to join them on his Djembe drum.

"You didn't agree to represent my brother, did you?" Lora asked, concerned. They were alone and Archie had downloaded the details of his lunchtime in the park with Dom.

"No, I didn't, dear. And I probably shouldn't be discussing this with you."

Lora wrapped her smooth fresh-smelling arms around him and held him close. "Of course, you're not representing Dominic. Let's have a drink. Tell me what's allowed."

They sat down on the upholstered stools at their wooden tiki bar that separated the cottage's living room from the tiny kitchen. Archie retrieved a bottle of local multi-distilled vodka from the freezer and shook up a batch of martinis.

"Your brother didn't actually say to me any of what I'm about to tell you," he said. "So, I'm not betraying his confidence if I give you my theory," Archie went on, while pouring the pearly mind-numbing elixir into their favorite glasses. "I think Dominic gets his allowance from the legal offshore gambling proceeds generated in your father's office building on Mauritius. But it also sounds like a couple of Sal's online-betting tenants were running an identity theft ring on the side, with stolen credit cards and hacked bank accounts."

"What's my brother got to do with international bank fraud?"

"Some of those funds were traced to his account."

"Maybe this cyber theft ring was another profit center for my father's business?"

"You know something I don't?"

"Just speculating, Archie. Same as you."

"Well, I think the government is going to squeeze your brother into cooperating against your father. In that case, I don't even want to be standing *next to* Dominic's lawyer."

Chapter Ten

"If I Were Two-faced Would I Be Wearing This One?"
"Honest Abe" Lincoln

In urban criminal courtrooms the spectator gallery is often larger than "the pit," the arena of judgment inside those ubiquitous swinging saloon doors. Ever since frontier judges rode the territorial circuits on horseback, conducting trials at the local tavern in towns without a courthouse, most modern American temples of dispute have retained this traditional design element.

When Radon Jaalaba and Archie Krafter walked down the long center aisle in Department 29, approaching the Honorable Judge Deena Norwell's altar, the packed chamber buzzed with press and too many curious local folks having nothing better to do on a Thursday morning in late August. Radon's presence was required for Judge Norwell's pretrial rulings and to hear her ground rules for jury selection commencing on Monday. Nevertheless, the proceeding threatened to become more about seat selection, as the line of wannabes in the hallway had stretched all the way to the elevator.

Cameron Wheatley and Bryan Marten stood together, leaning against the railing of the empty jury box, rapt in discussion, the likes of which Krafter could only imagine. After ushering Radon to his seat at the defense table, leaving him alone and jittery, Krafter hurried over to keep Bryan from inadvertently blabbing something confidential to the prosecutor. "I thought we agreed not to talk unless I was included," Krafter griped, mostly at Bryan.

"We're not talking. Are we talking?" Bryan sarcastically asked the DA. "Are you *talkin'* to me?"

"Now, A*rr*chie. We're all in the same fishbowl," Cameron offered in her soothing drawl, a sharkskin pant suit and pointy dress heels complementing her lanky frame. "I wouldn't engage Bryan on substance without *you*."

"Actually," Bryan spoke out, "we just started discussing whether the jury should get a reasonable doubt instruction if Radon doesn't testify."

Krafter had to admit Bryan always looked sharp, his big mouth notwithstanding. Marten's scrubbed, doughy face and curly ginger hair matched nicely his burgundy pinstripe suit, pale yellow shirt and violet silk tie embossed with tiny scales of justice. Bryan's skin hadn't aged despite his ongoing appreciation of alcohol in all manners of consumption. For he had also assiduously applied the toniest facial moisturizers available, since he'd left his father's parquet flooring business in the Irish section of St. Louis, a quarter century ago, to attend law school in San Francisco.

Bryan's eventual specialization in the nuance of forming and protecting the intellectual property of multi-national corporations had led to his association with professional athletes, performers, and their multi-million-dollar promotion contracts. He'd secured the hillside house facing the Golden Gate Bridge that he shared with his slightly overbearing wife Susan and Simon, their sprouting teenage nightmare. Make no mistake; Susan's California pedigree fueled their heady civic and social positions. Having contributed major clients to his law firm, as well as faithfully supporting Bryan's wackiest ideas over the years, Susan continued to drive the family bus towards their twentieth anniversary.

"Don't ya' think it's premature talking about reasonable doubt?" Krafter asked the DA, trying to back away from Bryan's remarks. "Judge Norwell's probably gonna toss this mess before Radon even has to think about testifying."

"Maybe you're right, Archie," Wheatley placated him. "Everybody can't wait to hear Mr. Jaalaba's big explanation. Ben & Jerry want to name a flavor after him."

"I hope they ask for permission," Krafter returned the quip. "By the way, I received an e-mail from the Worriers' attorney that you're withdrawing your subpoena for Radon's medical records?"

"Mr. Crocker persuaded us that Radon's team files are protected by the physician-patient privilege, as they already existed long before the homicides."

"Great. So, you're dropping the subpoena for Dr. Dewhauser's records too?"

"Sorry, Archie," Cameron oozed it out like toothpaste. "Mr. Jaalaba was present during an armed robbery that led to a double homicide. We have a duty to prosecute any murder case with the most relevant information available. If Dewhauser's treatment records prove Mr. Jaalaba was addicted at the time, Judge Norwell is gonna let us look at them."

"Seriously, Cameron?" Krafter replied testily. "What's the difference between the team's medical records and *his* treatment records? How can some arbitrary cutoff date cancel my client's rights to the same doctor-patient privilege?"

"I'm not trampling anybody's constitutional rights. I just want to tell Officer Trower's eight-year-old kid that I made every reasonable attempt to examine the evidence explaining why his father died."

Krafter struggled to hide his disappointment at the District Attorney's choosing a *ménage à trois* with Charlie Crocker and Perry

Dunbar over him. "Did you happen to ask the team's lawyer about the team doctor's history of prescribing opiates?"

"Don't worry A*rr*chie," Cameron toyed with him again, demonstrating how she'd been elected twice. "I'm guessin' Perry Dunbar understands the legal consequences if their team doctor knowingly facilitated his addiction."

"ALL RISE," the bailiff intoned when the Honorable Deena F. Norwell literally swept onto the scene, her flowing black silk robe nearly touching the floor. Tiny feet, clad in barely visible stacked heels, briskly propelled her up a customized, carpeted step into her padded-leather chair overlooking the courtroom. She wasn't a little person, per se; at sixty inches tall, Deena Faye Norwell was perfectly proportioned and apparently well-endowed within her petite frame. However, her burgeoning Napoleon Complex didn't always harmonize with her duty to be objective.

"This is case number 1-1-4-5-7-8-9; State of California versus Radon Jaalaba," Judge Norwell declared, beginning her customary litany. "Please be seated. The People are represented today by the District Attorney. Good morning, Ms. Wheatley."

"Good morning, Your Honor. I'll be assisted by Mr. Nogato from our office."

"Alright. Good morning, Mr. Nogato. I see Mr. Jaalaba is present and represented by Mr. Krafter and Mr. Marten. Good morning, gentlemen. Before we start, I want to state on the record that I have been a Worriers fan for more years than I'll admit. Especially since the day Mr. Jaalaba was drafted. Ms. Wheatley, I have never met this defendant before he was assigned to my court, but if you have any hesitation about my ability to give the State a fair trial let me know and I'll step down. That goes for you, too, Mr. Jaalaba. Say the word and I'll return this case for reassignment."

Krafter was aware that Deena F. Norwell had not come upon her exalted post by accident. Having begun as an incubator baby, eventually fed with growth hormones, her brain had grown too big for her britches. Nevertheless, Deena had excelled on the balance beam in high school, medaled at coxswain in college skulls, graduated Boalt Hall, summa cum laude, and went to work for a well-connected labor law firm representing the Bay Area's largest employers. After cutting her teeth on insurance claims from disabled employees, the firm had sent Deena on a nationwide educational circuit, alerting brick and mortar employers to the dangers of ADA non-compliance, while hawking their best-selling desk manual: *Employer's Guide to Workplace Management.*

Having made partner a decade later, Deena had ironically spent her pro bono hours mostly representing displaced families from bankrupt employers. Her community contributions and the firm's donations to the DCCC caused Norwell's nomination to the superior court, where she served with distinction for six years, first in juvenile and then in criminal court. Lately, though, Judge Norwell has lobbied to preside over civil trials in the courthouse next to City Hall. Mastering this Radon Jaalaba circus was a huge opportunity to make that happen.

"Your Honor," Cameron Wheatley replied, having stood in response to the judge's offer to recuse. "I'm a Worriers fan, too. Like most of us here. The State is confident you will give the defendant a fair trial."

Krafter rose at the defense table, noticing that Radon was not mustering his usually charming public personality. "My client also believes you will be fair and impartial," Krafter declared, while Radon managed a weak smile up at the judge.

Bryan leaned over and said something to Radon, sotto voce, and Jaalaba went off at Krafter as soon as he sat down.

"This *little* bitch is gonna lynch me," Radon whispered angrily.

"What the fuck, Radon." Krafter replied, covering his mouth with his hand, fighting to restrain himself.

"Let's proceed with the motions to quash production of Mr. Jaalaba's medical records," Judge Norwell declared amiably. "I understand the People are withdrawing their subpoena. Is that correct, Ms. Wheatley?"

"Yes, Your Honor," Cameron replied from her chair. "We won't demand production of the defendant's records unless they are directly related to the charges before the court. But Dr. Dewhauser's records are certainly within . . ."

". . . Please excuse my interruption, Judge," Krafter popped out of his seat. "I wonder if we may take this up in my chambers?"

"Ms. Wheatley?" Norwell inquired without expression.

"Yes, of course," the DA conceded, while shooting Krafter a look saying, "You owe me one." Wheatley signaled to her condescending and narrow-lapelled assistant, Chris Nogato—who'd taunted Krafter in the office, and those three followed Judge Norwell out a rear door toward her private office. Radon remained with Bryan at the defense table.

"Thank you for not insisting we air this publicly, Ms. Wheatley," Judge Norwell said, once they'd gathered around her mahogany desk, which rested on a Native American area rug in her otherwise drab book-lined county office suite. "I'm sensitive to Mr. Jaalaba's right to an impartial jury trial," Her Honor went on, while hanging her robe on a standing wooden rack in the corner behind her desk. "Some prospective jurors are probably in the courtroom now." She stepped onto a small, carpeted riser beside her worn brown leather executive chair and sat down. "The jury summonses to report on Monday went out weeks ago. Who *isn't* following this case?"

"Kudos, Cameron, for not tainting the jury pool," Krafter spoke up as soon as they were seated, side-by-side, in the office chairs facing Deena Norwell's desk. "Judge," Krafter continued, "it's also important to maintain my client's right to privacy. So, if you decide that Mr. Jaalaba's treatment records should not be turned over to the prosecutor, I hope you'll also consider sealing them from the public."

"Sadly, Mr. Jaalaba has tarnished his own reputation," Wheatley jumped in, her turn to kiss Judge Norwell's diminutive derriere. "The defendant was seeking drugs at the scene of a double homicide. With respect, it's relevant and the jury should hear it."

"Madame District Attorney," Deena Norwell responded decisively. "I've given this considerable thought. Even assuming Mr. Jaalaba is an addict, whatever that means these days, Dr. Dewhauser's records might be relevant if they somehow proved the defendant was under the influence at the time of the offense. I will read those records *in camera*. But I'm not inclined to let you or anybody else see them *unless* Mr. Jaalaba decides to testify in his own behalf and does so inconsistently. *Comprende?*"

"Thank you, Judge," Cameron Wheatley said, according to the barrister's secret code of eating shit with a touch of sarcasm.

"Excellent," Judge Norwell pressed on, standing up at her desk and retrieving her judicial robe from the rack. "Shall we discuss jury selection here while we're comfortable? Mr. Krafter, kindly ask your client to join us and I'll call in the court reporter. We might even go home early today."

When Radon, Bryan, and the court reporter had joined the cramped group assembled around the judge's desk, Her Honor explained on the record that they were conducting this hearing in her private chambers to avoid potential jurors and any reporters who might be in the courtroom. Then she announced: "I've ordered one hundred for the initial jury pool, and I'm reserving all next week to select twelve jurors and two alternates, unless either side intends to drag out the trial. I usually conduct the voir dire, but I'll consider a joint request to question the panel. Finish your proposed jury instructions over the weekend, and any other scores you want to settle . . . Mr. Jaalaba," Judge Norwell focused directly into Radon's seriously stressed, greenish pupils. "Do you have any concerns you want to address before we adjourn this hearing?"

"No, Your Honor." Radon answered wearily, no longer paying attention to what they were haggling over. He was focused on the deepest regions of his soul, wherein resided the inviolate decision to honor Russell's life.

"Go home and take your lawyers with you," the judge decreed. "Get plenty of rest and we'll see you on Monday morning."

Bryan and Archie hustled Radon out through the back door of the courthouse. They dodged the gauntlet of media on the street and dove into a waiting limo. Radon leaned back in the perfumed leather upholstery, took a couple deep breaths, and unable to relax, he finally said, "This is worse than I even imagined. I am so fucked."

"Au contraire, my friend," Archie assured him. "We got 'em right where we want them."

But Radon kept hearing the damndest thing bouncing around inside his head. Sam Cooke was singing: "Ooh . . . ahh . . . Ooh . . . ahh," and Radon realized he was in danger of losing the plot right then and there in the company of the most important keepers of his freedom. They certainly weren't his enemy; there was no point to press with either one of them, as they silently rode alongside him. "Ooh . . . ahh . . . Ooh . . . ahh, that's the sound of . . ." Starting inside Radon's gut, a different pain suddenly seared through him; surfacing in waves, an unforgiving ache thrashed wildly against the seawall of shame and guilt over Russell Marchetti, struggling to face the horror his hubris had set in motion.

Chapter Eleven

Who's Kidding Whom?

Lora feared this evening might arrive after Archie had returned from a recent meeting with Radon and told her that he suspected Radon may be using again. Though her husband has never wavered in pursuit of Radon's acquittal, and despite Archie's terminal optimism, Lora hoped Archie wasn't naive enough to think Radon was going to wake up one day and suddenly realize the path to his own redemption.

Not being a natural schmoozer, Lora was grateful for her friends and the opportunity to entertain charitable causes. Socializing required her to be "on" while she'd rather be home playing the piano. Hosting a sit-down dinner was draining; hours were spent prepping, cooking, and remaining interested until the last guest went home. But tonight promised to be the mother of all energy suckers. For Lora, with Archie's reluctant permission, was facilitating a last minute, pre-trial pep talk gathering of Radon's inner circle with "mocktails" and tapas. The evening will likely include a full-court press, convincing Radon that he ought to admit his relapse, renounce his denials and finally face the music.

When Michelle Garroway and Marina Ramirez arrived together Lora was relieved. "How nice to see you," she declared, while guiding them in the front door, across the wide foyer. "Bryan and Susan are here. Radon is on his way."

"Thank you for helping my son get with folks who understand." Michelle's taut copper-toned skin defied her fifty-six years, while complementing her sleeveless salmon sheath. "I owe you and Archie a lot,"

Michelle added, taking Lora's arm in hers as they entered the parlor. Marina followed, and Lora could read Marina's worried face, fearing Radon's reaction to being confronted this way.

Archie stood at their wet bar, listening to Susan and mixing her a non-alcoholic cocktail. Bryan got up from the couch to greet Michelle, who walked over to Krafter first and gave him a warm hug. "You're helping my baby," Michelle said softly into his ear.

"I'm doing my best. Radon will probably disagree when he figures out what's going on here."

"Something to drink, Michelle?" Lora stepped in. "How about you Marina?"

"Sparkling water is fine, thanks." Marina Ramirez was too anxious for alcohol anyway. Her guilt weighed on her, so she was grateful that Michelle had endorsed this get together. Although Marina and Michelle often met to promote the Jaalaba Foundation's good works, by the time Michelle had trusted her enough to discuss Radon, Marina had been holding her tongue for so long she didn't know where to start. In addition to Radon's legal problems, the foundation had lost nearly a million dollars in sponsors and donors, she has irritable bowel syndrome from the stress, and she keeps finding clumps of hair in her bathtub drain.

An electronic bell subtly sounded once, and Lora headed for the front door. Archie met her exiting the parlor and together they crossed the foyer.

"Please answer it," Lora implored him.

"Getting cold feet?"

"I know it's my party. But your load will get lighter too if Radon responds."

"Do you know how ethically weird this is for me?"

"It's impossible to help him, Archie, unless he accepts responsibility for what he's doing to himself."

"He has the right to demand they prove his guilt beyond a reasonable doubt."

"I'm talking about saving his life, not getting him off the charges."

"I'll answer the doorbell, but please stop squeezing my balls like a Dellacozzi."

A stony silence ensued, allowing Archie to usher Radon inside with a quick hello and a firm bruh-hug. Radon's face had a neon tinge, like toxic waste wrapped in a John Varvatos sweater. Still, he was upbeat and engaging, and he made a point of thanking Lora for encouraging his mother to fly up early for his trial.

"I'm glad Mama came," Radon said to them in the foyer. "I have some things to discuss tonight that might surprise y'all."

As soon as Radon entered the parlor and started toward the group on the other side of the room, Michelle descended upon him. "C'mon, Radon honey; gimme some sugar."

Mother and son embraced, holding on in silent recognition of their ties that would forever bind. In due course they stood back, and Michelle examined Radon's eyes, hoping for confirmation that the warrior she'd raised still had game. Radon shared an extended hug with Marina and kisses on both cheeks. Then Susan latched onto Radon around the waist, smiling up into his eyes. Finally, Bryan declared, "I love you, man," and did his elbow-bump, karate-chop, handshake thing.

After everyone had refreshments and the preliminary mingling wound down, Lora directed the group through the adjacent dining room toward the patio deck. The French doors were open on this balmy, windless night and they strolled outside to a string of pier lights glowing beneath Coit Tower, stretching along Fisherman's Wharf toward the Golden Gate. For the next forty-five minutes, gathered in one configuration or another, they discussed: Charlie Sheen's tiger blood meltdown, "Rolling in the Deep," and Kim Kardashian's ten-million-dollar wedding to Kris Humphries, who Radon had played against in Dallas. They talked about the killing of Osama bin Laden, homeless encampments, dirty needles all over Market Street and the repeal of "Don't Ask Don't Tell."

A Mediterranean buffet of appetizers and small entrees in silver-plated warmers awaited, and following trips to the bar and the restroom, eventually they all turned up around the votive candle-lit dining table with a plate of food in hand. Marina and Radon were the last to sit in the remaining empty seats on Lora's left, while Michelle had already settled on her right, with Archie anchoring Susan and Bryan at the other end.

"May I have your attention, please?" Krafter eventually called out from his chair, while clinking his water glass with a fork. "I want to say something about supporting Radon during the upcoming trial. First, I want to thank my lovely wife, Lora, for getting you all here; and for being the special sauce in our spaghetti." Archie glanced across the table at Lora, who smiled back at him affectionately, while mouthing: *"Sauce in our spaghetti?"* A round of thanks went to Lora, all the same.

"Based on my experience at trials," Archie said, "nothing is more important—except evidence of course—than my client having his family and friends behind him." Glasses were raised around the table. "So, let's toast to Radon's acquittal."

Everyone clinked their glasses and took a gulp. "Whatever God you pray to," Krafter went on needlessly. "Whether you're religious, or you're a spiritual person, you have to believe the jury system won't fail us."

"Why're you making this sound like a funeral?" Radon chafed. "We got this. You'll prove I didn't rob anybody without me getting up there to say so."

"Why is it so important you don't testify?" Susan wondered aloud, emboldened by the group. "If you're found innocent, won't you be able to play next season?"

"Hold on a second," Krafter jumped in. "Radon, this conversation is not confidential. If any of you end up testifying as a character witness, I don't want the prosecutor hearing any of this. 'Cause the DA *will* ask whether you discussed the case with Radon."

The ensuing silence seemed to last forever, until Bryan seized the vacuum to advance his agenda's version of legal wisdom.

"He's right, Susan. This discussion is not confidential. But in my hypothetical opinion, if Radon's testimony exonerates him, that would go a long way toward rejuvenating his career whenever the lockout ends. Radon voluntarily sought treatment so the team can't legally fire him for admitting his past drug use in court as long as he remains clean."

"Is that true?" Michelle wanted confirmation.

"Mama, that's only half the story."

"OK, that's enough," Krafter spoke up again. "Bryan, you are way out of line."

"I'm so sorry, Archie," he replied snarkily. "Didn't you create this genius defense plan in the first place?"

"Bryan, shut your pie hole!" Susan suddenly let loose, realizing she'd opened this festering wound.

"What's the rest of the story, Radon?" his mother asked softly, soldiering on.

"I really don't want you to explain any of this now," Krafter implored him.

"I know you got my back, Archie."

Then Radon Jaalaba searched around the table desperately reading each one of their sympathetic, pitying faces; really, for the first time.

What was he looking for? He was exhausted, tired of lying. The superhuman strength that had carried his team, yes, even lifted the City of Oakland, evaporated in his mother's eyes.

He examined his own trembling hands, calling up his special inner reserve: the laser focus built up over many years in the white heat of the last shot; the hero or the goat, all or nothing; carry it on your shoulders, millions in revenue dangling; worldwide approbation or unrelenting scorn. Calming himself while the walls crashed in around him; a mind trick he'd learned from Coach Nellins during a fourth quarter huddle at *the critical moment* in Radon's cherry year; another story from a different time. Finally, he stood up and clinked his water glass just as Archie had done.

"There are some things I have to say for *me*." Radon knew he was about to dive from a high cliff into a churning sea. "Marina, I apologize for lying about using for too long. You deserve a better partner. Please forgive me enough to keep running my foundation and helping those sick kids, no matter what happens to me."

Radon turned to Michelle without waiting for Marina to respond. "Mama, I made some mistakes when I came off my second knee surgery. Because I was taking prescription painkillers again, I started using natural stimulants and cocaine to help my physical therapy along. I know I have an addictive personality. So, I will never use cocaine again. In case you're wondering, I haven't had a drink in six months. If y'all think I need an intervention, that's cool."

Lora was startled by Radon's openness. Unless he was full of shit, which seemed more likely to her, considering his addiction had led him to Shenkman's apartment in the first place. Radon's *mea culpa* sounded pat, and Lora noticed that Marina was obviously pained being dragged back into his world. Michelle wiped away tears streaked with disgrace, obviously being shared with her son during the lowest point in his life.

Lora clearly understood that her province at the moment was silence. She looked over at Archie, trying to be the team player he'd always encouraged her to be. Bless his soul, Archie raised his handsome eyebrows and cocked his head, signaling in their secret spousal language, cautioning Lora to follow her instincts this time, and *shut the hell up!* Thankfully, she was saved from herself when Michelle stepped in.

"Was I such a terrible mother?" she asked him. "How did I fail that you have to kill yourself with drugs?"

"I haven't taken drugs because you're a terrible mother. The team treated my injuries with prescription pain killers over the years, and now I may have some residual damage."

"I don't understand what you're saying, son."

"Mama, even if I'm acquitted, I'll probably never play again. Exonerating Russell's good name is really all that matters. He went into that apartment to get cocaine for me after we were binging all night."

"Then you have to get up there and tell them the truth."

"You know I'm gay, Mother . . . And you know I never would have been drafted if they knew. If I get up there, I'd have to tell them about my true relationship with Russell. There are still no players out in the NBA." Radon looked at the others. "This never leaves the room. You all hear me?"

"Darling, Radon. You were always a handful." Michelle couldn't help feeling relieved to hear him address this.

"I'll bet you don't remember waiting at Riyadh airport coming home to LA," she went on. "When you were just five? You were wearing a kid-sized, No. 32, Lakers jersey that your daddy gave you, and you were already practicing dribbling a basketball through your legs and behind your back. On the opposite side of the boarding area, two Saudi women were standing together watching you. One was young and pretty, dressed in a colorful designer *abaya*. Her almond face was done-up with lipstick, eyeliner and thick lashes, while her companion was completely covered in her *burka* with eye slits . . . Son, you asked me if the lady in the *burka* made up *her* face too. Then you wanted to know if men also wore make-up underneath *their* clothes? Do you remember any of this?"

"I remember the men wore those ugly hooded wool robes and all different kinds of masks that used to scare me."

"Then you informed me one day you could wear make-up in the NBA. Do you remember *that?* When I asked you, 'Where on earth did you get such a thing?' Do you know what you told me? You said, 'Dennis Rodman wears make up.' . . . So, I already knew you were different."

Chapter Twelve

A Call To Arms (And A Leg)

"I'll understand if you knew and couldn't tell me, Archie."

"Whaddaya want from me, Lora?" Archie was irritated. It had begun the night before after everyone had departed, the leftovers were packed away, and they'd nearly finished cleaning up.

"I wish he would take the deal," Archie had confided as Lora turned on the dishwasher. "Gino Trower was already honored by the Police Commission and according to Cameron they won't complain too loudly if Radon is sentenced to home confinement for six months, community service and a long probation. Provided Judge Norwell is willing to approve it."

"She's *Cameron* now?"

"Ha, Ha. Wait a minute . . . Radon thinks the judge wants to hang him. Would Norwell be more sympathetic if she knew he was gay?"

"Do you really believe that's how women think?"

"I think a male judge would probably hold it against him—the macho athlete who ran away like a . . . a . . . coward."

"You mean like a *girl*? . . . Don't worry, Archie. I'm grateful for you. Even on the days when I'm not."

"Thanks, Sweetheart. But how's this for irony? By the time they settle the lockout, Radon could be the first player in NBA history reporting to training camp wearing an ankle bracelet."

"You really think he'll play next season?"

Krafter hadn't known what to say. He *had* held onto hope that Lora's home-baked intervention might convince Radon to end the game of chicken he was playing with his life. Despite everybody's best intentions, Archie was selecting a jury come Monday morning, and Radon's continuing refusal to testify had finally gained a little traction within the defense team.

Consequently, Krafter was still annoyed the next evening as Lora had agreed to sit in with George Hardy and his latest trio at a North Beach cafe bar. Being a last-minute addition to B-flat's gig, Lora expected Archie to accompany her for moral support. Well, he thought at first, she was only singing two jazz standards in a café while he was preparing for the trial of the century in less than forty-eight hours. But then, of course he was a proud fan, having attended all of Lora's performances since they'd been together. Was *he* ready for war on Monday? Wasn't that the real issue irking him?

Nevertheless, Lora and Archie sat at a small round table near the makeshift stage in back of the café. They were waiting for George to get started at the upright piano against the wall, to be accompanied by silent Marty on bass guitar and hairy Stu sitting behind his drum kit. Archie bristled anew when suddenly Dominic walked in with Andrea Steiner and stopped at the espresso bar inside the entrance. "Why didn't you tell me your brother was coming?"

"I'm so sorry. I thought you wouldn't come if you knew he might show up."

"Aren't I here for you?"

"You're right . . . I told Dom to stay home."

"Well, Dominic and Andrea are walking over here with flowers for the chanteuse."

"I owe you a big one for this, Archie."

"Oh, I'll remember."

"Hey, Lora," Dominic said, handing her a large summer bouquet. "Andrea chose these for you." He embraced Lora and then wrapped his arms around Archie, while Lora hugged Andrea. "Thanks for your lovely thought," Lora replied, addressing both of them, wondering whether Andréa might be a diversion so Dominic could corner Archie into discussing his legal problems. "The music's about to start," she told her brother. "If you're staying, grab a couple seats at the table over there."

So began Archie's selfless evening of fun, as Dominic retrieved two chairs from the adjacent table instead of sitting there and proceeded to squish them all in together. B-flat's trio soon took off on an interpretation of "Duke's Place," eventually leading to George's swinging solo, and somehow morphing back into "Take the A Train." The cafe was filling up with regulars and walk-ins, all of whom applauded enthusiastically when the medley ended. Nevertheless, within a minute after B-flat was into one of his original compositions, Dominic tapped Krafter on the shoulder and leaned into his face.

"Gimme five minutes, Archie," Dominic whispered, while subtly jerking his bony thumb in the direction of the front door.

Krafter ignored him. Dominic tapped him again, and Krafter whispered back, "After the show." Then he saw desperation mounting in Dominic's eyes. Despite his first instinct, Krafter got up and followed him, winding apologetically through the annoyed audience of fake smiles clogging the aisle all the way to the front door. Outside Dominic ushered them toward his waiting town car and Krafter stopped. "You want me to go for a ride?"

"That's funny, Archie. *Please* ride around the block with me and let me pick your brain. I talked to the attorney you recommended and, I gotta say, Boynahan is not you by a long shot." Dominic ushered him inside the smooth leather passenger compartment of his vintage guzzler and reassured him. "I know you can't take my case, Archie. I'm even willing to pay this guy's huge retainer, against six hundred an hour . . . Just not for bad advice, you know?"

"What about Lora? Aren't you here for her performance?"

"We'll be back in ten minutes, I promise," Dominic countered. Then he directed Marco, a soft-spoken, beefy young fellow in a short-sleeved white shirt and narrow black tie, to drive off. "Archie, tell me if I should listen to Boynahan," Dominic went on. "He's Irish, and my father's long-time lawyer is jittery about him. One quick stop around the corner, OK?" as Krafter's face registered growing concern. "There's somebody I want you to meet."

The sun still shone in the western sky at the opposite end of Broadway when Marco, who Krafter had never met before, stopped at the valet entrance to Pullouts only a few city blocks from the café. Krafter followed Dominic inside the upscale "gentlemen's club" that Archie and Lora often passed during their afternoon constitutional through the infamous night life district, dotted with nudie bars, restaurants and music venues, along their way to the waterfront.

At the far end of Pullouts narrow lobby, thick purple drapes opened into a huge high-ceilinged room with tables and chairs on two levels surrounding a stage in the center. A long chrome bar, velvet ropes, sticky perfumed carpeting and Vegas lighting collapsed night and day into another dimension. Dominic was met promptly and reverently by a pie-faced, fortyish man with dark curly hair, in a grey wool suit. "Victor" directed them to a banquette table away from the stage, upon which two bare-breasted women were slithering in erotic competition on side-by-side stripper poles. Krafter hesitated again when they reached the table.

"Strike two, Dominic," he said. "First, you kidnap me. Now you expect me to miss my wife sing while you force me to watch this?"

"Jeezus, Archie. Lighten up and have a drink. Victor's my man. He's Slovenian. Victor knows the Klitoff twins who got busted on Mauritius . . . Victor, this is my brother-in-law, Archie. He's the 'Naked Lawyer' blogger."

"We only got women here," Victor replied. "I'm sure they'll love you in the Tenderloin. What can I get you fellows? . . . Dominic, you know your money is no good, right? Whatever you guys want," he went on, making a sweeping gesture toward the stage, apparently intending to include all the "perkies" in the place.

"Bring us three Blue Devil specials," Dominic answered without waiting for Archie's input. "You know how I like 'em, Victor. And one's for you, so come back. I want to ask you something."

Victor snapped his fingers twice and a chunky, bright-eyed Caribbean woman with curly, bronze-colored extensions appeared, wearing a pink nightgown and scant panties, the upturned nipples on her youthful breasts pushing through the sheer fabric. Victor gave her the drink order and she whispered something to him. "Meet Angela," Victor said to them. "She is summa cum loudly from S&MU. Angela will get the drinks, and the rest is up to you . . . I'll be right back, Dominic."

"I want to get out of here," Krafter said, as soon as they were alone.

"Hold on, Archie. I need your advice. The Klitoff brothers are in the Port Saint Luis jail awaiting extradition and Boynahan thinks somebody should bail them out."

"Your father's offshore gambling tenants? The hackers whose loot ended up in your account? Bailing them out sounds like the advice John Mitchell gave to Nixon about the Watergate burglars."

"Who's John Mitchell?"

"Never mind. Bail is usual for non-violent crimes. But you're talking about a federal indictment with help from the British Extradition Treaty of 1931, allowing the US Attorney to prosecute them in

Sacramento. Unless those brothers are lawful residents of Mauritius with legitimate ties to their own homeland, I see the Feds fighting to keep them in custody until they're transported here for trial. Anyway, this is between you and your lawyer."

"See, that's what I mean about Boynahan. He wants me to take care of them, so they won't roll over. Like you said, he thinks the government wants to make a conspiracy case against me. If they don't come back to testify, there's no case."

"OK, Dominic," Krafter rose from the table. "I'm outta here."

"It's not what you think, Archie. This is strictly about raising bail money. I have no friggin' idea where they're from. Like I said before, it's an office building I visit twice a year; I did not know they were doing anything besides licensed online gambling until you first read me the charges against them. If they post bond and decide to go home rather than come to America and face trial, how is that my goddamn fault?"

"As long as their lease has been terminated, and you don't pay for their lawyer or their bail . . . You want my advice, stay away from the Klitoffs."

Angela's nipples reappeared with the drinks, which she seductively served separately, Dominic first, by setting out his special martini before him, ceremoniously bending over him, turning around and twerking her taut, glittering butt in his face before gently lowering herself, briefly, on his lap. Angela turned to Krafter, who snatched his own drink from the table and held it up in a toasting gesture instead.

"Balls in wife's purse," Archie declared with a mixture of pride and wistfulness. Angela deferred, taking off as soon as Victor sat down at the other end of the leather banquette and grabbed his waiting martini.

"So, Dominic," Victor followed up, likely assuming his loyalty was being questioned. "What do you want to ask me?"

"Ya' know what, Victor? Forget it."

Archie was never exactly sure when he realized his drink must've been sprinkled with Ecstasy. Still, within minutes of Dominic's sudden decision to clam up on Victor, their short ride back to the cafe bar was punctuated by Archie's mild case of the grins, thereby indicating things had begun to go awry.

Back inside the cafe, they were unable to penetrate an overflow crowd standing in the tiny aisle between the tables leading all the way back to the musicians. Lora was midway through "Round Midnight" in front of B-flat's trio. Her voice reigned over a silent sea of enchanted initiates filling the normally noisy venue. When her moody, sensual rendition was done, Archie gave a four-fingered whistle through the vibrant applause that drew Lora's attention, along with everybody else in the county.

Lora's brief scowl demanded to know, "Where the hell have you been?" But any further silent discussion was tabled, as Lora heard the opening chords of: *"My love must be a kinda blind love, I can't see anyone but you* . . . and she was off into the song, becoming "Miss D" . . . *Are the stars out tonight? Don't know if it's cloudy or bright. 'Cause I only have eyes for youu, dear."*

Lora's self-referential shtick actually helped her focus when she sang without sheet music. After her mother died and Lora was left with Olivia's piano, and her own imagination, she'd eagerly transformed her lonely existence into an alternate reality, where Miss D's self-confidence was nurtured, and her talent was adored. Consequently, Lora brought her life experience into the room laid out in the octaves and the audiences embraced her.

Archie and Dominic had made their way back to the table by the time Lora's song was over and the clapping ended. She replaced the mike in the stand, hugged George at the piano, thanked the other band members and approached Archie waiting to embrace her.

"You smell like vodka," she said, after a brief kiss. "Where'd you go?"

"You sounded incredibly wonderful. I teared up on that note near the end, Lora, I swear. You totally rocked."

"Either you were flirting with a woman or you're on something?"

"You don't want to know."

Lora drove them home with mixed emotions running high. She was totally jazzed about her performance and the audience's reaction, while she continued to be appalled by her family. Dominic's opportunism was bad enough, but her brother didn't even care to hear her sing, having snatched her husband, and dosed him instead. In a further reminder of her brother's handiwork, she was presently dealing with Mr. Happy seated next to her, kissing her neck and stroking between her thighs, as she navigated their car into the garage. "Okay, Archie, come up for air. We're here."

"You're irresistible," he responded, looking into Lora's eyes, while persisting in the nether region. "You feel so warm and tingly. Let's do it right here."

"In the garage? . . . You're *really* tripping."

"What's wrong with the car? Corinthian leather used to be fine. Remember that night in the China Beach parking lot?"

"I remember the police drove up, you freaked out they'd smell the weed, and you were gonna lose your law license. It's time to go upstairs to bed, Archie. You have the trial of the century on Monday."

Chapter Thirteen

Trial And Error

"Just look at his *beady little eyes*," Bryan whispered into Krafter's left ear. "That Manjy can't wait to stick it to the government."

The three of them were seated at the defense table in the crowded courtroom. Krafter in the middle, Radon sitting stone-faced to his right, while they *Googled* social media information on Bryan's laptop about the fourteen potential deciders of Radon's fate currently occupying the jury box. Surprisingly, their pending selection had progressed rather smoothly.

Out of the large first pool, Judge Norwell had dismissed a slew of unfit prospects for reasons ranging from "it's a police set-up," to those folks who already believed he was guilty. Considering the wavering hero-worship of Radon Jaalaba, Cameron Wheatley had deftly used most of her preemptory challenges to exclude those most likely to be caught up in an authority versus celebrity dynamic.

On the other hand, Krafter had sought out individuals capable of blaming the police for overreacting, while sympathizing with a victim of circumstances who also happened to be an easy target. Nearing the end of day four, the parties were left only with choosing the second alternate juror. He or she was required to sit through the entire proceeding but would only deliberate if two of the other twelve members were unable to finish the trial for any reason.

Krafter rose from his chair and headed toward the podium, choosing to walk around the prosecution table—where Cameron Wheatley sat with her human torpedo, Chris Nogato—in order to pass in front of the nine women and five men seated in the two-tiered box. Archie had already exchanged friendly banter with most of them over the course of the *voir dire,* so he immediately focused on Mr. Manjy in the second row, end seat.

"I'm sure you accept the presumption of innocence?" Krafter queried the weathered-skinned, pony-tailed, letter carrier, whose Facebook Page had revealed that Wilfred Manjy graduated from Balboa High School thirty years earlier. His hobbies were fishing, bowling, bug-collecting and baking, as evidenced by too many photos that Wilfred had posted of pies, cakes and breads.

"Suppose my client doesn't testify in his own behalf?" Krafter had waited to pose the question that addressed the elephant in the room, wanting every member on the panel to 'fess up if they would hold their hero's silence against him. "Mr. Manjy, what if you hear a reasonable version of the evidence that is consistent with Mr. Jaalaba's innocence?"

"Well, I guess if I heard a witness say one thing, and you said it happened another way, I'd want to hear Mr. Jaalaba's side of the story."

"Suppose the Judge instructed you that my client doesn't have to prove anything at the trial, and the law requires you to follow that instruction. Would that make a difference?"

"I object Your Honor." Cameron Wheatley woke up after the proverbial barnyard animals had already vacated their enclosure. She couldn't hide her displeasure at being skunked. "This line of questioning invades the Court's province," Wheatley went on, rising respectfully and directing her remarks at the fourteen expectant faces hoping to be installed before their personal biases betrayed them. "Mr. Krafter is attempting to give these folks your instructions before they hear the evidence."

The Honorable Deena Norwell picked up her gavel and pointed it testily in Krafter's direction. "Yes, counsel, please save that for closing argument."

Judge Norwell was feeling the effects of a greasy *chimichanga* brought in from the corner food truck at lunch, while she'd worked through the rest of her cases on the daily calendar. She had prepped for the trial with an appropriately severe new hairdo. "Ms. Wheatley's objection is sustained. Mr. Krafter, confine your questions to the jurors' qualifications for service."

"It seems to me, Judge," Krafter pushed it, while keeping one eye on Mr. Manjy. "Following your instructions on the law, even when a juror may not personally agree with the principle, *is* a requirement for service."

Krafter retreated to his chair at the defense table, figuring he'd pay later for sassing Her Honor after she'd already sided with the DA. Still, he hoped the jury panel got his point.

"Bounce this guy," Bryan suggested. "He's obviously prejudiced against Radon."

"I think we have to keep him," Krafter replied. "I already singled him out, and I don't want the rest of them thinking we aren't willing to follow our own rules. What do you think, Radon?"

"The dude looks like he can't wait 'til I'm strapped to a gurney and they put me to sleep. It doesn't matter whether you keep him. I'm beginning to think if I don't get up there, nobody's going to believe you."

"Your Honor," Krafter spoke up in time to avoid Judge Norwell's impending hammer. "The defense accepts these jurors and tenders the panel to the prosecutor."

"Very well then," Judge Norwell said, removing her wire-rimmed reading glasses and peering down at Cameron Wheatley.

The orderly manner in which the trial was progressing amidst such a frenzy of public scrutiny had helped the judge's gastric issues subside. Deena Norwell hated the limelight, including all these professional media vultures who begged for seats in the front pew only when the most sensational carrion turned up on her roster. She looked at those fourteen inscrutable faces in the box, randomly plucked from their mundane lives, suddenly infused with power over the liberty of another citizen; in this case, someone way more powerful than any of them will ever hope to be. And she marveled at the humanity attending such a brilliant necessity. Nevertheless, having presided over more than a hundred jury trials, she also cringed over the lack of humility too often attending those same jurors' transformation into the role of the Almighty.

"Unless I hear a further challenge from the state," Judge Norwell declared, "we have our jury . . . Members of the panel, please stand. Raise your right hand and the clerk will administer the oath of office . . . Uh . . . Mr. Mangy? Raise your other right hand, please."

When it was done and they were seated again, and the murmur over this new development had passed through the gallery, Her Honor continued. "We've made good progress today, so I'll let you folks go home . . . We'll resume tomorrow morning with opening statements and your initial witnesses, Madame District Attorney . . . Ladies and gentlemen of the jury, remember not to discuss this case with your family or your friends and neighbors. Don't watch any news reports about the case or read any online stories, no newspapers, and especially do not peek at the check-out counter."

* * *

Mike Prey made his move in Yelapa. He had come to believe that Tanya Radishoff had wisely skedaddled on down to Mexico, trying to put the double homicide in Lonnie Shenkman's apartment behind her. Mike had first learned from Russell's grieving older sister that Tanya had introduced Russell to Shenkman in the first place. After more than six months of digging, through blind alleys and droughts, Prey had discovered that Russell hooked up years ago in the Castro with Peter "Scotty" Newton, a pudgy, dotcom phenom who loved to entertain.

Small world: turns out Tanya had also started hanging around with Scotty Newton's crowd not long after landing in America from Croatia. Newton had invested some of his profits in a series of real estate development deals, including a residential estate in Yelapa, with a separate brick and stucco casita off the rear garden. When Prey had finally caught up to Scotty in the lobby bar of his new boutique hotel near Union Square, Newton was affable and genuinely seemed surprised to be asked about Tanya Radishoff; although she had been all over the news. But then Scotty had also said he couldn't remember whether he'd ever met her before.

Based on Mike's semi-informed hunch that Newton had lied, and fueled by Krafter's expense account, including authentic "Tommy Bahama" tropical wear, Prey flew to Puerto Vallarta, made some inquiries of the local real estate brokers and learned there were a number of luxury rentals in the hills above the river. The consensus was that the casita Mike described had been "occupada antes de Marzo" by a skinny female with an Eastern European accent and short, spiky black hair, who, maybe, resembled the photo Mike showed them.

Mike took the ferry over to Yelapa and walked from the town pier up to Scotty Newton's property via the map with hand drawn annotations by one of the brokers. There he came upon Tanya Radishoff napping topless in a hammock on the screened-in porch off the rear garden.

"Am I busted?" Tanya asked, without bothering to cover up. She appeared relieved to see a civilian rather than the police who she'd probably been half-expecting to show up anytime.

"They're not bad from where I'm standing." Thankfully, Mike's brain had instructed his penis to refrain from saying this out loud. In the old days, he would've been all over the situation. Let Tanya seduce him into thinking he won't turn her in. Get her to spread open her visa problems before him, and then he'd penetrate any impediments to safely navigating the legal consequences awaiting her in San Francisco. Tanya was attractive, and the twenty years between them didn't bother this "Loose Guy," the dubiously enduring moniker hung on him way back in college.

In fairness, though, Mike had invented the persona at open mike nights in a local comedy club on campus, trying to break into stand-up, after perfecting his routines in the sorority house dining room while he was supposed to be working as a busboy. Like most children without siblings, Mike had grown up unrestrained, seeking attention and love for as long as he could remember feeling alone.

As a young man traveling through India, he'd rediscovered his spirituality and migrated to California. Consequently, after many failed associations, Mike recognized this was the biggest case of his life, and he couldn't afford to get caught with his tongue in the honey jar. "The smaller the gap between satisfying one's desires and doing the right thing, the happier one will be." He silently recited the mantra. Thankfully, he'd retained one important divine lesson over the years.

"I'm not a cop," Mike finally answered Tanya. "But I do have to bring you back to testify about what happened. As long as you tell the truth you might not be deported."

"Are you kidding?" Tanya sat up and lithely disengaged her long legs from the hammock, still baring her breasts with what he noticed to be large pink nipples pierced by tiny diamond studs. "I don't going anywhere without immunity."

"You learn that on TV? . . . Pretty cool, Tanya. Except, you're lucky I found you first. Your best hope for staying out of jail is to return voluntarily before the police catch you. Lady, nobody is better than Archie Krafter on your side. But only the District Attorney can promise you immunity. If I were you, I'd be thinking about what to pack for the trip, and deciding what story you're going to tell the DA."

"What *story* am I telling? You cute guy. But don't mess around me, OK? . . . Lonnie and Russell had screaming fight over how much he owed when Lonnie lost it and starts swinging baseball bat. So Russell takes out gun to defend himself. I'm calling 911 and the basketball guy showed up."

"There was no marijuana robbery?"

"What marijuana? I see police coming from the front window and decide I don't be here, so I leave through the patio and basketball guy was in kitchen. Maybe he try to stop fight, I don't know. But I don't lie if I have to come back."

"Why would anyone believe you after hiding out all these months?"

Tanya beckoned him inside her casita. The room was draped in white, from the fabrics on the rattan furniture to the pulled-back curtains exposing long jalousie windows. She snatched a lacy shawl cover-up off the cushioned divan at the foot of her platform bed and walked over to her ivory writing desk, illuminated in the afternoon sun. Reaching into the top drawer, Tanya delicately withdrew a gold chain with a skinny metal key hanging from it. "This key opens box containing all proof anybody need."

* * *

Officer Daniel "Dan" Yancy, SFPD, nervously tugged on the knot of his skinny, navy-blue necktie, while shifting his twitching buttocks in the witness chair. Just thirty-six years old, handsome Dan has a three-year-old daughter he doesn't see enough, and his career was already marred forever by the frickin' coward sitting at the defense table. Dan fumed at the sight of the entitled druggy acting so contrite. Jaalaba had passed up the deal of the century and now he was going to pay for making Dan go through this torture *yet again.*

First, he'd given a gut-wrenching accounting of his partner's death to his District Commander, then a sworn statement to Internal Affairs and another to the District Attorney. Then he had to testify before the Grand Jury. It was bad enough Dan hadn't been allowed to touch his weapon since the day the unspeakable had gone down. He'd been reassigned to wander around the district, processing intake forms. Worst of all, nobody else really cared about Gino anymore.

Yes, Mayor Lee had attended Patrolman Trower's public memorial service, along with the Police Chief and most of the force. How incredibly difficult it had been for Dan, facing Gino's wife, Barbara, and their two teenage daughters, barely acknowledging him, neither of whom would look at him as he expressed his condolences. After all, he and Gino had been partners for three and a half years, and those sweet kids don't have a father because that superstar's supplier turned a gun on Gino trying to escape. Blessed Gino had answered a call for help, the two of them firefighters in blue rushing into a burning building. Yet, here he was again, being required to relive the entire humiliating nightmare in front of the universe. Especially Jaalaba's lawyer, who's trying to blame the entire sad episode on him.

"I told you it happened in a matter of seconds," Dan Yancy said into the long thin microphone protruding from the witness stand, as Krafter had begun his cross-examination by carefully leading Yancy back over his story. "I heard a gunshot and advanced from the yard toward the concrete patio," Officer Yancy continued, looking directly at the jury. "I saw a person inside with a shiny object I concluded was a gun. I drew my weapon, moved closer, then I heard two more shots and glass breaking, and I hit the ground. When I looked up, I saw the shiny gun again and the defendant was running out through the patio. I believed I was being fired upon and I fired back."

"Were you able to identify the person you first saw inside the patio with the shiny object?"

"Well . . . I know now he was Mr. Marchetti . . . right before my partner downed him. The next two shots came so close after that—just as the defendant came running out through the patio—I thought Marchetti was covering their escape, so I returned fire."

"You assumed it was the same gun and the same person?"

"Yes."

"One of the robbers?"

"Yes."

"Although you couldn't see who it was?"

"I was aiming at the gun."

Krafter seized on that remark, moving from the podium toward the witness, just not enough to require the Court's permission to approach him directly, yet closer to the jury box. "You fired even though you hadn't witnessed a robbery, had you Officer?"

"We responded to a home invasion, and one armed individual shot at me while another was escaping after my partner had gone in to investigate. I didn't have time to ask, 'Hey, is this a robbery?'"

"Turns out, though, you wrongly assumed the armed individual who shot at you was Mr. Marchetti, right?"

"How could I know that?"

"Turns out Mr. Marchetti's gun was never fired, was it?"

"I'm not a ballistics expert, counselor."

"Yet, you fired blindly into a residence at someone with a gun, although you knew your partner was also in there? . . . And you knew *he* was armed."

Dan Yancy struggled to retain his composure, taking a deep breath, and gripping the metallic arms of the cushioned witness chair, while the dam threatened to burst. "Nobody feels worse than I do. But it was Marchetti and your client . . ." Yancy caught himself, as he pointed a dagger-like finger toward Radon Jaalaba. "It's *their* fault."

"Alright, Officer Yancy," Krafter probed a different vein. "Let's talk about this alleged robbery for a minute. When you first entered the patio what did you see?"

"Officer Trower was on the floor, leaning up against the bar divider between the kitchen and the dining room, not far from Mr. Marchetti's body lying in the broken glass near the patio door. Gino . . . Officer Trower was bleeding badly in the stomach region, and I managed to staunch the wound with kitchen towels. He was alert enough to tell me the victim was still in the apartment. I called for an ambulance, moved into the long hallway and noticed a dark plastic garbage bag that later turned out to contain six pounds of high-grade marijuana flowers. Then I was met by Mr. Shenkman, who was clearly upset."

"Approximately how many feet from the garbage bag was Mr. Shenkman when you first encountered him?"

"The bag was on the hardwood floor a few feet from the kitchen entrance, and Mr. Shenkman was down the hallway near the bathroom, probably eight to ten feet away."

"You don't personally know how the marijuana got there, do you?"

"I didn't personally see Marchetti drop it, if that's what you mean?"

"You also don't know if Mr. Shenkman put it there, do you?"

"I know it was there when I walked into the hallway, and I know what Shenkman told me."

"Well, you aren't allowed to tell us what Mr. Shenkman said. The jury will have to hear from Mr. Shenkman directly. But isn't it true, Officer Yancy, that Officer Trower never told you Russell Marchetti had dropped the bag in the hallway before he shot him?"

"I was trying to save my partner's life, so I didn't ask him about the bag at the time."

"Well, isn't it also true the only evidence a robbery occurred is Alonzo Shenkman's word for it?"

"Counselor," Officer Daniel Yancy replied, looking over at Radon Jaalaba. "If your client wasn't part of the fracas, why didn't he halt when I ordered him to? He ran right by me, and it's a good thing I recognized him, or I might've shot out a kneecap to slow him down."

Krafter realized one question too late that he'd just asked one question too many. He staggered back to the defense table searching for anything to end this examination on an up note. As Krafter picked up a folder on the table and pretended to look through the police reports for a crevice into which he could crawl, Bryan suggested, "Grab a seat, Archie, unless you wanna see if your other foot fits in there."

"I knew that guy recognized me," Radon offered no help. "Whose side are you on, anyway, Krafter?"

As soon as Archie informed the court he had no more questions for the witness, Cameron Wheatley sprung to her feet, sensing the momentum had shifted. Rather than re-direct Yancy over the weak points exposed on cross-examination, Cameron moved in for the kill. "Thank you, Officer Yancy," she declared, excusing him with a gracefully knowing smile. "The People call Alonzo Shenkman."

Krafter watched as handsome Dan exited through the swinging doors, avoiding eye-contact with Alonzo Shenkman who passed him on his way to the witness box. Krafter's stomach churned in a stew of nerves and seething adrenaline, hyper-focused on exposing Alonzo Shenkman to be an opportunistic liar who took advantage of a tragic misadventure to cover up his cocaine dealing. That suddenly seemed a slipperier slope to scale than Krafter had anticipated, as Shenkman took the oath clad in a Men's Wearhouse suit with power tie and slicked-down hair, bearing more resemblance to an investment banker than an underground pharmacist. Krafter was left to wonder whether the jury would swallow this veil of respectability orchestrated by the DA.

"He looks a lot different than when he attacked Russell," Radon whispered to Bryan, who was searching their database for any updates on Shenkman that Archie might use during cross-examination.

Alonzo turned his chair to address the jury, as Cameron Wheatley directed him through his personal history, including Shenkman's employment with a licensed non-profit cannabis dispensary in the Lower Haight District. Then she moved on to the events on Christmas morning.

"They both definitely scared me," Shenkman declared. "I only allowed Mr. Marchetti in my apartment because he was a dispensary patient, and it was closed on Christmas. When Mr. Jaalaba walked in later, I didn't know who he was, and he didn't say. Obviously, I'm not a basketball fan. But he acted weird right off."

"Your Honor, I'm loathe to interrupt," Krafter said, standing at the defense table, as counsel's had leeway to lead the witness through the history. But I must object to any personal characterizations of my client's conduct."

"Yes, Mr. Krafter, we finally agree on something," Judge Norwell said with a wink at the jury, letting them know she was in charge with a sense of humor. "Your objection is sustained. Mr. Shenkman, please confine your answers to your personal observations and experiences. Not your thoughts or conclusions."

"Thank you Judge," Cameron Wheatley stepped in, getting her examination back on track. "Mr. Shenkman, can you tell us what you actually observed that caused you to characterize it as 'weird?'"

"Russell Marchetti sent me a text needing to come over on Christmas morning, and I texted back that he had to clear his debt to the club if he expected any help. As soon as he walked in, he started complaining about the prices and how much he already owed. He started getting belligerent and I told him to leave. Mr. Marchetti took a gun from his jacket pocket and pointed it at me. Then the defendant shows up," Shenkman said, gesturing toward Radon. "Marchetti tells me to give him the weed now or he's going to shoot me. My girlfriend heard them threatening me and called 911. That's how the police got there in time to stop them."

"Mr. Shenkman." Cameron Wheatley's voice boomed out across the room. "Did you fear for your life when Mr. Marchetti pointed the gun at you and demanded your medical cannabis?"

"Oh, man," Radon whispered into Krafter's ear. "Is the jury buying this?"

Was this a stupid plan? Krafter couldn't help thinking the question was more rhetorical. Was Radon about to go to jail for obstinately refusing to testify? *Check.* Was Krafter the bigger fool for listening to Radon? *Check!* . . . For the next twenty minutes, Krafter was relegated to making futile objections, trying to break up Wheatley's rhythm, as she coaxed Alonzo Shenkman through a rousing recap of the shootings and Radon's dastardly disappearance from the scene. For one moment, Archie thought, upon hearing such damaging testimony in open court, Radon might decide he needed to testify in his own defense after all. But a sideways glance at the rocky hero, beads of sweat dancing off his pulsating forehead, convinced Krafter that Radon would not get up there when his turn came.

Meanwhile, Alonzo Shenkman comfortably leaned back in the witness chair, finishing his bedtime story to the jury. "I never saw Tanya Radishoff again," he said.

Cameron Wheatley snapped shut her trial book with a touch of bravado and floated her fine frame toward the prosecution table, where she declared: "Your witness, Counselor."

Judge Norwell rapped her gavel twice, resuming control of her courtroom amidst a buzz once again spreading throughout the gallery. "It's nearly lunch time, Mr. Krafter," she offered without expression. "Unless your heart is set on starting your cross-examination, let's recess until one-thirty." Then she raised her meticulously drawn eyebrows heavenward, as if to say to him, "You're on your own, pal."

* * *

Mike Prey reached for the house phone on the Queen Anne bedside table in their suite at the Nob Hill Fairmont. "Okay. Thanks," Mike said to the operator delivering an 11:00 AM wake-up call. Mike and Tanya had made their long journey in a drive-away rental—with Arizona plates and an import sticker—from Puerto Vallarta to the border at Nogales. A thousand miles in just over two days, heeding the warnings not to travel at night, to stay on the Mexican toll roads and arrive at the checkpoint bright and clean around noon. The US Customs agent had examined Mike's license and passport, asked him some questions about their beach vacation and why they were driving home. Then he also stamped Tanya's passport that she had paid her "Cousin Sasha the photographer" fifteen hundred dollars to forge, including a birth certificate and driver's license, before she'd fled to Mexico.

After switching rentals in Tucson, they drove another two hours to Phoenix. The thought of crashing a few hours with a desert spa massage treatment had been tempting, but they'd decided to grab a burrito and go on to LA. Nevertheless, lack of sleep had weakened Mike's defenses, allowing his libido to take over when they'd approached Pasadena, and he suggested they check into a hotel room with a hot tub, room service and porno. Tanya had wisely refused.

Instead, they made the turnoff for Highway 5, pressed on to San Francisco, taking turns behind the wheel, and they'd crossed the Bay Bridge at 3:35 AM, arriving under the Fairmont's famed portico ten minutes later. Prey had phoned Archie as soon as they had safely crossed the border, and Krafter's connection at the hotel had secured an empty tower suite with some privacy from any media vultures hovering about.

Tanya was duly impressed that Mike had safely delivered her this far. She was also thoroughly exhausted. She took a quick shower and fell asleep on the king size bed. For a moment though, when the sun rose, she'd gotten up and walked over to the floor to ceiling picture window in the bedroom and pulled back the thick silk drapes. The iconic view facing Fisherman's Wharf and Alcatraz with the glorious Golden Gate beyond only made her think of going to jail again. That's when she'd finally succumbed to the Loose Guy's charms.

Presently, following their wake-up call, Tanya sat up in bed and said to him without inflection: "I hoped my last meal would be satisfying," only serving to confuse him. She retrieved from under the covers her lacy thong which, a scant few hours earlier, had been wrapped around Mike's curly-haired noggin.

He couldn't decipher whether she was commenting favorably on her orgasm, or she was being cruelly ironic. Rather than ask her: "Did you or did you *not* come?" Mike tried unsuccessfully to reach Krafter and Marten on their cell phones, while she pulled on her skinny jeans. "They must be in the courtroom," he said, wisely dropping the subject.

It was 11:50 AM by the time Mike parked at a commercial meter across from Wells Fargo's main branch in the Financial District. They rushed inside the glass-walled history museum entrance, passing the collection of pristinely preserved Pony Express stagecoaches, down the long wide corridor to an elevator bank connecting the branch on the other side of the vast main floor.

"Airports, they don't rent lockers anymore after Nine-Eleven," Tanya informed him as they rode down to the basement. "I try storage all over before I leave for Mexico," she explained.

Mike followed her into a waiting area, across from the private banking receptionist stationed at the large open vault. "Safety deposit box is only small private space you can rent long term," she went on. "I don't know when I'm coming back so, How you say it? I bite the gun? . . . I fill out application, pay one year, and we are here."

Tanya removed from around her neck the key she'd showed him in Yelapa and walked over to the young Asian woman with a bob hairdo wearing the bank's navy-blue blazer. Tanya signed the registration book: "Stella Zabrisky" and was buzzed inside the counter; she followed the employee to a room off the vault entrance, out of Mike's view. He sat nervously waiting in one of the low, thinly cushioned office chairs that flanked a stale-smelling coffee machine stand, with a home loan interest display banner hanging above him.

Following seven minutes of suspended animation, "Stella Zabrisky" emerged from the private room, signed out, and promptly banged her hip into the counter while hurrying over to Mike. She waited until they returned to the car and extracted from her purse a rolled-up plastic wad, four inches wide, wrapped in masking tape.

"I wish I never agree to take from Lonnie's apartment. Soon as I get home, I tape up bag that day, and carry it around for a week, until I stash it here and go to Mexico."

She started to unwrap the tape, but Mike stopped her. He removed a thick plastic evidence envelope of his own from one of the interior pockets on his fancy new beige island jacket.

"I figure three-and-a-half ounces of cocaine in Ziploc bag," Tanya said, while Mike gingerly took custody of the package and slipped it into the envelope. He sealed it, wrote his initials, and scribbled the date over the seal, then retrieved his briefcase from behind the driver's seat and locked the bulky envelope inside. Krafter and Marten's cell phones went straight to voicemail again, so Mike drove off toward the courthouse, barely one mile away.

Big rig construction detours backed up traffic most of the trip. Blessedly, a limousine pulled out of a parking space in front of the bail bond office down the block from the courthouse, and Mike eased in. "Sit here," he told Tanya, exiting the driver's seat and handing her his iPad. "Pretend you're working on this and keep your hat on. I'll be back in ten minutes."

Prey was halfway up the wide steps to the courthouse doors when Krafter's number finally appeared on his phone.

"We're recessed for lunch, Mike. Where are you?"

"Who's the *baddest motherf-er* you know? . . . Here to save your sorry butt from embarrassment. Just walk straight to the elevator and out the front door . . . Holy Shit! I am so excited I can barely contain myself, Archie . . . Archie? Can you hear me? . . . Hey? . . . Archie?"

Krafter darted from the elevator on the main floor, made his way out the front exit and hurried over to Mike, who embraced him on the courthouse steps. Prey beamed with self-love as he silently led Archie down the block to the rental car.

"Archie Krafter meet Tanya Radishoff."

Krafter struggled to contain his own delight, having often thought he might never encounter this crafty Croatian herky-jerky in the flesh. But before he could introduce himself, Mike gushed on.

"She's willing to testify that Shenkman and Russell got into a violent argument over a cocaine transaction and there was no marijuana robbery."

"Ms. Radishoff . . . May I call you Tanya?" Krafter asked. "Everyone is grateful you returned voluntarily . . . Let's be honest with each other, OK? You're a fugitive witness, a possible accessory to murder and an illegal immigrant with an expired student visa. You're facing a pissed-off district attorney who'd rather not believe you than scrape the egg off her face. You have placed yourself in serious peril."

"Mr. Krafter," she said; Tanya knew how bad it was. "By the time Mike find me, I'm relieved is over. Basketball guy shouldn't get blame for what happened. I call 911 to stop Lonnie and Russell killing each other in first place. Stupidly I agree to take Lonnie's coke out of the apartment to protect him getting busted."

"I'll try to help,' Krafter said, chewing over how much of what she just said was true. "Be prepared to repeat everything under oath from now on."

"I don't lie for Lonnie in court. I see on television Russell and policeman killed but I don't going back to return cocaine. I decide is better go to Mexico."

"You know Shenkman will deny it was his. After running away, why should the jury believe you?"

"Archie, my dude," Mike jumped in. "I'm sure Alonzo Shenkman's fingerprints are all over the sealed Ziploc bag that's inside this briefcase. The bag's been sitting in a safe deposit box, and this will be the first time anyone sees the contents since she wrapped it last Christmas.

But I'd wait until the DA is present when you open Tanya's present, 'cause it's gonna be way better than Al Capone's vault, I promise."

"All right." Krafter had heard enough. "I'll need thirty minutes to set up a meeting with Wheatley. Stay where you are and wait for my call. Then bring Tanya and your briefcase to the DA's office on the third floor and leave everything else in the car for now . . . Tanya, we'll help you get independent counsel, something the court is going to require. But I hope you're ready to spend some time as a guest of the county until this gets sorted out."

"Maybe you find me a lawyer who don't get me deported."

Krafter found Bryan and Michelle in the conference room next to the courtroom, where the attorneys and court personnel had carved out a safe space from the press and the "looky-loos" during trial recesses. As ecstatic as they were to learn about Tanya, Bryan remarked that they hadn't seen Radon since the break. Radon had rarely left the building for lunch, except with his mother who sat with him in the courtroom every day.

Michelle went looking for him, while Krafter and Marten headed out to locate Cameron Wheatley and try to arrange Tanya's voluntary surrender before Judge Norwell reconvened the afternoon session at two. Following ten solid minutes of Krafter's cajoling, borderline begging, and appealing to Wheatley's highest sense of justice, she agreed to interview Tanya Radishoff. An hour later, the DA was compelled to request Judge Norwell send the jury home for the day, while Cameron submitted Tanya's physical evidence to the lab for comparison and she conducted another interview with Alonzo Shenkman.

Upon hearing this request in her chambers, the Honorable Deena Norwell nearly levitated out of her swivel chair. She silently thanked divine intervention for delivering this last-minute witness and saving her from judging harshly a tortured soul of a sinner and one heck of a basketball player.

Judge Norwell returned to the courtroom and feigned reluctance to the jury while recessing the trial forty-eight hours for "a court matter" without revealing any specifics, and thereby allowing the DA to assess this new evidence. Nobody complained out loud when Radon had failed to return promptly after lunch. Having learned that Tanya had surrendered in a text from his mother, Radon turned his car around and slipped into the courtroom just as Judge Norwell was announcing the delay to the jury.

By the following afternoon, the bag of cocaine had come back from the lab with Alonzo Shenkman's fingerprints all over it; and it was all over for Alonzo Shenkman. He didn't last fifteen minutes with Wheatley before admitting that he'd staged the cannabis robbery to protect himself after Russell and Officer Trower were shot.

Consequently, the next day, Judge Norwell ordered a mistrial and granted the state's motion to dismiss the charges against Radon. She discharged the jury with gratitude for their service, assuring them they had each contributed to justice being done in the case. The judge also agreed to take under submission Tanya Radishoff's proposed guilty plea to aiding and abetting a false police report, negotiated by her court-appointed attorney, thereby allowing Tanya to apply for legal status after six months of community service.

When Judge Norwell had announced the state's dismissal to the stunned gallery, Radon was the epitome of humility. He asked to address the court and thanked the judge for treating him fairly while, choking back guilty tears, he expressed regret over "two good souls who senselessly lost their lives." Then he hugged his mother, who rushed to the defense table, followed by hugs with Archie and Bryan, along with Marina and Lora. Cameron Wheatley walked over to shake

Radon's hand. "Good Luck, Mr. Jaalaba," she said. "I hope we see you in a Worriers uniform again whether you cooperate or not."

Upon leaving the courtroom, Radon and his entourage were met by the crush of fans, media, and county employees who followed them through the hallway to the elevator. Bryan tried to keep out as many folks as he could until the doors closed and they rode down with a raucous group congratulating Radon, reaching out to touch him in close proximity.

Marten and Krafter led the charge outside the building and down the courthouse steps, where it became obvious that Jaalaba had to say something before the press would go away. Bryan herded together a group of reporters with microphones on the sidewalk at the bottom of the stairs and directed Radon to step up and say something, "Sweet and short; you're not getting an award."

"I'm grateful this ordeal is over for my family and my team," Radon spoke to the crowd spilling into the street. "Most of all, I just want to thank the fans for your support and encouragement . . . I know things can never be the same . . . But I'll never stop trying."

Krafter stepped in, saluting the District Attorney for her professionalism and lauding Tanya for coming forward with the truth. He said Radon was going home to rest and think about getting ready for the pre-season, whenever the lock-out ends. Then he asked for folks to respect Radon's privacy, as Radon would not answer any questions at this time. He thanked everyone for their concern and walked away from the microphones.

They finally escaped the most persistent in the audience by returning inside the courthouse until the group could safely disperse. Archie and Lora accompanied Radon to the sheriff's office, where they waited another hour and a half for the code that unlocked Radon's ankle bracelet.

"Why did the DA sound so sarcastic with me?" Radon asked Krafter as they sat on the bench in the sheriff's reception area.

"You heard those reporters' questions. Wheatley's getting pressure to charge Shenkman with perjury. If you don't cooperate with her, you could be charged with contempt."

"I knew this wasn't going to be over."

Archie and Lora drove Radon back to his condo, where Michelle and Marina had decided to host an intimate victory toast. For the first time in too many months they all relaxed together, released from the legal collar surrounding Radon, the moments of joy being subdued nonetheless by the underlying tragedy. Following several rounds of praise, and a couple rounds of vodka, Archie felt a little light-headed and Lora whisked him off to a romantic dinner celebration she had planned for them.

By the time they returned home, sated, yet aroused, the adrenaline of the case had begun to peel away. Archie stepped out of the shower, refreshed, imagining Lora waiting for him in bed, wearing one of the costumes she'd occasionally brought home from the theater. Maybe Vanda's sexy gown from *Venus in Fur?* Archie dried himself off, put on his pajama bottoms and a fresh tee-shirt, walked over to the bed, and promptly fell into a deep sleep for the first time in two weeks.

On the other hand, Radon had barely weathered the party in his own apartment, and sleep was not an option. After all the guests including Marina had left and his mother went off to bed, the adrenaline still raged. Radon rode the elevator down to the garage, got into his car and took off for anywhere else. He didn't have to come back. No longer tethered to the sheriff for the first time in eight months, Radon drove to the coast and disappeared.

Chapter Fourteen

Spilled Milk Awards

Archie and Lora got away for two weeks on Maui to enjoy the court victory, at the villa of a former client and friend with whom Archie had stayed in touch over the years. Rick had e-mailed Archie the front door code, left a stocked refrigerator and a stellar selection in the climate-controlled wine cellar while he visited his ailing mother in Chicago.

Twenty years earlier, when Krafter still lived in the Windy City, Rick was a successful commodities trader and hard-partying bachelor, often entertaining guests at his Gold Coast brownstone. He'd been referred to Archie following his arrest for allegedly possessing several ounces of ecstasy discovered inside the cushions of his posh living room sofa. The police had torn up his place with a search warrant based on the word of a "confidential informant," who Rick believed was a vengeful former playmate with no knowledge that any drugs were on the premises for at least six months. After Krafter had attacked the warrant's reliability in court and the cops refused to reveal their informant's identity the charges had been dismissed.

Having come within a lawyer's tongue of going to jail, Rick had gotten the message and moved to Hawaii in order to turn his life around. It wasn't long before he'd conceived and brought to market an herbal energy drink called "Surf's Up" combining Hawaiian pineapple juice and a South American root known for its sexual potency enhancing properties. "Maui Macha" or "The Big Swell"—as the late-night television ads proclaimed—had made Surf's Up an instant success, attracting venture capital and eventually being acquired for a smidge north of a hundred and fifty million. Rick had repaid his undying gratitude to Krafter many ways over the years, this time offering his oceanfront estate to the decompressing couple.

Archie and Lora have long reveled in tropical white sand and sea wherever they managed to find it. One of their reasons for not having kids was that they traveled well together as a cult of two, whether on a rowboat along the Ganges at sunrise or walking down the hill from home to the neighborhood produce market. Neither one of them has expressed a strong enough biological urge to stress test their formula for success. Lora has also rejected motherhood out of fear that she was predisposed to die during childbirth like her mother; or that maybe her offspring would inherit her father's worst traits?

At the moment, though, they were free to enjoy each other above Paia Beach without itinerary or personal agendas. Plenty of space allowed Lora to work out her latest songs on Rick's grand piano in the living room; while Archie sat at a deck table next to the infinity pool overlooking the calm turquoise Pacific, outlining on his laptop the next installment of *The Naked Lawyer*.

They might've stayed longer in Hawaii. More than a week away from Swami strained their comfort level. Despite the caramel-striped tabby's feigned indifference at his first sight of the couple returning from every prolonged absence; invariably, within hours, their irritated child drew his bloody revenge, biting the first uncovered arm or leg he could ambush on either one of them. Still, in the little bastard's defense, their long-time caretaker, Alex, was also a neighborhood dog-walker and Swami had to cope with the canine smell on Alex's clothes while they were gone.

Moreover, Lora and Archie had also returned for her father's eighty-sixth birthday party in the private dining room of Sal's favorite

Italian restaurant. Following much discussion, they attended mostly at the behest of her brother but also to keep their enemies closer.

A dozen folks were seated at the linen-covered rectangular table—one short of *The Last Supper*, and on both sides. Dominic had arrived solo and sat at the far end, with Lora and Archie to his right. Sal slouched in the high-backed chair at the opposite head next to his personal aide, Cousin Zeda, who lived at the venerable Presidio Terrace house where Lora and Dominic had grown up. Cousin Zeda used to travel to San Francisco visiting her mother, Aunt Rose, who'd taken care of Lora and Dominic from the time their mother had died until they'd both moved away. Being Olivia's only sister, Rose had stayed on to manage Sal's household, and Cousin Zeda had eventually relocated to be near Rose during her last years. When Sal came home from rehab following his stroke, Zeda, a tough spinster of little humor and big faith, had been the perfect choice to move in and care for him.

Sitting next to Zeda was Paul "Paulie" Dellacozzi, Lora's first cousin and Vince Dellacozzi's grandnephew; he reported directly to Sal concerning worldwide distribution of Dellacozzi Farms branded products and services. At Paulie's side was his loyal wife Antonella; savvy in a Chanel suit, she traveled with her husband keeping him current on international market trends and presentable at business meetings. Filling out that side of the table was Harry Mongo, Sal's dentist, longtime poker buddy, and a shoo-in for owning the world's loudest sports jacket. Joined by his wife, Janice, she too was no stranger to wearing vivid, randomly matched colors.

Across the table, packed with grand plates of antipasti, formaggi and prosciutti, Paul's younger sister, Betty, sat at Archie's right, next to her thickly handsome husband, Tony Costo, who bragged that he was in marketing *and* collections. Lora and buxom Betty, currently decked out in D&G, were first cousins, close in age and a resemblance around the eyes and nose. Yet, they no longer knew each other. It seems Paul and Betty's mother, Aunt Anita, had had a falling out with her older brother Salvatore over their inheritance, and Anita had retaliated by keeping Paul and Betty away from her brother's children for most of Lora and Dom's formative years. More than two decades of estrangement later, Sal had been invited to Betty's wedding and came with a generous gift. While Anita and Sal have co-existed ever since, Anita cordially declined to attend his birthday celebration.

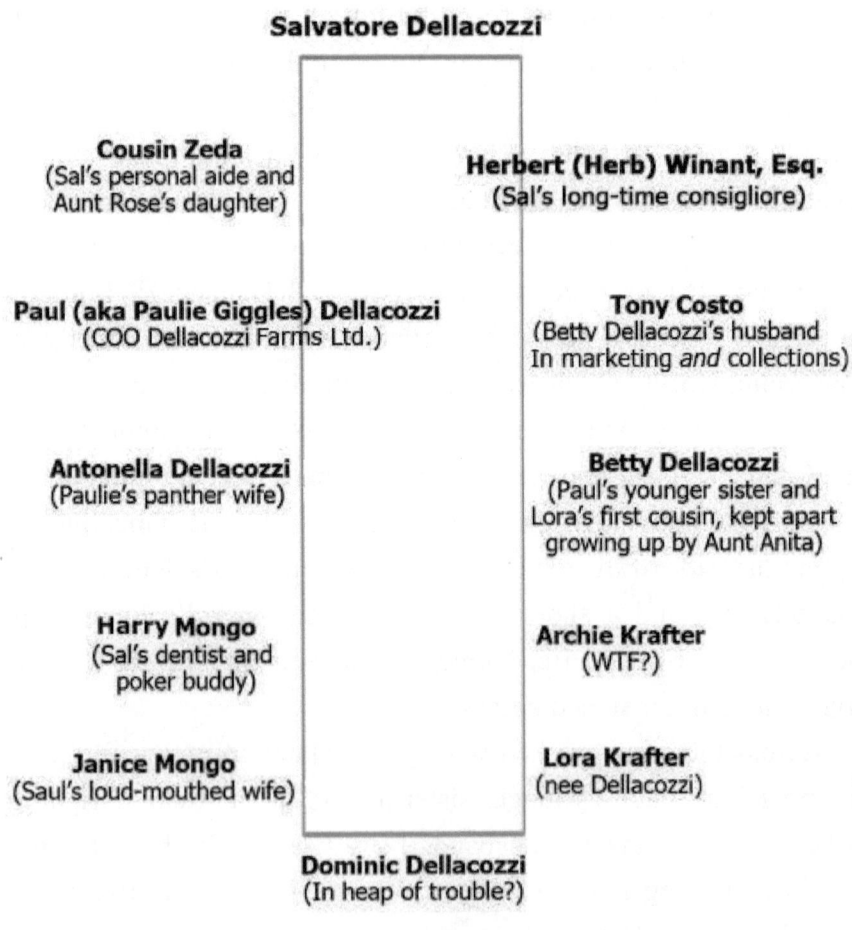

Herbert S. Winant, Esq. occupied the twelfth chair, to Sal's left, having remained Sal's closest business advisor since the late seventies. Forever dapper, Herb was a former Miami, Florida, district attorney who'd turned toward the dark side after coming to California and billing by the hour. Winant had made news by winning a not guilty verdict in one of the early anti-pollution corporate criminal cases prosecuted by the Justice Department. This brought Herb to the attention of John Ehrlichman at the Nixon White House, who'd asked Bebe Rebozo to check him out because of their South Florida connection.

Wealthy banker Rebozo—Nixon's close personal friend for nearly fifty years—had recommended Winant's law firm to some of Bebe's most important associates, including a new drilling client silently controlled by Carlos Marcello, head of the New Orleans mob. It wasn't long before Winant had answered a telephone call from Mickey Cohen in L.A., suggesting that Herb might hear from Salvatore Dellacozzi who had a problem up in "Frisco."

The FBI has been surveilling mafia activity since J. Edgar Hoover first got his panties in a bunch. Technological advances in snooping and post-Watergate anti-crime legislation had supported bugging in public places where subjects were known to meet, while transmitting and receiving from a stationary van located up to two hundred yards away.

Vince Dellacozzi's sudden death in a Chinatown restaurant, within months after Lora's mother had died, had thrust a sad and angry Salvatore Dellacozzi atop the family heap, back into the limelight for the first time since he'd been suspected in the Sacramento roadhouse murders. FBI field agents with powerful zoom lenses had begun videotaping Sal outside Vince Dellacozzi's crowded funeral at SS Peter and Paul's church; and they didn't let up, tailing Sal for over a year until he'd finally called Herb Winant.

Herb had seized upon the legal precedent set by Sam "Momo" Giancana, head of the Chicago Outfit. In one of the earliest attacks against what has since become known as "government profiling," Giancana had quite brazenly sued the FBI for a civil injunction to stop following him twenty-four/seven—frequently on the golf course—without any evidence that he was about to commit a crime.

His creative lawyer, who later became a federal judge, was among the first to win a harassment claim by asserting a violation of Giancana's First Amendment right to a "zone of personal privacy," even though Momo was a notorious public figure at the time. Herbert Winant had literally followed suit to halt surveillance on Sal Dellacozzi, eventually having secured a settlement agreement with the US Attorney keeping the FBI away from Sal except in cases of public safety and other emergencies.

Sal has since called on Herb Winant for advice and counsel often enough to keep him on retainer. By the time Herb sat beside Sal at his 86th birthday dinner, Winant had come to understand over the years that the main difference between his civil and criminal clients wasn't always about character. The bigwig corporate CFOs usually paid late and always complained about the fees, while criminals were uniformly appreciative and brought an envelope stuffed with cash.

"Great job on the Jaalaba case," Winant had said, complimenting Krafter at the bar before they sat down to dinner. Having known Herb since she was eight years old, Lora introduced them when they'd ended up next to him ordering drinks. Herb's curly coiffed hair crowned a craggily skinned face, the bottom half covered by a bushy Orange County mustache hanging over his disappearing chin. "Dominic told me he values your advice, so I know I can discuss this with you," Herb had continued after taking a healthy swig of scotch, neat. "I assume

Dom mentioned the indictment and his arraignment coming up in Sacramento?"

"No . . . Actually, we didn't know," Lora had replied, looking at Krafter, who nodded in agreement, as they silently sipped their Negroni con vodka.

"Well, the charges are sealed until he surrenders so the press doesn't know either. I'm sure Dominic will discuss this with you tonight. But Mr. Boynahan did not effectively oppose the Klitoffs' extradition to Sacramento, and I've been asked to step in as your brother's defense counsel."

"You mean they've agreed to testify against him?" Krafter asked.

"They both signed plea offers detailing their participation in a system of hi-jacked bank accounts, credit cards and a whole lot more, to the tune of over four million dollars last year alone. The government is claiming Dominic received regular profits from a continuing criminal enterprise."

After everyone had been seated and the opening chatter subsided, inspired by the pasta fagioli, Paul rose to honor his Uncle Sal's birthday and for continuing to preserve the history of the family name. Harry Mongo got up and said Sal had bridges in his mouth older than the Dunbarton. Then he retold his story about the time Sal had him do a root canal without anesthesia just to see how it felt. Luckily, before Dominic was forced to say something, the servers cleared off the antipasti plates and set down huge portions of angel hair pasta, platters of veal saltimbocca, chicken parm and baccala, and the specialty of the house: porchetta with rapini.

Dominic waited until everyone was silently ingesting the feast and leaned across his sister to address Archie about the indictment. "Isn't Herb something else?" Dominic asked coyly. "He's pre-arranged minimal bail. I'll have to spend a couple hours inside for processing and he doesn't want me to worry about any of this. He says he'll destroy those Russkies in court."

"If they're lying, I'm sure Herb will expose them," Krafter replied, maybe a little too cutely.

"What's that supposed to mean? You don't believe I had nothing to do with their friggin' business?"

"OK, guys," Lora cut them off, noticing that her father's attention had been drawn to their conversation from the opposite end of the table.

Having recently suffered a milder second stroke, Sal had been relegated to pushing an aluminum walker on two tennis balls, still dragging his left leg along defiantly. This led Sal to mostly refrain from speaking unless asking or answering a direct question. He had instead enhanced his already intense concentration and focus through his eyes, speaking volumes with a simple look. Lora had instantly connected Sal's seeming reversion to survival mode with the time following her mother's death when her father had coldly turned away from her.

In some ways, Sal's fearsome stare, accompanied by a two-fingered command using his good arm, was as intimidating to the recipient as any verbal order he'd ever given. While she recognized all the cracks and hadn't feared or even loathed him for decades, Lora couldn't help marveling over how he still shuffled along with relative impunity.

During the inevitable birthday *Sacripantina* presentation at the end of dinner, everyone stood in place and clapped as Sal mostly blew out the candles, with a little help from Zeda at his side. Not until everyone had said their goodbyes did Lora have an opportunity to address her father in earnest. She'd waited along with Dominic and Archie to help Zeda fold up Sal's walker and assist him into the shotgun seat of his Cadillac.

"I'm so glad you were able to get out again, Dad," she said, leaning into the open passenger window.

"Okay ... you ... too ... bizzy ... for ... fava," Sal spoke slowly, softly, without turning his head. "I'm ... no moron. You ... don't ... want this business."

"You're right, Dad. I don't."

Sal shifted his right side in the leather bucket seat, enough to look into his daughter's eyes. His upper lip quivered with emotion, then instantly turned down, his mouth forming its crooked half-smile. "Brofa needs ... you ... look ... after him."

Then he summoned Dominic with his two-fingered gesture, letting his only son know he continued to support him. "Stay ... strong ... son." Sal fixed on his weaker offspring, grabbing Dominic's arm through the open window, while catching his breath. "You ... know ... Stay strong."

* * *

Over the course of Radon's first week without bail restrictions, he'd escalated to multiple vodkas and too many Red Stripes. He realized he'd better get farther away from temptation if he hoped to be in playing shape whenever the shutdown ended. Having decided that his father's farm in southwestern Morocco was as isolated as it gets, Radon committed himself to twenty-eight days of self-imposed detox. Physically and mentally, he would cleanse all cylinders, cells, organs and orifices, retreating to the fertile property in North Africa that he'd helped his father purchase.

Ramin Jaalaba had never returned to America since his voluntary departure to avoid deportation when Radon was seven years old. As Michelle hadn't allowed her minor son to leave the country, Radon didn't see his father again in the flesh despite their exchanging letters, videos, and eventually e-mails until Radon had traveled to Africa during the summer following his sophomore year at Cal.

Back then, Ramin had recently retired from the Moroccan Royal Air Force with a small pension and was working as a dispatcher for an executive limousine service in Casablanca. Radon still remembered the visit warmly. Getting to know each other after a decade had passed, his father had been contrite and proud that his son was an American college basketball star, having installed satellite TV on his apartment building roof and invited the neighbors to watch Radon's Pac-10 games. His father's acknowledgment that he'd abandoned Radon for his own addiction stuck with Radon. He had returned five years later, a multi-millionaire, able to provide Ramin's down payment on forty hectares of verdant land midway between Marrakesh—at the base of the Atlas Mountains—and Essaouira on the Atlantic Ocean.

Ramin Jaalaba was still lean and handsome then, his dark curly hair and straight chin sprinkled with gray. Having declined to remarry, he preferred instead the uncommitted life without responsibility for the physical or emotional sustenance of others. Except that Ramin had always maintained his professionalism on the job. Indeed, he was a high-functioning addict believing it was inherent to his culture regardless of all that pious anti-alcohol rhetoric. The majority of Moroccan men grew up smoking *kief* or chewing *khat*, while most of those guys graduated to opium or to snorting heroin.

All the same, following two years of "parental duty" in America, upon returning home, Captain Ramin Jaalaba had been welcomed back into the RAF without demotion. Having resumed flying missions well into his forties, at fifty he'd chosen retirement over his mind-numbing desk job. But Ramin never thought he'd still be routing traffic at a livery service when out of the blue his world-famous son had asked him what he wanted most in life? Ramin hadn't hesitated to recite his list: a working farm with orchards and olive groves, maybe a small vineyard and even some sheep and other grass-grazing beasts, not to mention, a cannabis patch for processing into hashish.

Radon drove his rented Renault along the perimeter road to the wrought-iron entrance gate displaying its familiar sign: *Ranch de Jaalaba*. The undulating rows of vines, normally lush with ripening Grenache grapes just before the September harvest, seemed somewhat sparse. Tomato plants, anise and fennel, having spread contiguously over the vast front yard during previous years, were gone. Radon observed that even the unshorn sheep seemed forlorn despite being raised for wool, not food.

He motored the last five hundred meters to the main house, flanked by desert palms and eucalyptus. Then he spotted Ramin sitting in his wicker rocker on the front porch. Radon felt a shudder in his twice-repaired left knee, akin to a change in the weather, and his resentment roiled as he exited the car and walked over surprised to greet this gloomy, tired-looking old man—*his* old man.

Ramin's dream was manifesting nicely during the initial growing seasons since he'd taken over. The sun and rain had cooperated, the well-tended land had responded with plump grapes, olives, mandarins, tangerines and juicy apples adjacent to bushy marijuana plants in the brightest corner of the immense fields.

Ramin had tried hard to thrive, having retained the selling family's long-trusted ranch foreman, Tayseer, and his crew, while Ramin had studied how to manage his son's benevolent gift of opportunity. Sadly, though, Ramin simply couldn't keep it together when it came to being the decision maker, the one in charge of the operation. Throughout his military career Ramin had acted responsibly, when he was being told what to do. Too many problems arose almost every day on the ranch. Even his own *kief* wasn't doing it, and the Moroccan poppy straw extract he'd been distilling was serviceable enough for a while. Afghan was of course far superior; it was cheap and always available.

Consequently, when Radon showed up seeking some peaceful self-reflection on sobriety and freedom, it was obvious that life on *Ranch de Jaalaba* had taken a wrong turn.

They hugged in the afternoon heat, Radon surprised by the odor coming off his father—just like his own sweat. Ramin smiled proudly, and Radon saw that his teeth had begun to yellow and crack. They walked into the house and Radon was greeted by their cousin, Sayeeda, who Ramin called his "Mikaila," after the Islamic Angel of Mercy known for nourishing the heart and soul. First cousin to Ramin on their fathers' side, Sayeeda was also his cook, housekeeper and bookkeeper, commuting six days a week to keep too many of Ramin's balls in the air for what she was being paid.

By mid-afternoon, on Radon's fourth day, his father had yet to emerge since he'd stumbled off to bed the previous evening in a rage before dinner had ended. Sayeeda had prepared and left for them a tajine of chicken, olives and lemon, and Ramin had essentially lost the plot minutes after they'd sat down at the table. During an unsolicited litany of rambling excuses for the meager harvest, at the end of a rising crescendo, Ramin heaved his plateful of food into the fireplace. Radon had reasonably concluded that his father must be hooked on something.

But it takes one to know one, doesn't it? Nevertheless, rather than politely thank Ramin for his hospitality and leave the next morning, Radon was determined that the toxic environment somehow, against all odds, become his inspirational counter irritant. By focusing on his father's physical health, Radon would also have another reason to keep himself healthy. Challenging himself to gain his father's trust, even if he couldn't convince him to get clean, Radon resolved to at least engage his father in part of the daily physical training routine that Radon had practiced since arriving.

Previous owners had converted one of the barns into a gym and exercise room for the seasonal workers. Every morning Radon did ninety minutes of lifting on fairly modern machines, next to the squash court fitted with a regulation hoop and backboard that he drilled on for another hour. In the late afternoon, when the remote desert sky was cooling orange, he ran fifteen kilometers up and down the vineyards, through the orchards on the road around the property, and along the main road towards the coast and back.

Over the course of the next ten days, Radon persuaded Ramin to jog the first five kilometers with him, while they mostly found a way through each other's bullshit. His father agreed to apologize to Tayseer and ask him to come back; his foreman had finally quit after Ramin had made Tayseer look bad for months, stiffing vendors and some of his crew. Remarkably though, as Ramin's night sweats, stomach cramps and crawlers subsided, the combination of their structured exercise routine and having someone else to level with had a noticeable effect on Ramin. He was recapturing the spark of the dream that brought him here, and he promised his son he would assiduously protect this life-saving gift forever. Ramin also vowed to stick to his home-grown tincture from now on, and not partake until dusk.

On the other side, Radon described his stint in rehab and answered his father's questions about the trial. Radon even mentioned Dr. Dewhauser's therapy, and his brain scan results. Then he promised Ramin he would be in the Worriers starting line-up on opening night whenever the lockout ended.

Radon didn't tell his father that Russell had been more than his friend. How could his father ever understand that Radon loved another man intimately? The *Quran* would not permit it. Radon had grown up around naked boys and men in locker rooms and saunas, as comfortable around them as being naked with women.

He'd wondered about his sexuality for as long as he'd had erections. By the time he'd reached college, at six feet four-and-a-half inches tall, Radon was a handsomely chiseled hunk among civilians. But on the court, he hadn't been the tallest boy since high school. In the NBA, he was a tiny twig among redwoods, effortlessly shoved aside by brawny bulging arms, abused and bruised by cement hips and flailing legs as big as oak tree trunks. To survive in this pituitary stew of strength and stamina, Radon's highly developed hand-eye coordination helped him perfect the quickest release in the league, resulting in an unstoppable outside shot from just about everywhere on the court. His ambidextrous control over the basketball at maximum speed, not to mention his incredible tolerance for physical pain, made him appear reckless to opponents, who became wary and respectful, if not just a tiny bit fearful of what he might do.

When Radon's high school coach had told him that a player with his talent should think long and hard about whose NBA jersey number he would be proudest to wear during his organized basketball career, Radon immediately chose #22 after Elgin Baylor, Hall of Famer and "the best corner-man ever in the NBA," despite that Mr. Baylor had retired before Radon was born. Such was the legend of NBA greats who lived in the hearts of every little boy dreaming of wearing an NBA uniform.

Radon had first encountered Mr. Baylor at the old LA Sports Arena during Radon's junior year at Cal, after the USC game where Radon went off for 37 points and 12 assists in front of his South LA homies, including a game-sealing stand-up jumper from the corner straight out of Elgin Baylor's playbook. "Good spacing, Sonny," Mr. Baylor had said, introducing himself after Radon's postgame courtside interviews.

Of course, Radon knew who he was, not to mention that he was the Los Angeles Clippers' general manager in charge of developing players. "Keep your nose clean," Mr. Baylor had added, "and you might play for the Clippers someday."

Radon's celebrity has resulted in young women and men throwing themselves at him for a decade. After all, he was used to preening and strutting in short pants before nineteen thousand screaming fans in the arena as millions more watched on television. His singular athletic talent and user-friendly good looks naturally attracted his legion of adoring followers and sponsors. However, basketball confidence and knowing yourself were quite different things.

Having first responded to ambiguous sexual urges by twelve, Radon had gone along *wilding* with his Torrance playground *gangsta* wannabes. A pack of four or five pubescent boys roamed the neighborhood on bikes at dusk, sometimes descending upon vulnerable girls and women they happened to encounter alone, allowing any one of them to quickly jump off his bike, grab their protruding breasts through their clothing, and ride off. After witnessing two of these assaults, Radon was repulsed rather than feeling emboldened to grab some strange girl's breasts, never equating male domination with sexual gratification.

Disgusted with himself for having participated at all, he withdrew from cruising in packs and doubled down on balling, while repressing his adolescent sexual stirrings. Every spare moment of his Torrance high school days was already devoted to basketball, and his few friends were teammates or connected to the game in some way. Being rather shy and socially awkward despite his athletic prowess, Radon rarely dated and first had sex with a female classmate who seduced him in his mother's bed during an afternoon study session. In his junior year, after a grueling team practice, the senior power forward had masturbated him in the showers, and they secretly hung out a few more times.

By the time he'd met Russell, Radon had never felt so comfortable with another person; or as understood as Russell had made him feel. Until he had brought Russell into the emergency room and locked eyes with Marina standing over the gurney. Their "it was meant to be" connection had sent Radon off to explore a new immersive romantic vision of sharing a "normal" life together . . .

"Yeah, and how'd that turn out?" Radon mused aloud, slapping himself back to reality. For if the NBA owners ended the lock-out tomorrow and the Worriers reinstated him, Radon wasn't sure his teammates would ever welcome him back. Lo, if any of them found out about Russell, he knew that would spread to his next team the moment he was traded or released. The stigma still held throughout the league and Radon was not about to sacrifice what remaining hope he had to ever play again.

The night before Radon returned to California, Ramin arranged a farewell party in the private dining room of a chateau along the highway towards the coast; a place where Ramin could celebrate his son in front of the locals and reestablish Ramin's own reputation. On the ride back to the ranch, following their elaborate feast, he thanked Radon for visiting at this important time for both of them. He reiterated his three solemn promises: to remain reasonably temperate, مەﮋ أشاﺪال (Praise Allah), to stay on top of their business, and to contact his son at any sign of trouble.

For the first time in nine months Radon wanted to resume his life. Bryan had arranged workouts at the Berkeley Pavilion, alongside the Cal team and a few NBA players, practicing on their own with the union's informal blessing. Radon would benefit from some pro competition and maybe his first positive press since the tragedy. He was sober, stoked, and itching to play basketball as he drove his father up the gravel driveway to the main house in his freshly washed rental. As

Radon was heading to the airport early in the morning, they stopped in the living room to say goodnight and goodbye. Ramin waited until their final hug to bite the hand that fed him, however unintentionally.

Maybe it was all the years of self-hatred, or resentment over Radon's phenomenal success? Maybe he was finally sober enough to hear the truth from his son?

"Something ain't right," Ramin said. "Are you being honest with me about why you left your dying friend like that?"

Chapter Fifteen

Collaboration Is Key

The elevator door closed on the ground floor of Perry Dunbar's Victorian apartment building, as Lora and Archie leaned up against the burgundy-striped velvet wallpaper. They rode up to Felicia's office at Dunbar Holdings LLC, where employees worked in the converted third floor apartments of the residential building. Felicia resided on the fourth floor in a spacious two-bedroom unit with views while Perry inhabited the entire fifth floor. One level above, the elevator also opened into his private office where his pretty personal assistant sat vigilantly behind her desk facing the lift. Little wonder her position frequently turned over as a result of refusing to do the same. Archie had heard from Bryan that Dunbar stayed up late watching the security video of everyone riding in his elevator that day. That's how Perry was able to remember all the folks he'd met with, and also keep an eye on any visitors his minions on the third floor were seeing behind his back.

When the elevator door opened, Felicia greeted them in the third-floor foyer. "I'm so glad you both came," she said cheerily, and they followed her down the carpeted hallway into one of the reconfigured apartments. "Let's discuss leasing your theater for a benefit." Felicia tossed it out casually as they walked past a receptionist desk and into her private office, no doubt at one time the formal dining room, with polished wood floors and intricate wainscoting encircling the walls.

Lora and Archie sat across Felicia's executive desk, apparently organized by neatly stacked colored folders. Felicia's wild curly hair had been cropped, better complementing her big round eyes and wiry frame, presently hot-wired in motor-mouth mode.

"Look, folks, I'm not gonna lie. As long as the lockout drags on, this conversation is just speculation. But you probably know Worriers' management doesn't believe there's a big dispute with *our* players, anyway... And Perry thinks it will be over in time for the pre-season schedule. We're wondering if *K*raftworks is available for a fundraiser during Thanksgiving Weekend. I'm proposing a joint gala evening, and I don't suppose the Jaalaba Foundation would object if the Dunbar Foundation underwrote it with a hundred-thousand-dollar donation?"

Lora and Archie turned to each other, their mutual surprise striking them momentarily mute, while Felicia gleefully went on before either could muster a reply. "Your occupancy is only one-twenty-five, right? Well, I figured a dozen tables, fifteen thousand each... I'm aware this is short notice for a charity event. But you gotta admit, it's already been a weird year for all of us, and Perry will bring some heavy hitters."

"Wow! Felicia, what a generous offer," Lora finally responded with one tiny reservation. "Can we back up a second, 'cause I can't help thinking something's missing here. You've asked the folks at Radon's foundation to co-sponsor this, right?"

"Lora," Archie interjected, "that's the reason we're here. Isn't it, Felicia? You want us to get them to agree?"

"I see why you married this guy," Felicia said.

"Why won't this violate the strike rules barring communications between players and management?" Archie pressed her.

"Our lawyers already checked with the league office. Since the fundraiser is sponsored by two independent non-profits and not related to basketball they're willing to look the other way." Felicia turned to focus on Lora. "I did my due diligence. Both foundations fund neurological research, so we've got a good collaboration here. The Jaalaba's do childhood brain diseases and Uncle Perry is into concussive disorders. It doesn't get any better than that . . . Well, you understand what I *mean* . . . Archie's right. I want this to happen, and you both are the shortest distance between two points for me."

"We'll noodle this and pitch it to Radon's team," Lora said, using Felicia's lingo.

"I chose you two," Felicia came back heavy, probably sensing their reaction to being stuck in the middle. "You're uniquely situated to host a successful fundraiser under the circumstances."

"The circumstances being that the event may never happen," Krafter replied, bad cop weighing in. "What does everybody do if the lockout isn't over by Thanksgiving? I read yesterday that the owners are discussing holding out 'til the end of the year and cutting the season in half. Both foundations will be embarrassed if they have to return a bunch of donations. We could get stuck with an empty theater and a hefty catering bill. Why would any of us agree to this?"

"Well, that's a mouthful, Archie." Felicia was unfazed. "What if Uncle Perry still pays your bill and pledges fifty thousand dollars to the Jaalaba Foundation in case the event has to be cancelled?"

"We're really grateful you're offering us this opportunity," Lora jumped in, good copping her. "Suppose we talk with Radon and his foundation folks?"

A door behind Felicia opened and Perry Dunbar scurried in wearing a royal blue crew neck sweater, with a yellow polo shirt collar sticking out, and the team logo embroidered over his heart. Dunbar's bushy grey hair had been sculpted atop his Mediterranean salad face: olive complexion, classic Greek nose, mischievous Italian smile, and his octopus eyes capable of searching around the room with no blind spots. Considering Perry's eightieth birthday was imminent, the squat mogul was a Tasmanian devil, eruptive, intimidating and yet, by turns, charming and even, by some accounts, seductive.

"Don't let me interrupt your meeting," Perry said sweetly, advancing around Felicia's desk. "I only want to chat for a minute . . . Lora, dear. What can I say? You're more gorgeous than ever. If you ever ditch this guy," Dunbar made the *call me* sign with a closed hand, thumb and pinkie extended, to his ear. "Archie," he went on, turning to him, "I'm impressed with the job you did for Radon."

"Thanks. Sometimes it's better to be lucky than good."

"I'm not sure about that," Dunbar replied. "It's a clever phrase, anyway. Which Lefty Gomez said a long time before you."

"Pardon my ignorance," Lora asked. "Who's Lefty Gomez?"

"He was a Hall of Fame baseball player back in the thirties and forties," Archie answered, "who grew up in the Bay Area."

"Unfortunately, I'm old enough to remember watching 'El Goofo'—that's what they called him—play in Yankee Stadium when I was eight years old," Perry elaborated. "Vernon Gomez pitched on five World Championship teams and still holds the World Series record for six wins and no losses. OK? But guess what? He never earned more than *twenty thousand dollars a year!*"

"No way," Lora said, pretending that she wasn't already sorry she'd asked.

"Like most kids in America, I idolized Lefty Gomez, but then my father told me he was under an unbreakable contract to Yankees' owner, Colonel Jake Ruppert. That was my very first lesson in business, 'cause I believed my dad when he said the Colonel and his manager Joe McCarthy had the right to recognize the moment any player stopped performing up to their individual standards, and to adjust their salary accordingly."

"The fans must've hated those guys," Lora said.

"Oh, but the system worked. Before there was collective bargaining, of course. Now players sign these vulgar multi-year guaranteed contracts, and it no longer matters how they performed last year. And then these ridiculous strikes only drive the fans farther away . . . There I go, talking business again. I just stopped in to wish you well with Felicia's charity benefit for Radon. To tell the truth, Archie, I didn't think he'd beat all the charges. Off the record, I hope he's staying in shape; and off the stuff?"

"Last time I saw him," Krafter thrust cautiously, "he was sober and clear-eyed as the judge who set him free."

"Sounds terrific," Perry parried. "Does that mean he's in *basketball* shape?"

"As far as I know, Radon works out every day at the Cal gym, anxious for the lockout to be over so he can get back to camp with his teammates. By the way, Perry, Lora and I are grateful for your generous donation and for thinking of us to host the benefit."

"Well, Felicia manages the details of my foundation things, even though she doesn't always tell me what she's doing."

"You know I tell you everything, Uncle Perry. All day long. You don't hear half of it, and you ignore the other half."

"I know our *star* missed almost two seasons with knee injuries," Dunbar invoked the final word. "And most of last season on trial. Forgive me if I'm not crazy about guaranteeing another twenty-one million for the next three years, just to find out if he's going to show up."

* * *

For Mike Prey an intimate dinner at the Krafters was a rare occurrence. He was invited to their annual *Kraftworks* "Fall Schedule" party, which Mike usually attended along with other friends and core theater supporters. Lora also invited him to fundraisers, mostly as a joke, he thinks, since he hardly ever showed up. Not that he's too cheap to cough up some bucks for a good cause now and again. Mike never fancied himself the swanky type, though, and the women he meets at Lora's soirees are mostly married. The single ones take one look at his sneakers and run away. But a sit-down dinner at Archie and Lora's meant a surprise homemade dinner from any number of cuisines infused with Lora's creative touch.

Mike has known Lora ever since Archie brought her around for his approval soon after the couple had met. She was good-looking, polished, and approachable, if a little too trim for Mike's own tastes. Lora was also smart, loaded, and sang like a bird, which seemed incongruous with that Mafia thing—spoiling perfection as if a hairy mole graced her lovely chin. Mike had to admit though that Archie had been tamed by love, or something similar, as he was committed and selfless when it came to Lora. Why not? Together they were obviously more than the sum of their parts. Mike had watched them grow closer and stronger as time went on, while they championed each other's careers. Then Lora's family started taking advantage of Archie's legal acumen.

During Mike's initial report to Archie about Dominic and the Klitoff brothers, Archie had hinted at feeling pressured to help his brother-in-law. Then Mike's friendly former paramour, and current paralegal in the US Attorney's office, had alerted him to an apparently unsuccessful kidnapping attempt on Yuri Klitoff's three-year-old daughter, obviously intended to shut him up. Mike became concerned about Archie's safety for the first time.

Not that Lora would ever consider or endorse aiding her brother in any nefarious way. Yet, Mike knew what Archie knew when Archie had signed up for this: wise guys, mobsters, mafiosi, Cosa Nostra or whatever you call them, do not stop until they get what they want, going all the way back to the Italian Renaissance of Popes, Machiavelli, and beyond.

At the moment, though, Mike was unable to read Archie's level of concern while they sat in The Krafters' comfortable parlor sipping artisanal vodka Martinis, nibbling on fresh caprese and spanakopita appetizers. The sounds of Lora vocalizing and B-flat on the piano wafted over from the opposite end of the room.

"I appreciate the heads up about Klitoff's daughter, Mike," Archie said. "I'm trying to stay out of Dominic's case."

"Herb Winant plays hardball. I'm not sure you understand what will happen if you're asked to . . ."

"Enough! . . . I'm forever grateful for your concern. Let *me* tell Lora about this."

"OK, Archie. You're the genius. I just want to be able to keep getting paid to make you look good."

"Yeah, I noticed your Mexico expenses included making you look good, too."

"Hey, guys," Lora called out from the piano bench on which she and George sat together. "Dinner is ready whenever you are. But first I'd like to try out a song we're working on for my solo show. OK? . . . C'mon over here. I'll explain."

Lora stood next to the piano and B-flat began playing the soft background melody. "This song appears early in the piece," Lora said. "'Sophia' is a young woman in the throes of a battle between good and evil while she comes to grips with being the offspring of a notorious gangster . . . Hey, I know, it's a stretch. Yet, Sophia is learning to transcend her shame, and her rage, by making her dream career come true—I haven't decided whether she's the owner of a spa and fitness center or a pharmacist. Either way, she does it with a little help from the dark side.

"I'm leaning upscale fitness spa that her father financed as a gift. As Sophia's business becomes successful more locker room space is eventually needed, prompting her to discover an unaccounted-for locker that nobody seems to claim. But when she cuts off the lock and looks inside, she finds a freezer bag containing a somewhat decomposed left hand . . . It's a work in progress," Lora acknowledged. Then she nodded to B-flat who played the first few bars, and off she went:

Daughter of Rain
Despite all the gain
Don't know what you're made of

This bloody fascination
Don't swallow your imagination
To be free from your own

Hang the devil's sword above you
Anchored in the truth of love
Daughter of rain
You know what you're made of

Corruption is the norm
Destruction but another storm
Won't let it bring you down

I'm a daughter of pain
Carrying this refrain
To be free I'll look to love

Daughter of rain despite all the gain
What are you made of?

Chapter Sixteen

The Home Stretch Lurks Around The Corner

With a nod to Lemony Snicket, it had been a series of unfortunate events that left Dominic Dellacozzi fit to be tied, maybe even fitted for an orange jumpsuit when all the dust finally cleared. What had literally begun as a week at the beach on Mauritius, at the end of Dominic's semi-annual international schmoozing tour of Dellacozzi Farms Ltd.'s vendors, had eventually turned into the quicksand of his father's deal to bankroll the Klitoffs' offshore betting service. The particulars of which Dominic had known absolutely nothing. For Dominic had paid much more attention to his regular excursions through some of the finest wine regions in France and Italy, dotted with countryside eateries, fresh verdant produce, glorious cheeses, and sumptuous bakeries. He was studying at the source the newest European foodie trends in the preparation and pairing of ingredients.

Back in '04, Herb Winant had touted Mauritius as a modernized tax-haven island republic in the Indian Ocean, with barely a million people, legal gambling, and tight banking secrecy laws. Cousin Paulie had been dispatched to scout a gateway location for expanding into Asia, to find a clearinghouse for off-loading Dellacozzi branded products and profits.

Fortuitously, the steel and concrete building in downtown Port Louis had been available on account of the untimely death of its principal owner. After Paul had been introduced to the appropriate local officials, he'd negotiated with island bureaucrats and made a sizeable contribution to the municipal judge's re-election campaign. The rechristened "Dellacozzi Center" had re-opened with the present international bank on the ground level remaining as the anchor tenant and Dellacozzi Farms' newly adopted financier.

    While Paul was establishing the export-import headquarters, featuring the computerized legal offshore bookie establishment on the third floor, his raven-haired and thick-nosed fashionista wife, Antonella, was decorating the seasonal home she'd found in an exclusive enclave of Grand Baie oceanfront villas.

    Dominic had heard stories about the best beach in the world being steps from his cousins' back door, and he'd managed to stop on the island at the end of his second regular sales trip abroad. While enchanted by its beauty and old-world charm, Dom had been hooked on the climate and the laid-back attitude, so he'd decided to spend the final two weeks of his biannual European tour at the Mauritian villa. Considering that Sal had leased the entire second floor of the Port Louis building to the Klitoffs, Dom had agreed to accommodate his father by keeping an extra set of eyes on the legal gambling operation when Paul and Antonella weren't on the island. Nevertheless, over the next five years, having to endure the fifty-minute drive and a mandatory visit with the other Dellacozzi Center tenants, including lunch with the building manager, Dom had checked in on the Klitoffs twice a year for about thirty minutes.

    It had always been pretty much the same drill. Yuri Klitoff met Dominic at the elevator and escorted him into their offices, where Puri Klitoff was often not there. Even when he was, his head was always buried in the gambling numbers. They opened the safe in Dom's presence and offered to show him both sets of the books.

    Dominic wandered around among the rows of cubicles containing young white and brown-skinned men and women, including teenagers, sitting in front of computer screens wearing telephone headsets, placing and laying-off bets on nearly every professional sporting event happening in real time around the world. In hindsight, had he paid better attention, Dom probably would've recognized that the number of folks working on the floor had nearly doubled between visits; or, at least, he might have inquired about the two offices at the end of the hall designated "online merchandise sales."

Dominic had simply not known that the crew of male Slovakian geeks in the merchandise rooms was actually Yuri Klitoff's key-logging specialists. By the time they were shut down by the FBI, Interpol, and the Mauritian police, they'd managed to steal almost ten million American dollars, hacking into thousands of American customers' accounts in the three biggest banks. Sliding back and forth between Chase, Wells and Capital, they'd pinched two million in cash from each; plus, more than three million from fraudulent credit card purchases of high-end consumer products that the Klitoffs had repackaged and resold out of a rented warehouse near the commercial port.

Herb Winant had also informed Dominic that the Klitoffs' admitted all of the above in a plea agreement with the US Attorney in Sacramento, including affidavits along with financial records from customers at the defrauded banks. Of equal import, though, roughly twenty percent of the stolen identity revenue had been traced to one of his investment accounts for three years running. However, as far as Dominic knew, the deposits were dividends earned from his trust. If the Klitoffs testified in court, their evidence was damning, and Herb had suggested it might be time to start considering the alternative to a trial.

This did not sit well with Dominic, particularly as Herb Winant was the attorney responsible for administering the family trust where his money came from. So, Dominic again sought out Archie's legal advice.

He also needed to hear what his big sister thought he should do. Ever since Lora had first split to Europe, Dominic had been left to grow up suffering alone the attendant complications of their birthright. Sal had beaten out of him most of the rebellious behavior he'd learned at the same Catholic prep school from which his father had nearly been tossed. That's how Sal operated, grooming his son for the business by teaching him respect, the way his father had taught him, and his father before him. Respect and loyalty; then Dominic would be taken care of for the rest of his life. Nevertheless, he had escaped across the country to college in Miami, where Herb Winant's recommendation had secured his admission, and Sal had grudgingly paid his tuition, room and board.

Dom had easily attracted friends, making him quite popular, though he was mostly avoiding being alone. Partying had its downside, particularly when it came to passing his courses and paying for all that fun on his meager allowance. Dom got a job on weekends bussing tables in a barbecued rib franchise, gaining his initial exposure to food service. But he also turned to supplying whatever "under the table" items happened to be in demand on campus: untraceable phones, fake ID's, stolen tests, Adderall. Much like Sal had boasted about having done during the Korean War. Nevertheless, when the campus police eventually busted Dom, his father hadn't seen it the same way. Luckily, he was only nineteen and Herb Winant had ridden to the rescue, yet again. Dominic had skated on the criminal charges, but he'd withdrawn from the university and returned to the Bay Area determined not to live under his father's roof again.

Having managed first and last for a mother-in-law unit attached to a Sunset District bungalow, he'd enrolled in City College and spent four nights a week as a kitchen helper in a fancy steak house, where Dominic got to tenderize the meat with a mallet. He had also learned to order quantities of fresh fish, produce and flowers, how to use the correct herbs and spices—cooking with flower pedals and stems being the current rage—all the way to watching each dish plated with pride. After his twenty-third birthday, and sporting his bartender's license, Dominick had approached Lora with his plan to open a neighborhood restaurant and enlist his sister's financial support.

Lora had encouraged Dom by suggesting that he build up experience in the front of a like-minded establishment to learn the entire operation. In those days, Lora didn't have the money for a loan. Instead, she had hooked him up with "Paulina & Suzanne's," the caterers who Lora had often used for fundraisers at the cultural arts center. And Dominic had fit right in, helping "P&S" with food prep and schlep, setting up and serving. So much so that Dominic started secretly canoodling with Suzanne after four months on the job, although she was married. Not surprisingly, things deteriorated, and Dominic had been asked to leave a few months later.

Thereafter, Lora maintained some distance from her brother, while keeping in touch with his escapades: the restaurant he'd finally scraped together was destined to open on 9/11. It hadn't gone well. Then there was the first Oxygen Bar on Fisherman's Wharf. A great idea. Five years ahead of its time, considering Dominic's landlord refused to wait that long for the rent. So, Lora hadn't been completely surprised when her brother ended up working for their father. Sal had probably given Dominic the seed money for all his failed ventures in the first place. In any case, the gulf between siblings had widened over the years, until Sal's stroke brought them to communicate again.

Dominic didn't resent his sister for not investing in his restaurant. She was the primary parental figure during most of his first twelve years. Lora had inspired him to travel, to learn about himself and to strive for the art in things. But she had judged him way too harshly once she found out he'd become a vice president at Dellacozzi Farms Ltd.

She'd delivered a gut punch that still stings. Lora had lost interest in his life from that day forward.

Nevertheless, he had to admit that Lora came to the rescue while he was in France and their father was stricken three years ago. For as soon as Sal had recognized Lora standing next to his hospital bed, feeling her grab his hand and holding on to it for the first time since she was a child, their father had been invigorated, his will to live restored. Sal might never have recovered if Lora hadn't returned.

Presently, Dominic couldn't help wondering whether that had been such a great thing, after all. For Dom had found himself in Herb Winant's office three days ago, listening to the mastermind basically preparing him to take the fall for his father's crimes. While Dom had recently received his portion of their mother's trust upon reaching age thirty-five—more than enough to have a proper go at his lingering restaurant dream—unless he suddenly turned disloyal and told the truth, ironically, he wouldn't be able to enjoy his bequest for another two-to-four years, with time-off for good behavior. Maybe he was being paranoid?

Yet, he couldn't stop thinking that his father and Herb Winant had intentionally used his personal account as a slush fund to protect themselves. Especially, since Winant had suddenly floated this guilty plea scenario.

Dominic's heart raced as he hurried under the neon *K*raftworks logo marking the tiny theater situated between an artisan bakery and a "green" dry cleaner. Before noon, Jill Banitch worked the box office via an intercom to her desk, and she appeared from inside to unlock the glass entrance doors. Daylight streaked the patterned red carpeting, and a faint coffee odor hung in the air as Dominic followed her through the lobby to the offices in the rear. He'd been attracted to Jill for a while. They'd spoken on the phone over the years, and then he'd come around to the theater with Andrea, who'd dumped him shortly after he was indicted. Jill was probably his sister's age, yet she seemed desperate and alone, much like him.

"They're waiting for you," Jill said, feeling his sad, sexy eyes on her, evincing a tug between her job and desire, while she led him towards Lora and Archie's converted rear office and conference room.

"So, I was wondering," Dominic said, stopping in the hallway. "Do you want to grab dinner sometime?"

"What would Andrea think?"

"It's a long story."

"I don't think it's a good idea," she said, knowing more than enough about Dominic to deflect his foray in favor of keeping it her late-night fantasy. "I don't trust myself with you."

"Well, that certainly won't get rid of me."

Lora and Archie were seated across one end of the conference table. Framed posters from previous theater productions hung around the windowless rectangular room and neatly stacked bookshelves lined the far wall. Laid out before them was the current seating chart for the Jaalaba and Dunbar Foundations collaborative gala dinner in thirteen days, on the Saturday after Thanksgiving, along with the latest printout of confirmed attendees and their preference requests.

The NBA shutdown had dragged on for over four months. The regular season, scheduled to begin on November 1st, had already been postponed and would not start for at least six more weeks, according to the latest NBA sources. Nonetheless, invitations had gone out and the response was enthusiastic: *"The Night of Knights for C.B.T.R."* (childhood brain trauma research) was sold out. Twelve tables of ten, four dinner courses prepared by La Foliage, wine and spirits donated by Napa vintners and Peninsula distillers, dancing in the lobby to DJ Maestro. Five Worrier players and their wives had RSVP'd early.

Renewed settlement talks last week between the players' union and the owners had ended in another failed deadline. Yet, Felicia had remained upbeat, insisting her uncle believed that the strike would be over by Thanksgiving; and Perry usually knew what he was talking about. In any case, *The Night of Knights* would provide a temporary bridge between the players and management who were not otherwise allowed to interact, for a good cause. Of course, Radon Jaalaba would be the main attraction.

"Hi Dominic," Lora said, rising to greet her brother when he entered the conference room. "You're sweating. Take some water." She reached for one of the plastic bottles on the table.

"What's goin' on, Archie?" Dominic acknowledged his brother-in-law as he took the bottle from Lora, then hugged her and sat down between them.

"Are you alright?"

"No," he replied, unable to hide his despair. "I'm having a really rough time right now."

"Oh, Dominic," Lora said. "What can we do?"

"Nothing you can do." Dominic choked up a little. "I gotta make a decision and there's nobody else I can talk to. Unless I explain how that money ended up in my account, I can't defend myself in court. So . . . If I don't sign an early plea agreement in the next sixty days, according to Herb Winant, I'm going to lose a bunch of credit off any sentence I'll get if they find me guilty at trial."

"Why wasn't your cousin Paul charged in the case?" Lora asked. "Doesn't he run the gambling business on Mauritius?"

"Paulie's your cousin, too," Dominic reminded her. "Yeah; I talked to him about it. He swears that Sal made his own private deal with Yuri Klitoff for 'those merchandise rooms' —Paul's words. He also said whatever accounting they did was separate from the corporate business;

'cause the sports betting operation was not on the government's radar when they came in with the search warrant. They didn't have any reason to shut the betting room down. Within a couple of weeks, the FBI actually returned wagering records they'd scooped up during the raid."

"Wait a second," Lora said. "Are you asking for advice whether you should plead guilty, or testify against our father?"

"Well, I guess so; yeah."

"Then you may appreciate this precedent," Krafter said. "True story; earlier this year the son of the Chicago Outfit's South Side boss, Frank Calabrese, who headed Tony Spilatro's crew—remember Joe Pesci's character in the movie *Casino?*—well, Frank Jr. published his memoir detailing how he had his own sentence commuted after wiretapping conversations with his father for the FBI while they were both serving time in the same prison."

"Archie, that's just macabre." Lora couldn't contain herself. "You're comparing my brother to the Chicago Mob?"

"He's kinda right, Lora," Dominic said, having long considered his options. "If I agree to implicate our father, the government will probably let me go. I sure can't discuss this with Herb Winant."

"I have to ask you something," Krafter interjected. "Did you know somebody threatened to kidnap Yuri Klitoff's daughter?"

Dominic scowled, wiping the back of his neck with his saturated handkerchief, protesting. "How many times do I have to tell both of you? I did not know they were stealing from bank accounts of innocent people. My salary comes from a legitimate Nevada corporation, and I pay my taxes. I don't order kidnappings to intimidate witnesses."

"Archie," Lora cut in. "How long have you known about this threat?"

"Maybe a month or so?"

"*A month or so?*" She was fuming. "You knew my father was probably behind this and you didn't tell me for over a month?"

"Nothing came of it, Lora. I didn't see any reason to worry you."

"That's a crock, Mister."

"Well, it worries *me,*" Dominic said. "You don't really want me to turn him in?"

"He didn't look so good on his birthday," Lora said.

"Zeda thinks Sal could live forever. According to the doctors, his heart is strong. Anyway, I don't think I'll be able to do that."

"Isn't Herb Winant guilty?" Lora wondered.

"Oh yeah," Krafter concurred. "If you could prove Winant knew where the money came from. But agreeing to cooperate is a treacherous experience, Dominic. You can't just tell the government what you want to. It will get messy when they start asking questions about your life. You have to be ready to open the floodgates of truth and that might eventually swallow you up."

"You mean he'll have to go into witness protection; don't you?" Lora summed it up for her brother. "Assume a new identity, at least until Herb Winant dies; right?"

"Jeez. So that's the deal?" Dominic was shell-shocked. "I don't know if I can survive a new persona. I'm barely getting to know this one."

Chapter Seventeen

Tunnel Of Love

The Naked Lawyer
(Thursday, November 24th)

On the first anniversary of Wikileaks' monumental dump of secret NSA cables, albeit feloniously, the Arab Spring has turned into Civil War Fall. After Hosni Mubarak fell in Egypt, Qaddafi was terminated in Libya, a revolt began against Bashar al-Assad in Syria, and dissent was even taking hold in Iran. Middle Eastern citizens, connecting more and more on the internet, and spurred on by Wikileaks, began a promising year of pro-democracy protests in Tunisia, Algeria and Egypt, where massive demonstrations forced Mubarak's government to resign. Saudi Arabia finally granted women the right to vote (can you believe it's taken so long??) and Tunisia held its first-ever free election to form a new government and write a constitution. Millions of Syrians demanded political reform reinstating their civil rights, calling for Assad to step down as president.

But Assad will never resign. Instead, he's cracked down harder on his own people, responding to peaceful protests by killing hundreds of demonstrators, including detaining and torturing young boys—a thirteen-year-old was beaten to death in jail—for having written graffiti in support of the Arab Spring.

The Naked Lawyer believes that story obviously grabbed Vladimir Putin's attention, because Russia recently voted in the General Assembly to deny sanctions against Syria for Assad's ongoing atrocities against peaceful opposition by his own people. Now Putin was standing up for Iran's repression of individual freedoms, threatening to revoke Russia's support of the anti-nuclear ban imposed against Iran. Mainly, though, and here's the scariest part, Russia is aiding Syria and Iran in putting down their respective insurgencies by teaching them how to hack into the anti-government media and close off their people's access to it. *Control the access to information and you can control the content of news that your citizens are permitted to see and hear.*

Syria and Iran have already made significant advances to quell the dissent in their nations, and *Naked Lawyer* recently learned from the horse's mouth why the Soviet Union produces the best hi-tech criminals in the world. Heck, they've been waging cyber warfare against their enemies— and hacking for their friends—ever since Al Gore invented the internet. Of course, Putin used to be a minister of information (propaganda) for the KGB. It should be no surprise that if Assad and Ahmadinejad are ultimately successful at "winning over their people," it will depend more on Russia's surreptitious cyber aid than military weapons or troops.

Which brings us back to Wikileaks and the fate of Julian Assange, who has been living under house arrest in a remote country village in England. Assange is appealing a Swedish government extradition order to stand trial for two felony sexual assaults that he claims were consensual. He also faces serious espionage charges in the United States when he's done in Sweden. Herein resides America's dilemma: Is Julian Assange a valiant campaigner for the truth, a whistle-blowing hero who published secret CIA cables turned over by a disaffected marine techie named Bradley Manning, who'd been horrified viewing real time footage of eighteen Iraqi civilians slaughtered by US troops in a helicopter raid? Or, on the other hand, is Assange really a publicity-seeking, convicted hacker, who sacrificed the true whistle-blower, while endangering many more lives by illegally disclosing a trove of sensitive information to the public?

Well, folks, despite Wikileaks' criminal participation in disclosing our embarrassing secrets to the world, America needs Julian Assange and others like Bradley Manning to bring forth snowstorms of truth whenever a government represses free speech; arbitrarily controls and manipulates the content of news and/or other media disseminated to its people. Especially on Thanksgiving, when Sgt. Manning is in the brig awaiting a court marshal and many years in prison, while Assange is rumored to be seeking political asylum in a friendly South American embassy in London. This may sound extreme but *Naked Lawyer* thinks we should grant clemency to Manning and allow Assange to seek asylum in America. Put Julian Assange back under house arrest, here, while we make sure that future Wikileaks cyber resources do not end up in Russian hands. Assange may indeed be a bad actor according to our moral and legal standards. Nevertheless, lest we never forget, whoever controls the information controls the public mindset and, eventually, the soul of the people.

* * *

Radon Jaalaba was thankful for plenty on this Turkey Day. His knee remained strong, as far as he could tell, and he couldn't wait to test it under game conditions. During scrimmages at the university gym, he'd danced and twisted, regular stops and starts, backward jumps and sideways cuts, working it as hard as he could, with high confidence and no flare-ups. He was also clean and relatively sober: watered down wine, occasional vodka and beer; no illegal substances have passed through him since the trial, being ever mindful that he'd have to be medically cleared to play if the strike ends and the owners decide to reinstate his contract.

Right after he'd been acquitted, teammates who made up Radon's core crew, going back to "22's" electrifying rookie season, had sent encouraging texts and e-mails. Plenty of folks had reached out with their prayers to a lot of different gods, in addition to some not so spiritual slams from a whole lot more. Radon had also heard from the new head coach, Keith Stacko, hired just before the owners had voted to shut down the training facilities and still in the dark after four and a half months. Coach had called a week after the trial to informally introduce himself—basketball related contact with management being *verboten* under the labor rules—and to let Radon know he was stoked to get into the gym as soon as the lockout ended.

On the other hand, a much darker play had been whispering in Radon's ear ever since that horrible Christmas morning. His enduring guilt over Russell's death, made worse by relentless public reprobation, left him searching for reasons to go on if the season was revived and he didn't make the team. The economic numbers that mattered hadn't improved since his trial: thirty-five—*count 'em, 35*—sponsors had bailed worldwide, while only three promised to return after the strike ended. His metabolic numbers, so to speak, seemed iffy as well. Despite Krafter's confidence that he'd pass the insurance physical, Bryan Marten wasn't so sure about anything.

During their most recent meeting Bryan had laid those lost sponsorship figures on Radon, and worse. The opinion research was firm: everyone still wanted to hear Radon's explanation of how those two people had died in Alonzo Shenkman's apartment.

"Sixty-eight percent negatives are definitely up there," Bryan had said, sounding a little condescending. "Even China's over sixty against you, and they love American violence no matter who perpetrates it."

Behind Bryan's humongous desk, the sunniest corner was dedicated to a phalanx of small silver-framed family photos: Susan, Bryan and Jason posing with Radon, along with many other celebrities in various venues, the three Martens always wearing the same smug smile. Bryan ran his manicured fingers through his sculpted ginger hair, searching for the right tone. "Unless you do a public *mea culpa,* I don't know if I can stop the bleeding."

"What more do I hafta say? The world has figured out why Russell took me there."

"It's not a legal matter, Radon . . . How do I phrase this? Your image problems are monumental? You walked away from a double homicide; that's legendary stuff. Until you take the basketball court again, your sponsors will continue to leave you."

"Now the lock-out is my fault, too?"

"Well, it finally sounds like this Friday's mediation session might bail out the season. Then let's pray Liberty Casualty doesn't get a copy of your rehab files. Frankly, Radon, the front office is worried. With a new head coach and a new approach, I heard they're not sure how much of a factor you'll be after sitting out most of last season."

"Where'd you hear *that shit*?" Radon sat upright in one of the side-by-side padded office chairs facing Bryan.

"Look, Radon. The public buys the tickets and right now they're not buying you. If the owners are serious about ending the lock-out this weekend, you've got to be ready to declare yourself fit for whatever revamped schedule is announced, and then answer all the reporters' questions."

"I didn't bother to think about Russell until it was too late. I'm not going to defile his memory now."

"I don't mean come out in public . . . Oh, I'm so sorry." Bryan immediately regretted what he'd just uttered, while he sat up straight in his executive massaging chair and paused its soothing undulation. It was none of his business who Radon diddled. That was a different tin of exploding snakes Bryan had no intention of opening. He wanted Radon to own up to his extremely bad decision to flee the scene, as well as to publicly describe his transformation into a dedicated force for sobriety and charity.

Radon had left their meeting shaken by the unrelenting pressure on him to be something he clearly was not. As confident as he was about returning to the court and dominating the game again, Radon was finally coming to understand that he would never have the inner strength to live clean and sober until he was able to openly acknowledge the true nature of his relationship with Russell. For Radon was also beginning to accept what Dr. Dewhauser had suggested; namely, that he was consciously sabotaging his career by doing drugs because subconsciously he needed to stop lying about who he was.

Nevertheless, on this feathered holiday Radon woke up thankful, nibbling on sponge cake, in a king-sized bed next to Lars, a lithesome thirty-four-year-old software sales geek visiting from Australia, without the foggiest notion or concern who Radon was. After making brief eye-contact in the fitness center at their exclusive resort and spa near the Russian River—where Radon had retreated to be alone and invisible rather than accept Thanksgiving invitations from his mother and Marina—he'd run into this attractive bloke at the mostly deserted restaurant bar. Lars was easy and direct about his intentions. He'd finished his semi-conductor seminar in Sonoma, was sussing out the local cuisine on his last weekend in America, and wondered if Radon was available to join him for a blooming onion dinner? They'd decided on room service in Lars's suite instead.

* * *

At 3:30 AM on Saturday, November 26th, after fifteen hours of talks between NBA owners and the players' representatives, a tentative deal was reached on a new Collective Bargaining Agreement. If ratified, the 66th NBA season would fittingly be reduced from eighty-two games to sixty-six, commencing on Christmas Day. Until both sides could formally approve the settlement package, the owners would allow the players and coaches to conduct voluntary workouts at all team sites beginning the following Thursday.

Lora got the good news around 6:30 AM from Archie, who'd read it online and woke her from a weird dream: she was on stage at the theater, singing: *"It's a quarter 'til three, there's no one in the place except you and me. So, set 'em up Joe, I got a little story I think you should know . . ."* In the audience Bradley Cooper was seated with Michelle Pfeiffer, but she was paying more attention to George Clooney in the row behind, sitting next to Marge Simpson, hanging with Reese Witherspoon who was sporting the same vertical hairdo. Then Lucian Freud came up on stage in a brocaded silk bathrobe, carrying a portable easel and a stretched canvas; he gave Lora a big wet kiss, set up his easel and started painting her as she continued singing: *". . . We're drinking my friend to the end of a brief ep-i-sode."*

Lora was on fire: *"So-oh make it one for my ba-a-by and one more for the road."* When Lucian revealed to the audience his colorful depiction of Lora's intestines and heart in oil, Lenny Kravitz suddenly leaped from his seat and challenged Humphrey Bogart to a swordfight, shouting indignantly "I'll take her." Lenny walked on stage, grabbed Lora, and they kissed passionately—just when Archie woke her with the settlement news.

Tonight's gala will be joyful, Lora thought. What a huge relief. Timing couldn't be better, as she rolled over in their bed and felt the reality of Archie's stiffness; she took him inside, slowly at first, in their familiar fashion, throbbing, until ultimately, they exploded together. They usually remained in the afterglow while falling back asleep. But this day was about the consummation of a higher purpose, so Lora sprung from the sack in order to prepare for a hundred and twenty guests at fifteen-hundred dollars a plate.

They checked in early at *Kraftworks*, rolling the collapsible seating back into the rear walls of the theater and securing the few loose threads remaining in the office. Being the quintessential Libra, with a Leo moon, Lora still hadn't decided what to wear. They went home to relax and attempt a power nap. Too excited to fall asleep, the couple walked down the hill for some fresh air, shared a latte at an outdoor cafe table and eventually came home to dress for the evening. By the time they returned to the theater, "Paulina & Suzanne's" round banquet tables had fit in comfortably, each one gloriously adorned with custom linen, China and crystal, fall flower centerpieces, a bottled selection of Napa Valley varietals, smart mineral water and gift bags, all designed in royal blue and California yellow.

At a few minutes past 6:00 PM, DJ Maestro's smooth bossa nova riff permeated the theatre lobby, transformed into the gala's reception area and open bar, already starting to fill up. The interested pack of medical R&D heavy hitters, sports-centric society patrons and local celebrities was assembling to imbibe and mingle before sitting down to their dinner of seared tuna, filet mignon, or a mélange of vegetables pot pie. Along one wall inside the lobby entrance a red-carpet staging area displayed: "Night of Knights" and "The Jaalaba Foundation" in block letters, with "The Dunbar Foundation" in slate, each logo repeating across the length and height of the glittering backdrop.

Two Worrier teammates and their wives were playfully mugging on the carpet for the gaggle of photogs when Felicia's publicist first noticed Lora and Archie chatting with Marina Ramirez and summoned the couple to take their turn under the lights.

Lora steeled herself to preen, focused on staying in the moment, grateful for her link in this chain saving sick kids. But she also couldn't help tallying up the numbers for the cause: in addition to table sponsorships, when you threw in official team memorabilia and the season tickets, not to mention Dunbar's hundred grand, the Night of Knights could likely reach its half-a-million-dollar vision. Here we go . . . Click—Click—BIG SMILE! —LETS SEE THE DRESS—Shutter—Click—Click—Shutter. Truthfully, one side of Lora couldn't wait until everyone stopped looking at her and the night was behind them.

Archie didn't mind the limelight, especially for a worthy cause. He'd grown comfortable with representing high profile clients in court. So much had been out of his control that he essentially remained nose to the grindstone trying to be professional; to observe keenly and listen considerately without violating the confidence of clients or friends. He owned two tuxedo jackets and one black suit, which he bought for his father's funeral and was wearing this evening in defiance of Lora's edict about the propriety of specifying "formal wear" on the invitation, despite that the event was a one-off charity dinner.

For Archie's social savvy had derived from his childhood spent in and around his parents' retail clothing establishment. As a young teen he'd first learned to relate to adult strangers by studying their quirks and fetishes over selecting their personal wardrobe and shoes, like the ladies who stubbornly tried to shove their size 8½ foot into size 7 pumps. Or the dumbass men who'd pick a pair of 34 inch slacks, obviously sporting a 38 inch waist, refuse to try them on and have their wife bring them back for the larger size.

Lora and Archie's different outlooks on life had clearly been influenced by the household in which they'd grown up. Archie normally couldn't wait to get out of bed in the morning, while Lora approached each day with trepidation. Though Archie's parents had basically left him unsupervised by the time he was fourteen, they'd spun their parental dereliction with love by encouraging his independence and convincing him he could accomplish whatever he set his mind to. So, he'd set out to a life of accomplishments. Mostly for other people who came to him for help. Considering that Lora had also been left to a lonely youth, but mostly without encouragement, she was always looking over her shoulder instead, focused on exorcising her father's hubris from her life.

Archie understood how Lora could accept witness protection as a solution to her brother's case. Unless Dominic was willing to rat on Sal, he was likely facing up to eighteen months in federal prison. It was an easy choice for Lora, sacrificing her father to save her brother. On the other hand, Archie's parents were law-abiding and rarely argued with each other. Archie's father had only "whacked" him once— Archie was ten years old—for lying about having stolen a box of *Titleist* golf balls, of all things, from Walgreens. Archie couldn't help feeling a tinge of sadness for Lora that her family members were not encouraged to attend this grand soiree, which by all accounts was swinging along.

For the evening unfolded delightfully from the moment everyone sat down and took a bite of the truffle-filled dark chocolate mini-turkeys waiting in the small plates before them, poured their first glass of Russian River pinot and inspected their gift bags. The morning's news of a revived season was collectively sinking in, the tension and frustration of the unknown future finally lifting. Emcee Robin Williams began by riffing on the fancy wardrobes of the players sitting with their wives at the front tables, and how upstaging the ladies' fashion look was affecting "their scoring stats at home."

Emotions ran high all night. Tears were shed during the video tribute to children around the world suffering from severe brain trauma, two of them in particular who'd recovered, including seventeen-year-old Yuka Pong of Thailand, actually struck by lightning, her paralysis reversed by stem cell injections. She flew in for the benefit, played a

Bach cantata and "Walking In Memphis" on the baby grand piano they'd rolled onto the stage.

It got rowdier when Robin returned with a hilarious auctioneer spiel in several indecipherable languages exhorting the room to pony up a little more for the cause. Drinking and dancing occurred in between dinner courses, along with more mingling among the benefactors. By the time the dessert course was served, many folks found themselves at tables other than their own engrossed in all manner of fascinating conversation.

Radon was the personification of positivity. Clear-headed and approachable, he'd given himself over to Lora when he arrived in an elegant tux separately from Marina. Michelle was on his arm, looking gorgeous in her Mackie gown, hair extensions dropping to her open shoulders. Radon made the effort to meet the biggest donors, and he delivered a sober welcoming speech to the room, declaring himself: "Fit and ready to report on Thursday."

Krafter was duly impressed at how far Radon had come back, despite the constant drumbeat of people refusing to move on from his acquittal; the rumors still swirled in the wind, likely becoming an indelible stain. Now that the lockout was over the team had to make a decision on lifting his suspension. Radon was in rock solid physical condition and willing to be drug tested. If they allow him to suit up, the intense pre-season training schedule could reveal whether he can return to form after the long absence, not to mention if he'll even make the team.

Archie figured that he or Bryan would end up discussing this with Perry Dunbar at some point in the evening. Just not during dessert, when Dunbar impulsively called Lora and Archie over to his nearby table the moment he and Felicia were sitting alone. After conspiratorially rehashing the "grand benefit so far," Felicia's words, she and Lora set off together to ensure that the rest of the night went as smoothly. Perry wasted no time going off in gruesome detail to Archie about, of all things, his recent lifesaving colonoscopy.

"Holy shit! What's a pedunculated polyp?" Archie heard himself repeat, caught off guard by Perry's bizarre medical disclosure.

"Two basic polyps are found in the colon," Dunbar said. "A *peduncle* is an elongated stalk of tissue extending off the colon wall, while a '*sessile*' polyp attaches directly to the wall. Luckily, the pedunculated polyp is less likely to be cancerous if during the procedure the stalk is snared cleanly by the robotic probe passing through the corridors of our intestines. Anyway, that's what they told me."

"You're clean?"

"As a whistle." Perry smiled, his dark round eyes twinkling, while he tugged on a corner of his bright purple clip-on bow tie. "They said the biopsy was negative, but I think they recycle the same polyp they took out of some other sucker years ago just for the biopsy fee, whether they find one or not . . . Listen, I know I'm lucky," Dunbar added, finally exposing his true intent by this metaphor. "They removed the cancer before it could travel to the rest of my body. Like our team needs cohesion coming back from this long layoff, and a leader to whom the other players can look up. Not some divisive figure spreading negativity through the locker room."

"You aren't seriously thinking about releasing Radon?"

"Your client could be certified drug free, AA, and still not be insurable."

"Wait a minute. If he's allowed to join his teammates at training camp on Thursday and passes the physical, we both know he'll be the best player on the court."

"Not if he has brain damage," Perry whispered.

His statement was deafening. It pierced any remaining doubt that the confidentiality of Radon's medical records had been breached. Worse, it signaled that they were preparing to cut him loose. All Radon's hard work and desperate hope for a second chance about to be gone in the winds of a greedy and immoral flag that Dunbar had decided to plant in Krafter.

"My partners and I don't want Coach Stacko distracted out of the gate by a reclamation project. Radon is a handsome young man. He should think about retiring and going into broadcasting. I have a few connections. The way I heard it, anyway, your client's fried brain from the drugs is affecting his nervous system, and he won't be able to compete in a year or two, no matter how straight he is."

Archie Krafter was never more clear-hearted or in command of the ether, despite the personal consequences of his response. "Did your experts on Radon's brain damage also happen to confirm that your employee Dr. Leavitt addicted him to opiates in the first place?"

"So what?" Dunbar's reply feigned a lack of concern, while his tone warned that he knew exactly what Krafter was getting at.

"The experts also agree there's a causal connection between Leavitt's malpractice and the damage to Radon's nervous system."

"So what?" Dunbar repeated, impatiently this time.

"In my opinion, Perry, the team is legally responsible for that damage, and no judge will let you claim any diminished skills that may have resulted as an excuse to get out of his contract."

Dunbar did not reside at the top of the heap of genius entrepreneurs by allowing anyone to threaten him, especially this arrogant little shyster. "You've got one helluva legal theory, Krafter," he began with mild sarcasm. A smile still covered Perry's face, while his hand surrounded a half-empty wine glass resting on the freshly crumb-swept tablecloth. "That's OK for your Naked Attorney crap. But you'd rather be a famous writer than a lawyer, so I'll rely on my *full-time* attorneys who've promised an entirely different outcome in Radon's case."

The crossroads of Archie Krafter's career had come to a dead end. Krafter knew this wasn't the occasion to explain why Perry's legal minions were in fact woefully misinformed. Having gone way past his bedtime defying one of the town's most powerful elites, Archie maintained the priorities of the evening's mission instead. He rose from the table to extricate himself from the deteriorating situation while lifting his hands in an outward gesture of surrender.

"I gotta help Lora with the caterers," Archie declared. "Thanks for your colossal generosity, Perry. You and Radon accomplished a lot tonight together. Considering all the good things Radon's done for the Worriers organization and the community over the years, I hope you and your partners decide to let him earn his salary like the rest of the team. You never know, it could be a win-win."

Krafter reached over and shook Dunbar's hand as the owner had made no effort to get up from the table. "A grand evening, don't ya' think, Perry?"

"Yeah, we're all happy the season is back on. Felicia's happy about the vegetable pot pie. Right now, I don't know where she went, and my car is in the lot across the street. You validate here?"

"Gimme your ticket," Archie offered amiably. He started to walk away in search of Lora, but something inside him resisted: a growing rumble of discontent, unfinished business rooting his feet to the spot in defiance of the Devil. "Listen, Perry," Krafter said, leaning in close enough to watch Dunbar physically stiffen in reaction. Then he smoothly looked into Dunbar's octopus eyes. "We both know Radon's files will never see the light of day," Krafter said. "If you don't honor Radon's contract, I will hound you and your partners for as long as it takes to make sure you don't ever get away with it."

Chapter Eighteen

Chastity Begins At Home

Dominic drove up to the front gate of the house in which he'd first lived after incubating in the neonatal ward for eighteen days while they had buried his mother. The old Tudor Revival was ever imposing, set back from the wide residential street on a corner lot, with steeply pitched intersecting roofs, cross-gables, carved timbers and stone. Built in '34, his grandfather Vince had apparently paid twenty-two thousand dollars to construct the fifty-five hundred square foot affair near Presidio Terrace, mostly at the urging of Dominic's Nonna, Sophia, who'd grown weary of life on the valley farm.

Olivia's death had left Sal with their newborn and Lora, not yet seven, so Sophia had implored her distressed son to bring the children and live with her and Vince in the big house. But what had begun as a temporary fix changed forever only eighty-eight days later, when Vince had suddenly died too and Sal ascended to the head of the Dellacozzi clan unceremoniously. Without time to grieve for his wife or his father let alone to think about his children's needs.

Meanwhile, Nonna Sophia, clearly devastated by her husband's untimely demise, on the heels of losing her daughter-in-law, was in no shape to care for her grand kids. Sal's sister Anita had agreed take their mother home with her for a while, leaving Aunt Rose as Dominic and Lora's nanny, in what had abruptly become Sal's big house. Ensuing disagreements between Anita and Sal over Nonna Sophia's right to return to her own home had inevitably escalated, as Sal had dodged and deferred, and Sophia had remained with Aunt Anita until her final days.

One of Dominic's earliest memories occurred after Nonna's funeral, back at the house, where Anita got into a screaming match with Sal that had spilled out of the kitchen in a river of lifelong invective. Little Dominic had watched terrified as Aunt Anita, finally freed from her brother's financial control upon their mother's passing, had marched up to Cousin Betty, standing with Lora in the living room thoroughly engaged together discussing those most important matters between eleven-year-olds. Anita grabbed her daughter by the arm and dragged Betty out of the house where the girls had played together since they were toddlers. Aunt Anita's retribution had been swift and cruel, thereafter banning Betty and Paul from ever associating with their cousins again.

Family business had demanded otherwise. By the time Paulie reached eighteen, Dominic's older cousin had already begun delivering envelopes filled with cash to supermarket managers "in thanks" for placing Dellacozzi's products on their over-crowded shelves. Paul had grown up to become Sal's most trusted employee, often by way of Sal's derogatory comparisons to his own son. Dominic had been reminded of his inferiority enough to eventually succumb to it.

Just as Cousin Betty had given in too, marrying handsome and loyal Tony Costo, nephew of Francis D' Giorgio, a *cumpari* from Southern California. Sal and "Frankie Thumbs" had arranged the couple's first date with the idea that Tony might potentially fill a need in the company. Yet, Betty had truly fallen for the big lug, and in the end, Aunt Anita couldn't reject the serendipity of their pairing, so she made an effort at rapprochement by inviting Sal to her daughter's wedding.

Dominic thought that Anita had decided to behave, if only because she was more fiercely determined than ever to support her children. This was particularly true since Sal's stroke. Her son Paul was next in line to head the family business and Dominic was pretty sure that Anita couldn't help wondering about "someday," as most mothers would. When she could no longer navigate on her own, and her son was pulling the strings, Aunt Anita might even return to spend her final years in the big house where she'd grown up.

As Dominic punched in the gate code and drove up the circular driveway toward the front door he couldn't stop thinking, "So let it be written, so let it be done," evoking Yul Brynner in *The Ten Commandments*. Dom was not so much confirming a postscript to his family history as he was reflecting on the desert of lost hope enslaving him. Cast into this alternate zombie reality, he'd been shuffling around in a daze for weeks, unable to accept a fate he didn't deserve.

Dominic knew he wasn't one of the good ones, certainly not one of the smart ones, who always managed to stay one step ahead of the curve. But he never thought he'd become one of the bad ones: predatory and unfeeling, using succor and lies to climb over the back of anyone in his path. Though as much as he reviled himself for thinking such things, Dominic sensed his current situation was a different animal entirely. This concerned his very survival, really, an involuntary manifestation of nothing less than patricide.

Dominic was so freaked out he'd researched mythological references as far back as the Babylonian creation epic: *Enûma Elish*, where Apsu was killed by his son Ea in the struggle for supremacy among the gods. In India, Babruvahana murdered his father the Hindu god, Arjun, but Arjun was brought back to life by his wife, the snake goddess Uloopi. Cronus offed his papa, Uranus, in the Greek epic, to usurp his domination of the universe; until he was overthrown by his son, Zeus.

And of course, there was Oedipus, fated to snuff *his* old man, a king, and to marry his mother. Oedipus's parents had apparently been forewarned, having left their infant son on the side of a mountain where he'd been found and raised by a shepherd. Many years later, Oedipus met his father on the road by chance and killed him; having thereafter unknowingly married his mother to become king, and ultimately fulfilling the prophecy. No matter how hard Dominic tried to relate, mythologies, however instructive, had no practical application to his present homicidal thoughts of self-preservation.

He drove into the pristine four car garage and parked alongside Sal's shiny Escalade. The thick white rubber soles of Dominic's leather designer sneakers squeaked on the freshly surfaced floor as he strode determinedly to the rear pantry door. Although Dominic hadn't lived in the house since leaving for college, and while his father clearly didn't think much of him, he remained one of only two or possibly three souls with the private access codes to Sal's homes and wall-safe combinations, his safety-deposit boxes, offshore account numbers, and his hand-drawn maps of hidey-holes containing copious amounts of cash buried on the grounds of his various properties.

Another creepy feeling arose as Dominic traversed the vast kitchen, its old Venetian ceramic floor tiles still shining in the afternoon sunlight flooding the breakfast nook. Up until the seventh grade, Dominic had come home from school and either Aunt Rose or Lora would be waiting with a glass of chocolate milk, ready to make him a peanut butter and banana sandwich, or his favorite: grilled cheese on rye bread pressed with Nonna Sophia's old electric iron. Dom and Lora regularly sat at the round Formica table in the nook, on red leather and chrome diner chairs, discussing Dom's day at school, laughing in the afternoon sun's warm glow as he devoured his snack.

Dominic made his way across the entrance hall toward the first-floor parlor and library converted après stroke into Sal's primary bedroom suite. The irony of his father otherwise having to ride up and down the stairs strapped into an electric chair in his own home was not lost on Dominic. When he was growing up, Sal's stern directive: "Meet me up in the trophy room in fifteen minutes," was never too far from Dom's mind. The L-shaped office and storage closet was fashioned under the cross-gables between the second and third floor landings of the house's west wing. In stark contrast to those sunny afterschool sit downs with Lora, Dom's trips to the trophy room had inevitably led to dressings-downs delivered unpredictably and with varying levels of emotional and physical intensity.

Between the ages of twelve and fifteen, after Lora had moved away, Dominic started acting out against his father's cruelty and his feelings of abandonment by stealing cars and stereo equipment. Although he hadn't been nabbed by the authorities, Sal had always been informed somehow and had taken his son to task many times. Figuratively, Sal used lectures about how stupid Dom was to risk becoming indebted to the police, and he was making the family appear low class. Literally, Sal used the same worn-out leather barber strap on Dom that Vince had kept hanging from a hook on the back of the trophy room door for his own son.

"Hello; Dad? . . . Dad?" Dominic repeated over the drone of *Judge Judy's* screechy voice spewing from the massive flat screen TV monitor mounted over the striped wallpaper in the parlor. "How are you feeling, Dad?"

"Hello . . . Son." Sal was reclining in his over-stuffed leather chair, positioned directly in front of the screen. "I thought you . . . coming for dinner? The girl went shopping."

"I want to talk to you alone, Dad."

"You . . . staying strong, son?"

"Yeah, I'm staying strong . . . You may not like it."

Sal reached for the clicker resting on the arm of his chair and, clearly annoyed, muted Her Honor mid-diatribe. One did not interrupt

Judge Judy—same time every day —unless it was urgent. "Tell me . . . What's . . . up?"

"I've tried every way I know, Dad. Believe me . . . I'm sorry. I won't go to prison for you."

"Lemme ask . . . a question," Sal said, swiveling around to get his son's attention, face to face, while he struggled with the lever straightening up the chair. "Where you think . . . the extra two million come from?"

"From my mother's trust according to Herb. Which I paid the taxes on."

"How many times . . . I told you," Sal reached out, grabbed one end of his walker and pulled himself out of the chair, standing as straight as he could, defiantly addressing his ungrateful offspring. "Who you gonna believe . . . Herb . . . or Fatha'?"

"I don't know, Dad. Maybe I'll go away for a while, adopt a new identity and a new life."

"You know . . . I'll die . . . in there." Sal's upper lip quivered, his mouth formed its crooked half-smile, and his eyes watered over.

"Don't worry, Dad. I won't let you die."

Anyway, that's what Dominic told him. What was he supposed to do in the moment? Tell him the truth? Dominic didn't think so, considering he'd been planning to go over there and smother the prick in his chair with a pillow! It was hard enough letting his father think he couldn't decide between running away or silently doing the time. Dominic could only imagine how Sal would react if he found out that Dom had agreed to a one-on-one meeting with the United States Attorney concerning his knowledge of Salvatore Dellacozzi's unlawful offshore activities.

Chapter Nineteen

Head Lice

Radon realized the axe was poised to fall. During week one of the truncated training camp schedule, he had run the first team's drills over the last three days. The voluntary workout sessions had already produced a full roster of invitees and contract players, nearly all of whom couldn't wait to get back on the court together after five months locked out of their gyms. The team hadn't smelled the playoffs in three years; coincidentally, not since Radon blew out his knee late in the third quarter of the clinching game for their last post-season appearance. The core regulars had been there with Jaalaba before. If they'd grown wary of his character, they appeared to appreciate his return in playing condition and were starting to acknowledge his elevated performance thus far.

Management had permitted him to participate in training camp rather than fight over his contract, apparently realizing they'd better find out if he could still play, or whether he would bring value in a trade, before they dumped him. Now everyone seemed paralyzed by the possibilities. The beat writers were quite curious how he remained in the mix, as trade rumors flew, and they noted that the regular season opener against the LA Clippers on Christmas Night will mark one full year since Radon had been in the line-up.

The rookies who'd spent last season in the "D League" and the draftees with guaranteed money were all in with Jaalaba's on court methods and instruction, proven over eight years of experience, as they gained confidence from him in order to step up and learn the system.

Most of the coaches were new and welcomed Radon's steady hand while they got to know each other and evaluated the players on an accelerated timetable. Even the fans who'd attended open practices at the Arena were hungry enough for a winning team to forgive him in the moment. Their silence when Jaalaba initially strode onto the court had turned to applause by the time he'd scored the first bucket of the scrimmage at the end of the first workout.

Radon was therefore stunned when Coach Stacko pulled him aside following that afternoon's practice. He said Radon was not going to start against the Sacramento Kings tomorrow night, in the first of only two pre-season exhibition games, and he probably wouldn't get many minutes. Coach had clearly been following orders; his terse explanation merely repeated the GM's BS that they didn't want to risk a re-injury before the season started. Radon fumed during the car ride back to his condo. He had done whatever they'd asked of him. Already, he'd voluntarily given the team blood and urine samples, as the union and the owners still hadn't adopted a mandatory drug testing policy under the new Collective Bargaining Agreement.

Radon was clean, cleared to play and, thanks to Krafter, the insurance underwriters had no reason to deny covering the remaining years on his contract. Nevertheless, he was being shelved, most likely being repackaged as trade bait. When Radon walked into his condo lobby, he had to learn from Eduardo at the security desk, who was listening to KNBR, that the Worriers just announced the acquisition of a big shooting guard from Indiana to help defend against Kobe, Hardin and Westbrook during the upcoming shortened season. READ: to replace Radon Jaalaba.

He retreated to the far corner of the empty elevator, staring at his soft leather loafers, riding up to his elegant glass-lined prison in the sky, twenty-two lonely stories above the Bay Bridge. Desperately morose, Radon was on the verge of caving to the fakers in charge and walking away. All the paraphernalia was still there as, at one time, Marina had also possessed an appetite for it. But at what cost? He'd clearly taken advantage of her, despoiling their intimacy from the start with deceit. Inevitably, though, Radon had owned up to his failure to love Marina in all the ways she wanted, needed, and deserved.

In the kitchen he removed a bottle of Grey Goose from the sub-zero freezer and nearly filled the wine glass waiting on the slate countertop. Radon hoisted his drink into the air and toasted nothing, swallowing enough to propel himself out of the kitchen onto his small balcony off the living room. He peered out across the Bay at Oakland's bustling harbors and the vast rim of glistening hills beyond. So easy and simple to end this, he thought, as he held onto the railing atop the thick Plexiglas balcony wall. He experienced a vertigo panic attack, seeing himself jumping, and Radon rushed back inside sloshing his drink on the polished hardwood floor.

There was a super-secret Doomsday stash he had not considered in the four months of eternity since his trial. Having forgotten its whereabouts within the condo, he tried searching on his laptop for the "medical" folder in the locked Foundation files, but he couldn't remember the password. His old address book in the bedside table contained a handwritten list, including the code to open it, which ultimately reminded him that two grams of cocaine were buried inside a roll of adhesive tape, back of the cabinet, under the sink in his en suite bathroom ... So fucking what? Radon scoffed. He was far beyond the worst-case "base" scenario.

He rang Bryan again, wondering why he hadn't called back with some information in nearly three hours. Why hadn't Bryan heard about the new guard from Indiana? Radon sounded calmer this time, as he impressed upon his agent's voicemail the need to remove this uncertainty threatening his destiny. And while he hadn't told Bryan about it, Radon also couldn't stop fretting over the "faggot" remark, casually thrown at him by the drafted rookie out of Dumb Fuck State, with a guaranteed contract, during their first head-to-head practice two days into training camp. It hadn't registered with Radon as anything other than one of the usual insults that ballplayers hurled at each other all the time. Radon has heard descriptive derivations of every human orifice for as long as he's been hanging out in locker rooms.

Nevertheless, yesterday, during a defensive dribbling drill, Radon had dismembered Dumb Fuck, stripping the ball and demoralizing him. Dumb Fuck stood there for an instant, glaring; and he repeated, "Fuck you, Faggot." Jaalaba simply dropped the ball at Dumb Fuck's feet and calmly answered, "Not with your dick, little man," and Radon walked away to bow-downs from those within earshot of their brief encounter.

But if Dumb Fuck had heard something, that could explain why they were trying to unload him? Radon's main competition for the position was dogging his every move, searching for any weakness, including his personal laundry, while stealing his job at a fraction of Radon's contract. All of this was apparently with management's silent encouragement.

When that didn't work, they went out and purchased a starting player from another team to replace him. Radon wore the inevitability of exposure like a suit and tie in the hot sun, constantly uncomfortable, fighting to keep it buttoned up. He could think of a couple people who might have let it slip. Not his mother, who he decided to call, as he wanted to be the first to inform her that he wasn't starting in tomorrow's game and might never play in the NBA again.

Michelle's answering machine came on and Radon hung up, determined to prepare the magic powder he'd removed from under the bathroom sink. Cozy crystalline compounds cosseted him, calming his fears, while coalescing strength enough to weather the squall of public disgrace.

Radon unwrapped the hand-folded paper bindle and spread it open on a small ceramic tile resting on the kitchen countertop. Using a razor blade, he slid a sizeable portion of the solid-flake dream dust directly onto the square tile and, chopping the tiny pearl chunks finely with the blade, he resisted a strong urge, after so many months, to simply snort some lines. He focused instead on the basing ritual, of which he and Russell had last partaken during the day (and far into the night) before Russell had been killed.

Radon sifted into the crushed flake a smaller amount of baking soda retrieved from the refrigerator, scooped up the mixture with one of Bryan's embossed business cards folded in half lengthwise, and poured it down the center of a Pyrex test-tube, making certain none of the crystals stuck to the sides. Dripping the kitchen tap, Radon gingerly filled about one quarter of the test-tube with water, shook the test-tube, his thumb covering the opening, and turned on the gas-stove burner with his free hand. He clamped the test-tube with needle-nose pliers and placed it a few inches above the blue flame, keeping the liquid from boiling too far up the tube, while he waited for the murky, gooey residue to finally appear once the impurities had burned off.

"Critical mass," Radon said out loud, remembering that the secret was not letting too much water into the test-tube. He removed the Pyrex from the flame, the magical, phlegm-like healer settled at the bottom, and he immediately stuck it in a glass of water to cool. Using an unwound wire hanger fashioned with a tiny hook, Radon gathered the clump of goo at the bottom of the test-tube and painstakingly lifted the hanger out through the center of the tube. The joy crud stuck on the hook and hardened immediately upon exposure to the air. He chipped the pure crystalline hunk from the hanger with a razor blade and plopped it onto the ceramic tile sitting on the kitchen counter.

The ritual always ended with Radon slicing off a portion and placing the prized residue into a glassine pipe atop a wire screen. In the lurch of boozy anticipation, he religiously dipped a cotton ball taped around the other end of the wire hanger—resembling a marshmallow on a stick—into a container of rubbing alcohol, lit it, and placed the flaming rod directly over the precious crystal, drawing the smoked ivory substance through the pipe stem deep into his lungs . . . THIS TIME, as Radon was about to light the alcohol-soaked cotton ball, having already conjured those next steps in his likely demise, a shivering jolt of energy surged through his body, as an astoundingly simple realization washed over him. Something he'd heard from Krafter while preparing for trial. Part ancient scriptures, part aphorism, the concept finally took hold: Speaking the truth is always easier than lying. We expect the truth to be forgotten the moment it's uttered; but a lie is harder because we have to remember every lie we have told.

Radon found himself tossing the wire hanger into the sink, and he fell to his knees whimpering like a beaten dog. He began sobbing, deeply, painfully, finally releasing the frustration of denial built over so many years. It went on for several minutes, Radon curled up in the fetal position wailing for his life. "The truth is always easier," kept playing in his head. After all the pain he'd caused, and all that he'd endured to recover, Radon still burned to play again, and he realized the only way he could ever claw his way back onto the court was to fight just as hard for his right to be himself. He knew who he was and he was ready.

Simple as that. He decided to kill himself another day, and he dumped the cocaine in the toilet. Radon would bear his badge of cowardice instead, even as it overshadowed the uniform number inscribed above his heart. He'll show up tomorrow prepared to play better than anybody else in whatever role coach assigned to him. No longer would he hide behind some fake *hetrofficial* standard in order to keep his career no matter how much it meant to him. Radon punched in his mother's number again. This time she picked up.

"Hello, Son. What's goin' on?"

"Is somethin' wrong, Mama?"

"Not at all. I'm excited about coming to see you tomorrow . . ."

". . . Are you with someone?"

"Lemme' turn the TV down . . . OK now? I'm on the 2:40 from Long Beach. Is there a change in plans?"

"No. But about tomorrow . . . I might not play because I think they're trying to trade me."

"Trade you? Nine days before the season starts? I can't believe that, Son. After how you've been conducting yourself? What more do they want?"

"I dunno. You heard they just brought in a free-agent point?"

"What? . . . Who is it?"

"He aint hardly worth mentioning. . . Listen, I gotta say something more important to you. If I don't play again, I'm all right with that. You know I had a good career . . . I'm competing with the right approach now, Mama. Seeing the game for the first time again, and I know exactly how to play it. I know who I am . . . Make sense?"

"Yes, Son. You sound ready. And you know I'll always support you from my heart to yours."

"I'm gonna play somewhere as long as I'm better than anyone they throw at me . . . When I visited my father, we worked on getting us both into shape, but we still have some work to do . . . I hope you watch me get some minutes tomorrow. I don't want your trip to be for nothing."

"Oh, Radon. Don't you worry about it. You keep on playing as good as you been, with no more pain, and you might have your best years ahead of you."

"I'll be at the arena when you get here, Mama. You got your key?"

"Yes. Love you, Honey."

* * *

"Well, ain't that something?" Michelle put the phone down on the nightstand next to her bed, reached for her silk floral robe draped over the chintz covered chair, and covered her naked, still-toned bronze body. "Why do you suppose Radon brought up his father in the middle of the conversation?"

She turned to face Mike Prey standing in the doorway sporting tight boxer-briefs, sucking in his fifty-year-old gut. Mike had retreated to the bathroom following quite a tantric session between them, thereby allowing her to answer the phone. "Radon sounded suspicious," Michelle continued. "He couldn't possibly know you're here, right?" Then she joked. "Unless some investigator told him?"

"You're hilarious, lady. What's the big secret? You're a single woman and I just popped in on my way to Disneyland."

"I worry about my son, same as any mother. Radon has always been a special child. He's been living large for a long time and he's not thirty yet. A lot is my fault. I took care of things, so he didn't have to. That didn't help him become a man. You and me, though, we're mature enough to satisfy each other without expecting more . . . I trust you, Mike. When you leave in the morning, I don't know if we'll see each other again. That's OK. We'll be fine. My son sounded clear-headed and resolved about his future, but I'm afraid he's facing new challenges he may not be equipped to handle."

Mike went over to the bed and held Michelle in his arms. He had fallen into another one of those rare intimate encounters between two folks meeting under extreme personal circumstances. When he'd first contacted Michelle, searching for leads to Tanya Radishoff's whereabouts, Mike had immediately sensed a mutual attraction. Up to that point in his life, he had messed up almost every major opportunity. Nevertheless, Archie had taken a chance on him during the biggest media circus of Archie's career. Then Mike actually found Tanya in Mexico, convinced her to return and managed to seduce her in the bargain. What a difference a year makes!

Mike was amazed on many levels, albeit with a dash of: What the fuck took so long? His phone hasn't stopped ringing. Media savvy, security-minded companies have taken notice, and Mike Prey was indeed on his way to nearby Anaheim for a meeting with executives at Disney about tracking down the source of a pirated anime version of *Goofy at the Beach.*

Mike and Michelle had run into each other again at the Night of Knights fundraiser, where Lora had invited Mike to sit at their table in appreciation for having helped to spare the foundation's benefactor doing jail time. Mike had approached Michelle at the bar in the theater lobby, having remarked how lovely she looked in her gown. Then Mike had listened, eyes gleaming, while Michelle praised his tenacity and, of all things, his professionalism for following through on his promise to help Radon.

Later, they'd sat together for dessert and coffee, and Mike mentioned their first meeting, back in February, recalling how he'd been sent to Michelle's house to discuss the case. "You opened the door in exercise gear, no make-up, your hair tucked up under your Navy baseball cap, obviously on your way out despite making the appointment with me . . .. You know," he'd boldly added, "you looked just as lovely then without the glamour."

Michelle had beamed while they rotated forks into a scrumptious plate of tiramisu resting between them. That had sealed the deal. As soon as he'd mentioned he might be down her way in a few weeks, she'd invited him to call and see what happens.

Well, yeah. Mikey like it. Especially the part about no strings. Maybe this *was* the last night they'll ever spend together? He was OK with that, too. Except, Mike didn't really believe it. They'd made a hot connection, and he figured to be looping back around through Torrance for as long as he was working on *Goofy*.

"Fish gotta swim," Mike finally said out loud, ratifying Michelle's declaration, reclaiming his long-lost mantra.

Chapter Twenty

Penultimatum

Bryan Marten's befuddlement over Radon's descent from worldwide brand to pariah pending had long since morphed into anger—directed mostly toward Archie Krafter for prolonging Radon's failing career out of some misplaced sense of loyalty. Last year, half-a-million pairs of "*RCC*'s" (Radon's Camouflage Commanders), excluding post-Christmas returns following Radon's arrest, had dwindled to fifty thousand units sold through October of this year. In the final preseason game at Sacramento, Radon played nineteen stellar minutes, scored fourteen points, with seven assists and four rebounds. Nevertheless, Bryan had to advise Radon that management was exploring a trade, and having encountered little interest was now considering other options. Radon had apparently called Krafter in a panic as Archie had wasted little time accusing Bryan of knowing way more than he should about the team's plans. Bryan was irate. After handing Archie the case of his career, Bryan thought, Archie has the *cajones* to question his loyalty?

"Third time's the charm, my ass!" Bryan groused out loud over their failed associations, while making his way through the ornate lobby of the century old Olympia Club on Nob Hill. He had known it might be uncomfortable working with Archie again. But Bryan never thought Archie would turn on him, having insinuated that Bryan had colluded with Perry Dunbar to put his own financial interest ahead of Radon's—a serious breach of his fiduciary duty.

'Twas the Thursday afternoon before Christmas and Krafter had insisted they hash this out in person, just the two of them. Bryan had already shut down for the Holidays, preparing to fly the next morning with Susan and Simon to their Cabo timeshare on the Gulf of California. Consequently, Bryan had agreed to meet Archie for a drink at Bryan's Club, his regular respite from the rigors of making lots of money off other people's talent.

His tension fell away inside the genteel baroque palace of deep pile carpet and draperied walls, with its warren of parlors, meeting rooms and well-stocked library, plus the Russian steam baths and Olympic size pool in the basement. Nearly twenty years spent creeping up the membership ladder. Recommended for admission by a retired appellate court justice, having made his way with the traders, bankers and industry titans, who lately identified more and more as young nerds and techies, Bryan was finally entering the ranks of acceptability.

In a matter of weeks, he would officially join a more exclusive club, becoming a minority shareholder in the Worriers. No longer would Bryan be required to babysit self-absorbed, demanding athletes and performers. No more pandering to corporate sponsors, prima donna coaches and paranoid GM's. Or playing second fiddle to the likes of Archie Krafter.

Bryan had tried explaining to Archie that he was retiring from representing ballplayers as soon as the deal closed. But Krafter accused him of selling out Radon along the way. Hell, Bryan, thought. He'd offered to refer several clients to Archie, including Radon. But no. Krafter was too much like a dog with a bone who won't give it up because it soothes him to keep on chewing. So, Bryan agreed to meet in the bar before commuting over the bridge for the final time this year; his last-ditch effort to soothe Krafter's qualms and to set him straight.

Archie Krafter loved the ancient Russian baths in the cavernous basement of Bryan's club. Having had that perk when he worked for Bellicose, Marten & Fang, Archie had occasionally been offered a guest pass since leaving the firm. Then Fang happened to sink *his* a little too deeply into Bryan's skin one day; Bellicose intervened, taking Fang's side, and Marten had quit, taking with him his roster of famous clientele including Radon Jaalaba, the newly crowned NBA Rookie of the Year. Bryan had invited Archie to re-up as a consulting partner at Bryan's newly constituted management firm.

At the time, Archie thought it was a generous offer. After representing the deal to Lora, she'd expressed her belief that Bryan and Archie were on a collision course and lobbied Archie to decline. But Bryan was a whiz-bang financial operator; his connections with sponsors, retail chains and media outlets had been cultivated cutting his teeth on IP in the salad days of Silicon Valley. Having come to realize that he was essentially trading in the commoditization of people, Bryan nevertheless tended to view his clients in the same vein. Unfortunately, coddled millionaires didn't appreciate being condescended to. Thus, it turned out, Fang had left the biggest hole in the firm for Marten to fill: chief client 'splainer and cheerleader; a role handcrafted for Archie Krafter.

Archie had accepted. He should have listened to Lora. He wasn't naïve; he already knew Bryan's tendencies. Within six months, Archie had begun to feel petty jealousies and resentments; Bryan's frequent comments about being left out of meetings and imagining he was the butt of inside jokes whenever they all sat down with *his* clients—clients whose everyday management Bryan had assigned to Archie. After little more than a year, Bryan's persistent alcohol-fueled tirades had grown tiresome. Far too often, though, Bryan's attacks were personally directed at Archie. Or Bryan's actions were potentially harmful to the clients.

Radon had just gone down with his first knee injury before the All-Star Game, having been selected to the Western Conference team. He'd opted for surgery, out for the season. Yet Bryan had begun manipulating Radon into coming back too early during the late season playoff run, via steroid injections and Radon's first opioid seduction. Bryan's tactics included intimidation, having used his then fledgling relationship with Perry Dunbar to repeat things Perry had allegedly told him, such as: the team was growing impatient with Radon's post-surgery progress.

Too many times, Bryan's lack of empathy had been rewarded with huge financial packages that demanded superhuman performances bankable for an improbable number of years. Like livestock, his clients' durability and consistency were valued above all else. Krafter had let Bryan know that he didn't approve of the way he was "handling" Radon, and Bryan had reacted badly as Archie thought he might.

Thus, having realized that he too was contributing nothing to society other than keeping the entertainment too expensive for all the fans to enjoy, Archie had opted out of the people factory without much surprise or resistance from Bryan. Marten promptly replaced Krafter's team with a contingent of new starry-eyed believers and, alas, Archie had not been invited to the steam baths in four years.

When Radon had asked for help last Christmas, Krafter had little time to consider whether he was up to taking on the case, let alone that Bryan might eventually sit next to him at the defense table. After all, maybe he and Bryan were a little too similar of character for Krafter to admit? . . . Nah. They were worlds apart on the most important things to Archie. For one, Archie took seriously his duty to protect his clients' interests ahead of his own. Solving their problems filled him with gratitude more than the desire to collect. Money did not define Archie. He certainly maintained a decent ego and earned a comfortable living. Nevertheless, Krafter remained in awe of the power his law license afforded him rather than normalizing ways to abuse it.

Krafter probably couldn't prove in court that Perry Dunbar had rewarded Bryan in exchange for disclosing Jaalaba's confidential brain scan results and offering to deal his contract to another team. Yet, Archie was reasonably certain that the "quo" had definitely been given for the "quid." Why else would Dunbar have revealed to Krafter at the Night of Knights Dinner that he knew about Radon's potential damage to his nervous system? Perry had clearly assumed that Marten and Krafter were on the same raft selling Radon down the river.

If there was one thing Archie had learned about Perry Dunbar over the years, he simply didn't promote employees or consultants who were not his blood relatives. But not only had Perry personally endorsed Bryan's bid to purchase shares in the franchise, Dunbar had recommended him for a seat on the NBA's board committee on player development and marketing. This extraordinary gift had inspired Krafter to persuade Bryan to admit what he'd given Dunbar in exchange. The club's bar simply wouldn't do for an interrogation. Archie registered in the lobby as Bryan's guest and texted him to meet downstairs in what was steadfastly referred to as the Health Club.

"I barely have enough time for a drink," Bryan said when they met outside the locker room. "But you pushed your way into using the spa facilities."

"You must be punishing me for something you think I did to you in the past." Archie replied.

After settling on a steam and a swim, they sauntered into the brightly lit locker room, sat on the polished wooden bench in between the row of standing lockers and silently undressed. Clad in towels wrapped around their waists, they waded barefoot through the frosted glass doors, past the Jacuzzi, and into one of the interconnecting steam rooms, where the iron pipes running along the perspiring, white-tiled walls belched out blasts of hot mist.

Mostly naked middle-aged white men were variously reposed on the tiered pine benches lining the sweltering sweat chamber. Archie and Bryan ascended to the upper-level bench in an unoccupied corner, sat on their towels, facing each other with fake smiles and began *schvitzing*. Bryan managed to contain himself less than twenty awkward seconds.

"Why the fuck would you threaten Perry Dunbar at his own charity dinner?"

"It obviously worked," Archie said, watching Bryan's closely cropped ginger curls drip dew onto his freckled doughy forehead. "Radon passed the physical; he's playing great as ever. I had to bully Dunbar because you handed him a copy of Dewhauser's confidential files, *asshole!*"

"Jesus, Archie. That's a messed-up thing to say. As soon as mini camp opened, Matt Singer's team took over Radon's management in the office. I lost faith after we got him acquitted, I'll admit. But Perry Dunbar brought up Radon's neurology test results first. He said their experts determined that any definitive prognosis was too speculative and they're keeping it confidential to preserve his trade value."

"When?"

"When what?"

"When did Dunbar tell you he knew about Radon's brain scan?"

"I didn't record the exact moment, Archie."

"Before or after the lockout ended?"

"Really? . . . I'm not playing this game with you."

"Why would Dunbar tell *me* before he told you?"

"What difference does it make? You worried them enough to renew his insurance policy. They just don't want him on their team anymore."

"And what happens if *they* can't trade him?"

"I gotta go sit by the pool, Archie. It's way too hot up here."

Bryan's pink, sweat-drenched body wobbled as they descended the tiered pine benches through a steamy heat shield and trudged toward the multi-lane heated pool at the far end of the cavernous basement. Archie thought back to the Russian baths in Chicago, where his father used to bring him on Sunday mornings. The craggily faced old men, some with colorful cloth bandanas tied around their heads, filled weathered oak buckets with cold tap water and dumped them over themselves to cool off in the withering steam. They'd add a little soap, and using traditional, thickly bound oak-leaf brushes called *platza*s, the men dipped them in the soapy buckets and washed each other. Archie wished he could apply a *platza* to Bryan's skull repeatedly until *he* came clean.

"OK. I get your concern," Bryan said, reluctantly acknowledging his potential conflict of interest while they ambled along, side by side, towels draped over their shoulders. "A Chinese wall is already up at my firm. I'm officially removed from Radon's management list. We have no further business communications, and I have no input on efforts to resolve his status. It's also no secret the Worriers will have to eat Radon's contract if he's cut. Unless there's some legal reason to void it."

"You already know Dunbar's gonna try to stiff him, don't you?"

"Your insults are getting bizarre, Archie . . . I won't apologize for understanding why some people think Radon's baggage weighs too much to carry anymore."

"His baggage weighs too much? But you just said that's not your concern any longer."

"It's not a stretch to say Radon breached the morals clause in his contract. Between the drugs, the deaths and let's be real, the homo thing is another nail in his career. You know I don't condemn other people's personal behavior. Can't you sympathize if players aren't comfortable with the guy in the locker room?"

They were sitting, side by side, at the edge of the pool, toes in the water, watching naked men swimming, lounging and walking around together, reminding Archie of the sexually ambiguous Roman bath scene in the movie *Spartacus,* where Laurence Olivier asks Tony Curtis whether he prefers oysters or snails? . . . Archie wondered why on earth Bryan couldn't grok the cruel hypocrisy of his words, denigrating Radon's character and promoting discrimination?

"Whoa!" Archie grunted out loud, suddenly realizing that Bryan hadn't leaked Radon's brain scan results, after all. He'd done worse. "You told Perry Dunbar about Radon's sexual relationship with Russell Marchetti, didn't you?"

"I might've mentioned our intervention at your house," Bryan conceded without the slightest awareness of his betrayal. "I've only said that Radon was staying clean and in playing shape ever since . . . Face it, Archie. We both know his career was mortally wounded after that cop died. The retail numbers tell the story in spite of how he's played during pre-season. I'm sure this sounds weird, but if Radon came out publicly it might be his best chance to revive the *merch.* There are none—count 'em —zero openly gay players on any active roster in the NBA. So maybe the League isn't ready for this, Archie. And is Radon Jaalaba really the poster boy to front the movement?"

"Are you fucking serious? Do you not understand what you've done?"

"What?"

"What?? Disclosing Radon's most private confidence? Being financially rewarded for irreparably damaging his career? . . . Your conscience is what's supposed to hurt, Bryan, when all your other parts feel great."

"You hosted his damn confession with Hors d'oeuvres. Spare me the high-hat speech. Not everything is black or white. Y' know, Archie; you've always had a special capacity to focus on the wedge issue, grab it by the throat and rattle it in your opponent's face until the end . . . Guess what? You're still strangling the issue. Get over it. Does it really matter what side you're on?"

Considering the serious breaches of fiduciary duty that Bryan just boastfully acknowledged, Krafter was equally enraged by Bryan's indifference to Archie's true character, assuming that he too was corruptible. At what point does the desire to do good for others go extinct? . . . The lone takeaway from Bryan's monologue that stuck in Krafter's head was "strangle," and in the next moment Archie had his hands around Bryan's neck, squeezing tightly, jerking Bryan's body around toward the edge of pool, about to hurl him in. He saw Bryan's eyes widen, terrified by the surprise attack on his person, while the power surge bounced off Archie's brain like a pinball machine gone amuck. The message received, he quickly let go of Bryan's throat. The futility of his fury was embarrassing, yet he resolved not to sink to Bryan Marten's level.

"What the fuck!" Bryan exclaimed, struggling to get up without falling into the pool. He rubbed his neck with his right hand. Then he bent down, grabbed his towel off the floor and tied it around his potbellied waist. "OK, so you're a thug, just like your father-in-law?"

"Piss off, Bryan! The side you choose to be on makes all the difference in the world."

They stood towel to towel, close enough to spit on one another. "I've decided to do some pro bono work from now on," Krafter continued matter-of-factly. "Starting with Radon's lawsuit against you for invasion of privacy and violating your professional oath."

Bryan's shoulders arched high as he could raise them, and he stared into Archie's eyes, considering him anew, wondering how long Krafter had held such animosity toward him. "That's a relief," Bryan replied sarcastically. "For a minute, I thought you were gonna order a hit on me."

"You better hope that's just a clever remark," Archie said. "I get it, Bryan. You'd rather follow Perry Dunbar's formula for success. But remember, if you profit from betraying your client's loyalty, you're a thief."

Bryan walked off toward the locker room not knowing how to deal with this accusation. Krafter caught up and whispered into his ear: "What's happened to you, Bryan? Aren't we all judged by the same rules?"

Bryan Marten stopped, turned, and displayed his grim and sweaty silent face. Bryan knew Archie could never accept Bryan's point of view. He just wanted to get away. To retrieve his clothes without bothering to shower, get into his car and get home to finish packing for Mexico. He tried walking around the wide circular Jacuzzi to avoid Krafter, who stood directly in his path leading to the locker room doors. Archie persisted and Bryan was pinned in the narrow aisle between the whirlpool bath and the corner wall, trapped like a cockroach on the kitchen counter, the final escape route sealed off.

"Look, Archie," Bryan spoke up at last, tossing out a tiny crumb of compromise. "We can slug this out if that's what you want. When the dust clears, my insurance company will indemnify your insurance company and I'll get back to you, blah, blah, blah . . . Or we can co-exist. We don't need to tear each other apart. There's plenty of opportunity for you on this journey."

"All right," Krafter said. Having run through the options in his head already, Archie posited his final offer. "Let's consider this your last chance to do the right thing before moving on, Bryan. Convince Perry Dunbar to honor Radon's contract and protect his privacy."

An interminable silence followed, as they searched for any common thread still tying them together after all these years. Archie watched the decades roll by in reverse as Bryan's eyes darted about contemplating how he was going to flee. "C'mon, Archie," he said. "You don't really think they'll listen to me?"

"I dunno. Sounds like Dunbar's been listening to you too much, lately . . . So, there's one more thing. Swear to me you'll plant the bug in Dunbar's ear to put Radon in the starting line-up on Sunday. Other teams will want him if he's allowed to shine."

Bryan just snickered. He was feeling faint, likely dehydrated and definitely exhausted; he simply couldn't stand there any longer. "I don't think it's you, Archie, but I'm really gonna puke if I don't get out of here soon."

They could have been alien visitors meeting on the same planet for the first time and Krafter resolved that understanding may indeed be the booby prize of the universe.

"Puke on yourself," Archie said, as he shoved Bryan hard into the Jacuzzi and walked on toward the locker room.

Chapter Twenty-One

"Denouemint"—The Last Confection

When Lora awoke on Christmas morning, the predawn harbor lights stretched across the cobalt sky, the blanket of stars fading along with the night. She slipped out of bed to avoid disturbing Archie and Swami, curled up at their feet, who opened one eye, recognized Lora's penchant for early rising and went back to sleep. The creeping sun met the crisp windless air while Lora pulled on her Uggs and a fleece-lined hoodie.

The brass thermometer hanging from the rear deck post outside the kitchen door read forty-six degrees as she trekked down the back lawn to the cottage studio. Lora turned on the lights, plugged in the space heater and started the electric tea pot on the kitchenette counter. Then she went over to her old Kimball, sat down and began charting the music for a tune bouncing around in her head since Archie had come home from his meeting with Bryan and confessed to choking him in front of everyone at the club pool.

Although Archie said he was ashamed of himself, Lora mostly thought it was funny. She let him know he got some points for zealous client advocacy, not to mention Bryan Marten deserved worse than being thrown into the Jacuzzi. Archie rarely lost his temper. She'd never seen him raise a hand to any person or creature except household vermin such as mosquitoes, roaches and rats, but not spiders. It's bad luck to kill a spider.

Nevertheless, one positive theme among the gory details of Archie's encounter with Bryan had sparked a musical homage to her honorable husband, and the lyrics emerged from the phrase she kept repeating in her head: "Pro Bono Man."

```
F#M          C#M  C      Bbm
Met him      in the lobby    queue
F#M          C#M  C      Eb   F
Breezing past life's endless meal
F#M          C#M  C      Bbm
Didn't know  his karma      then
F#M          C#M  C    Eb   F
The icing    up his sleeve was true

F#M          C#M  C      Bbm
Had the      forked tongue gift of know
F#M          C#M  C    Eb   F
Couldn't let those issues go
G     Ab     G       D
Pro   Bono           Man
G     C#     E       D
What's in    the     worth

G     G#     G       Bm
When you're  hurt by the system
G     G#     G       Bm
Your life's  broken and twisted
F#M          C#M
He'll stitch you a letter
F#M          C#M
To fight for your better

C            Bbm
The madder   the hatter
C            Bbm
He's the last on the list
He's the last on the list

F#M          C#M  C  Bbm
To seek      a finer  soul
F#M          C#M  C  Eb   F
He           throws it  all away
F#M   C#M    C       Eb   F
Just spreads that gift of know
F#M   C#M    C       Bbm
Couldn't let those   issues go

G     Ab     G       D
Pro   Bono           Man
G     C#     E       D
What's in    the     worth
G     Ab     G       D
Had the forked tongue gift of know
G     C#     E       D
No black or  white of youth
G     Ab     G       D
Do    you    have the truth?
```

Sunlight pierced the rooftops of Russian Hill and poured in through the cottage windows. The music moving through her at the same time that nature's beauty warmed her soul was overwhelming. Lora was ecstatic with gratitude and love. She began to cry, pure joy encompassing this moment. Simultaneously, though, she also sobbed over the temporary nature of her happiness and good fortune. She'd found a life partner who encouraged her individuality after spending her youth mostly hiding from her own name.

Consequently, Lora often fretted her fate within the crucible of daily existence, feeling threatened by every manner of disease or genetics and other random acts of violence. She and her soul mate might both be gone tomorrow. Over the course of their years together, Lora has tried to hold back these dam bursts for her private moments. While Archie was a reasonably sensitive male, he has simply never understood how she managed to cry tears of joy and sadness at the same time.

Lora was also concerned with her brother's dire legal situation. As much as she'd kept her distance, she still felt guilty for moving away when he was just eleven. She supported Dominic's decision to meet with the prosecutors and truthfully answer all their questions. When it came to cooperating as a witness, Dom needed to find other counsel as Archie vociferously repeated to both of them his refusal to formally represent Dominic in the case.

Nonetheless, following some prodding from the wife, the *mench* promised to *think about* accompanying Dominic to his initial interview with the US attorney in January. Still, the wife was most concerned that Dom had recently confided he was leaning toward pleading guilty to avoid hiding in witness protection for who knows how long? If he refused to implicate anyone else, Herb had told him that he'd likely receive no more than twelve months in a federal minimum-security facility. Lora couldn't stop thinking that she didn't want him going to prison for something he didn't do, just to avoid testifying against their father and Herb Winant.

"Hey there, beautiful," Archie said, his voice breaking through her deep cogitation. He'd entered the cottage and approached Lora at the piano, carrying a tray containing her favorite breakfast: a spinach, mushroom and feta omelet with an avocado slathered slice of toasted *pain au levain* bread. Archie set the tray on the nearby kitchen divider as she hustled over to inspect her surprise. Lora's sparkling amber eyes lit up her face and her gleeful smile erupted, evoking the first moment Archie fell in love with her. "I didn't want to interrupt your music," he said. "Just wondered whether you've decided about going to the game this evening?"

"I'll go to support Radon, of course. It's opening night. But you know his seats suck, right? Right on the floor behind the basket. For a second, I was hoping you'd want to curl up in bed and watch on TV."

"Would snacks be involved?"

"Tai Chi delivers on Christmas. I'm just sayin'."

* * *

It was 1:15 PM when Radon exited his car in the players' parking lot and approached the Arena entrance. A crowd of kids and other not so young fans had already gathered, waiting to score an autograph, or to glimpse their favorite stars arriving for pregame preparations. Radon enjoyed this time best on game days; the personal connection with loyal fans making a point of being there from the beginning, waiting for their players to arrive. Obsessed, probably; yet almost one hundred percent wishing for the team to win. Radon always got a jolt from the interaction, helping him mentally prepare to enter the gladiator's arena. Most players don't like the familiarity and interaction with fans, ignoring all outside stimulus before the game, wearing noise-canceling headphones from the moment they leave the car until they're in the locker room.

Ever since the NBA became a steppingstone for its mega-stars to score broadcasting gigs, movie contracts and designer clothing lines, the largest group of fans and paparazzi regularly assembled for the post-game runway fashion parade out to the parking lot. Win or lose, sharply dressed players on every NBA team eventually emerged from their locker rooms freshly scrubbed and fluffed, wearing their latest eponymous clothing lines, and strut the concrete stadium corridors in their respective cities through a gauntlet of adoring fans and fashion photogs all the way outside to their exotic cars parked in the players' lot.

Radon usually arrived six hours before the opening tip-off of an evening game; for stretching, lifting, an informal skull session and the shoot-around—with a walk-through of pre-designed plays and defenses—then a light buffet lunch. All of it was intended to keep everyone together, to sharpen their focus and mentally prepare them to march into war on the court as a team.

Opening Night crowds were raucous and electric. The beginning of a brand-new season was like a playoff game, every team equal in the standings with the same shot at *The Finals*. This afternoon's fans appeared particularly hungry because game day had arrived nearly two months late. Radon immediately got their vibe as he made his way into the wide interior corridor of the arena, its thick cement pillars rising overhead to cradle the vast concrete walkway encircling the stadium. The hallway buzzed with employees and vendors. Like munchkins in Oz, they followed Radon to the team's private entrance door.

Inside, walking along the empty well-lit passageway, Radon nodded at his own action photo, relieved to see it still hanging among the gallery of players that lined the walls. Radon entered the locker room as regally as he could muster and marched across the spongy carpeting. A spattering of teammates lounged in their ergonomic office chairs, listening to iPods in front of their forty-inch-wide closet stalls. Lined up, side by side, the open cubicles ran the length of the room, each player's uniform number prominently displayed on the facing.

Radon went directly to his space, briefly acknowledging everyone he passed along the way, and hung his suit bag next to his game uniforms on the clothes rack in the rear. The wise veteran has returned for his eighth opener already having made his claim for a leadership role during training camp. With the new coach and only two roster players more experienced than Radon, his maturity demonstrated a keener sense of clarity and patience for making more effective choices with the basketball.

He had no idea whether he would play in this game or be traded in the morning. As far he was concerned, the best chemistry was rooted in unselfish professionalism and he put it all out there, as they say, for others to judge. Radon reached for his freshly-laundered practice sweats—folded and left for him on his mesh-backed manager's chair—and he sat down to contemplate the elephant in the room.

Him or them? Radon knows he will not be their leader until his teammates trusted him. He was prepared to pay for his cowardice the rest of his life, at the very least. Everything he has done to get back to this moment was in service to making it right with Russell. Radon understood his commitment would never be enough for the likes of too many to name, starting with Officer Gino Trower's family.

But the folks in this locker room needed to believe that Radon would always be there for them and, this time, he *would* take a bullet if that's what it takes to lead them on the court. Radon knew there was no way to prove this. He could only bless this second chance, be open and truthful whenever asked, and remain devoted to executing the game plan for as long as he was allowed. His teammates would have to let him know when they trust him enough to lead. "The wise veteran waits for the flock to assemble," Radon said to himself, unsure whether he heard it from Larry Bird, or he'd read it in a fortune cookie.

Soon after Radon settled in, Coach Stacko came over and Radon wondered if he was about to tell him he'd been dealt to Toronto. Coach wheeled "Number 4's" chair over from the adjacent stall, sat down and promptly informed Radon that he was in the starting lineup. "You earned it," Stacko told him. "I went to bat for you. Make us proud."

Radon's relief and utter joy over being invited back to the dance felt better than any high. مەأشادال (Praise Allah). During the shoot-around, Radon insinuated himself into the discussion with his teammates and the coaches. By the time they turned off the music and media in the locker room, thirty minutes before final warm-ups on the court, everyone sat in silent meditation, praying to at least seven different gods—by Radon's count—for strength and determination in battle.

He was calm and peaceful, thinking about the game plan to stop Chris Paul and Chauncey Billups, his roving assignments on defense. Radon had reasons to lead this team. Somehow, he had come through to the other side of hell on earth and would resist temptation so long as he remained committed to truly honoring Russell.

Radon felt a rare rush of belonging, beginning with gratitude for this second chance to relive his dream in whole. He knew that he still had a long way to come. That it would always be one day at a time. He was finally beginning to understand that whether his teammates or the NBA ever accepted him was really their issue not his.

Radon was the first player out of the tunnel jogging toward the Worriers' courtside chairs. The stadium was already filling with exuberant fans, their long wait finally over, particularly for season-ticket holders, their forty-one game plans unceremoniously reduced to thirty-three. During lay-up drills, Radon sneaked over to greet his mother, sitting with Marina in the floor seats behind the basket. All smiles, bursting with pride, Radon loved them up. His pit stop included Archie and Lora, who arrived in time to receive a special hug. Soon the pre-game hoopla was over, the national anthem sung, and the game buzzer sounded. House lights dimmed, the wandering search lights and sirens encircling the arena eventually came to rest. Radon walked to center court, where he greeted the Clipper starters and heard the referee's whistle calling like a coda.

* * *

"What do you think of *The Turnip Princess* for the title of my show?" Lora asked Archie during the first time-out, only four minutes into the game, called by the Clippers after Radon's third straight three-point basket.

"*Turnip Princess?* I like it."

"Really?"

"And since you asked, I really like the song 'Pro Bono Man.' Not so much 'Daughter of Rain.' I mean, I get it. But don't you think . . . Hey, your phone is ringing," Archie said, saved by the samba sound pulsating in Lora's purse resting between them on her padded folding chair. Lora pulled it out and looked at the screen. "Herb Winant," she said. "I'll call him back during halftime."

"Maybe you should answer it."

"Hello? . . . Yes, it's me, Herb . . . We're at the basketball game and it's very loud. I'm sorry . . . Wait; say that again . . . Oh my God! When? —My father is *dead*, Archie—Yes, I understand, Herb . . . Perino Brothers tomorrow at 2:30 . . . He did? . . . Well, he never shared any details from the family trust with me. You probably want to ask Dominic . . . Wait . . . What? . . . You can't be serious? . . . Oh, yeah. You bet; I'll tell him right away! . . . OK, Herb. Thanks for your sympathy."

Lora returned the phone to her purse, barely containing her excitement as she faced Archie. "You are not going to believe this."

"I'm sorry." Archie said, hugging her in sympathy. "Sal taught you what not to do in life and you took that lesson to heart. You're a good person, Lora. I'm proud to know you."

"Aww, Archie. That's so sweet. Right now, I'm just thinking my father was generous 'cause he left me alone. Cousin Zeda found him in his TV chair. They're assuming it was natural causes. But Herb said they won't know for certain unless they do an autopsy."

"You realize, Dominic can tell the truth now without worrying about witness protection. Herb Winant is going to be the government's fall guy in the case."

"You ought to know, Don Archie."

"What's that supposed to mean?"

"My father's will left everything to the Dellacozzi Family Trust, which names Arthur Krafter the Successor Trustee of the majority shareholder in Dellacozzi Farms Ltd. That is literally the funniest thing I've ever heard. Welcome to the Board, My Love."

Acknowledgments

Many thanks to Kurt and Erica Mueller, Nancy Rosenfeld, Erin Olds, Mandy Ballard, Nikki Lastreto, Byron Spooner and Judith Ayn Bernhard, Frances Dinkelspiel, Edward Guthmann, Robert Stricker, Bruce Crain, Michelle Jeffers, Evette Davis, Amy Kaminer, Evan Rosen, Katherine Hirzel, Stuart Weiner, Art Twain, Bob Bralove, Barbara and Jill Melveger, and special thanks to my wife Nancy Calef for the music and the inspiration.

About the Author

Jody Weiner wrote the acclaimed novel *Prisoners of Truth* (national IPPY award for mystery/suspense, (Council Oak Books, 2004, pb 2006) inspired by his experience defending criminal cases in Chicago. Weiner co-authored *Kinship with Animals* (COB, 2007) an anthology of true interspecies encounters, where he writes about serving as attorney to Koko the Gorilla. Weiner co-authored *Peoplescapes, My Story from Purging to Painting* (Babu Books, 2015) an illustrated memoir by Nancy Calef with Jody Weiner.

Weiner lives in San Francisco and collaborates with his wife and partner, American figurative painter Nancy Calef.

Read more online at: www.jodyweiner.com

Upcoming 2026 New Release!

JODY WEINER'S

Crime Therapy
The Krafters: Partners in Time
Book 2

Crime Therapy digs deeply into the making, care and feeding of the Krafters' enduring love affair, while taking the reader on a suspenseful, often hilarious roller coaster ride through the criminal justice system. Network sitcom star Leonardo "the psychic beagle" suffers a career interrupting brain injury when the autonomous vehicle he's riding in collides with a cable car while filming a Super Bowl commercial. Then a young woofer named "Rye" on a legal cannabis farm in Northern California kills a poacher he encountered trespassing too close to one of the grow houses on the forested property. Lora's brother Dominic once again finds himself in legal trouble. While Lora knows that Archie is the best man to also defend Dominic, it's the last thing in the world he wants to do.

Did Rye act in self-defense?

Has Leonardo recovered his astounding gift of interspecies communication?

Will Dominic manage to turn his life around or does his journey end badly?

**For more information
visit: www.SpeakingVolumes.us**

Now Available!
LUIS FIGUEREDO
WHEN CANARIES DIE
A Pierce Evangelista Thriller

**For more information
visit: www.SpeakingVolumes.us**

Now Available!

B. W. JACKSON

THE RISE OF THE LAZARUS
Book One

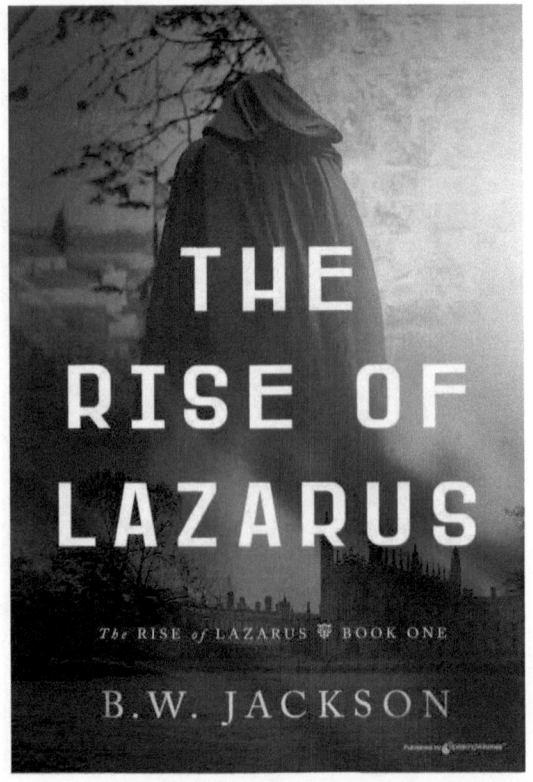

**For more information
visit: www.SpeakingVolumes.us**

Now Available!
MARK E. SCOTT

A DAY IN THE LIFE
Book One – Book Two – Book Three

**For more information
visit:** www.SpeakingVolumes.us

Now Available!

RAY DAN PARKER

THE TOM WILLIAMS SAGA
Books 1 - 4

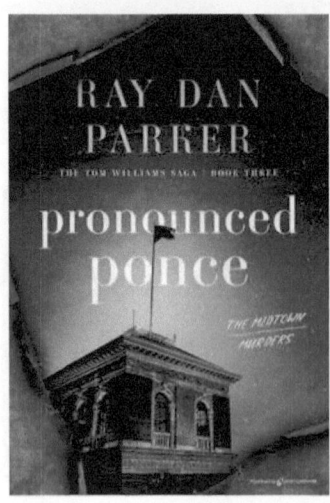
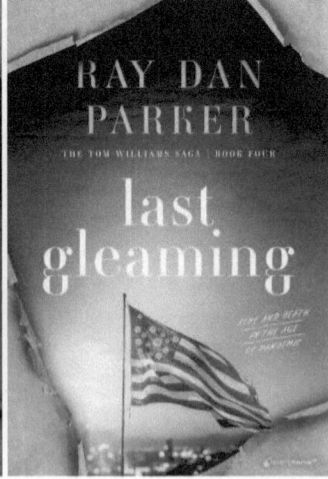

**For more information
visit: www.SpeakingVolumes.us**

www.ingramcontent.com/pod-product-compliance
Lightning Source LLC
LaVergne TN
LVHW041921070526
838199LV00051BA/2692